"Get the hell out of there, Alexandra. Get the hell out or I'm coming in," he warned through her earbud.

"Just stick to the plan," she hissed.

"I will if you will. Shit!"

She got to the first landing. "What now?"

"Neighborhood security. Damn it all to hell."

"Show your PI license." She cocked her head to the side. Was someone up here?

"I know that, princess, but I'm going to have to cut off communication so we don't get arrested. Get out of the house! Good evening, officers…"

Static filled her ears, and she slipped the earpiece out. There was no way she wasn't going up to the second landing. Jacob would have to get over it. The wood under her feet groaned; she cringed. She glanced up the last few steps. Nothing. She tiptoed into the hall; it looked like some creepy maze. Wonderful.

She walked with her back to the wall until she came upon the only room with light shining under the door. Putting her ear against the cool wood, she tried to make out any movement; again nothing. Dr. Drake didn't have any pets or girlfriends, so what in the hell was going on? She took off her goggles and hooked them onto her belt; she didn't want the light to make her hesitate.

She took a deep breath, put one hand on the knob, the other on the door, and pushed it open…

Praise for W.L. Brooks

The Secrets that Shape Us, McKay series book 2

"W.L. Brooks has given readers the whole package in this novel."

~ *Reviewer InD'tale Magazine*

Let the Dead Lie, McKay series book 1

"...you find yourself unable to put your eReader down until you get to the end. Because, it's that good."

~*The Romance Reviews*

The Truth Behind the Mask

by

W. L. Brooks

The McKay Series

This is a work of fiction. Names, characters, places, and incidents are either the product of the author's imagination or are used fictitiously, and any resemblance to actual persons living or dead, business establishments, events, or locales, is entirely coincidental.

The Truth Behind the Mask

Contact Information: info@thewildrosepress.com

Cover Art by *Kim Mendoza*

The Wild Rose Press, Inc.
PO Box 708
Adams Basin, NY 14410-0708
Visit us at www.thewildrosepress.com

Publishing History
First Edition, 2021
Trade Paperback ISBN 978-1-5092-3614-5
Digital ISBN 978-1-5092-3615-2

The McKay Series
Published in the United States of America

Dedication

For my nieces and nephews (most of whom are too young to read these books just yet)—
you are beautiful to me.

Chapter One

Jake Keller was not a happy man. Ten minutes ago, he'd been fucking ecstatic to be home. This case had taken only about a week, but he was tired of the long trips. The crazy life he led was catching up with him.

This last job had been the final hoorah for Sleuths, the private investigation agency he owned with his twin brother. Jake had planned on keeping the PI gig a little longer with a new partner, but taking in the state of his condo, that would have to wait.

Glass crunched under his foot, and Jake froze. He lifted up his boot and swore; the ceramic shards stuck in the treads belonged to his favorite mug, the one his grandmother had given him. *Damn it!* Of course that wasn't the only thing destroyed. Nope, his entire place had been smashed up, sliced up, and…*Were those bullet holes?*

"Damn it all to hell!" he mumbled, turning his kitchen table right side up. *What the fuck happened here?* It hadn't been a robbery. For one, there was no forced entry, and two, any intruder would have had to bypass his state-of-the-art security system. He sighed; there was no way in hell he was getting his deposit back.

Jake checked each room for signs of life. Even more important than his personal keepsakes was the person he'd been keeping here. She meant a lot to him too, though it would embarrass both of them to say so.

There wasn't a doubt in his mind this chaos had to do with her. Fletcher McKay attracted lunatics worse than shit attracted flies. Yep, the kid was trouble with a capital *T*. Not that he'd say that to her; she would kick his ass. Again.

Jake pulled out his cell and dialed the kid. His gut tightened; the call went straight to voicemail. "Damn it, kid, what happened? Call me when you get this." He put the phone back in his pocket and froze when his front door opened. He slipped his hand to his gun and waited.

"My Lord, who lives like this?" came the wispy voice of his uninvited guest.

Jake grunted, lowered his aim, and holstered his weapon. "What are ya doing here, princess?" he asked his brother's sister-in-law. Nearly two years ago, his twin had taken a job in Blue Creek, North Carolina, where he ended up meeting and marrying Casey McKay. Not only were the McKays a force to be reckoned with, Ryan had managed to marry into a family of hot ladies to boot.

"I'm looking for my sister," Alexandra McKay said, motioning to the mess. "She's obviously been here."

"What makes you say that?" He bristled under the scrutiny of her raised brow. Out of the four McKay sisters, this was the only one who made his damn jaw—not to mention other parts of his anatomy—twitch. Well, he didn't really get along with his brother's wife either, but one thing had nothing to do with the other.

"Hmm. Let's see, your apartment is in complete disarray. Now, I could be giving you more credit than you deserve by thinking this is not how you usually live, or it could be that my little sister has been here, and—as per usual—she brought catastrophe along for the ride."

He grunted, then started righting what was left of his furniture. She huffed, and he glanced at her out of the corner of his eye. Every inch of Alexandra's female frame was elegant. She always wore something fancy, and she looked it too. Fancy. Classy. Her dark red hair was in a precise bun on the top of her head, and her big blue eyes were looking at him like he was trash. Shit.

She crossed her arms over her chest. "Oh, and her truck is parked outside."

"Yeah, so?" Jake wouldn't look at her. She was the most judgmental woman he'd ever encountered. And there went his jaw…twitching.

"I need to find her."

"Maybe she doesn't want to be found." What he needed to find was a broom; it was going to take him forever to clean up this crap.

"What? Do you think Fletcher threw a tantrum, destroyed your things, and left without her truck? Though, I wouldn't put it past her—"

"Course you wouldn't," he accused, then looked up when she didn't defend herself. He stomped across the room to where she was holding a piece of paper, which surely belonged to him. "I'll take that." He snatched the note from her hand, ignored her tempting feminine scent, and read it.

Sorry for the mess, Jake. I cleaned up what I could. I'm going home to see Alexandra, so don't bother looking for me.

Sorry again,

Jamie

Jake cursed and dropped the letter. Alexandra picked it up and read it. He shook himself. For a moment, he would have sworn actual concern hovered in her eyes, but he had to have imagined it; the woman was an ice princess.

She bit her lower lip. "Could someone have her?"

"That's my take on it," Jake said. "She said she was going to see you, and she hates you; that's clue number one. Clue number two is she signed Jamie and that isn't her name, so we can guess whoever has her doesn't know her."

Alex rolled her eyes. "Jamie's her birth name. Our father changed it years ago. She uses J. as her middle initial."

She made a move to leave, and Jake grabbed her arm. "Whoa! Where are you going?" He dropped the hand she was glaring at and stepped back a space. He'd think about the name change thing later.

"I'm going to my hotel; then I'm going to make a few phone calls to see if anyone's heard from her."

"I have some questions for you first. If you don't mind, *princess*," he added to annoy her. "First, how did you know she was here? Second, who are you going to call? And third, who the fuck do you think took her?"

"Ryan told me she was here." She smirked. "What? Did you think he wouldn't cave?"

"That no good son of a—"

"I'm going to call my family," Alex continued, "and see if they've heard anything. And finally, I have no earthly idea who the 'fuck' took her, as you so eloquently put it."

"Okay, but you can't call home," he said, following

her outside. She'd gotten a new SUV. It was a beaut. He'd just bought a new ride himself. His brother had the same luxury vehicle and Jake had been drooling.

Alex leaned against the driver's side door. "Why?"

"Because they'll worry; then the whole crew will be up here putting their noses in and muddying up the damn waters!" They both knew it was true. There was no way in hell Emmit McKay would sit around and do nothing while his daughter was who knows where.

"They'll want to know." She looked at her nails, then murmured, "They deserve to know."

"If you say so." Jake did an about-face and began to walk away. He made it three steps when she called out to him. He smiled to himself, then turned. "Yeah?"

"Why did you give in so easily?"

"I mean, what the hell." He shrugged one shoulder "Tell everyone. It's your fault she's missing, and we all know it."

"What do you mean…*my fault*?"

"If it weren't for you, Fletcher would still be home, and this more than likely wouldn't have happened."

"Fine," she said between clenched teeth. "What do *you* suggest we do?"

"We look for clues," he said and headed back inside. He didn't have to turn around to know she was following him.

Alexandra's blood boiled. Why in the world did she have to be here with her brother-in-law's insipid twin?

Jacob Keller was a throwback to the caveman. His long brown hair was in one of those ridiculous manbuns, his jeans had holes in the knees, his black T-shirt had seen better days, and his leather boots were caked with mud. At least, she hoped it was mud.

"Okay. Which room was hers or"—she looked him up and down—"was she staying in yours?"

"Whatever you wish to believe, *princess*," he said with a bow and walked away.

Alexandra controlled her urge to growl and started searching through what was left of Jacob's things. She should be home right now. She had a bed and breakfast to run, for goodness' sake. Granny Vaughn's, named after her late grandmother, was doing quite well, thank you very much. Almost two weeks ago, despite it not being the most lucrative time of year, she'd had an entire tour group in residence. But now she'd had to close her business to pursue her little sister. Sure, she could have let someone else run things for her, but Alexandra didn't like other people taking control of her responsibilities.

She wouldn't even be here if she'd had a choice, but she hadn't been given one. Charlie, her best friend and slightly older sister, had given her an ultimatum. If Alex didn't bring Fletcher home, Charlie would elope with her fiancé, Craig, and there would be no wedding. Charlie deserved a wedding, a big beautiful event—the works—and Alex would make sure it happened. But more than that, it was up to her to bring Fletcher back because—and she was loath to admit it—Jacob was right; it *was* her fault Fletcher had left in the first place.

Though Alex hadn't acted alone, her suspicion of Fletcher's best friend, Sheriff Jasper Hart, had thrown Fletcher over the edge and out of town. In hindsight, Alexandra could see her error in judgment, but did this punishment fit her crime?

Her family put the brunt of the blame on her, which

she could handle; it *had* been her idea in the first place. But even people outside the family had been punishing her. Tiny Wellington, who was the head cook at the diner and someone Alex had known since she was a young girl, had burnt her food. Tiny had never burnt a meal in his life, until now, so she knew he did it on purpose. And Trixy Mae, who had been doing Alex's hair for as long as she could remember, had cut an extra four inches off the ends last week. *Four freaking inches!* Unbelievable.

Alex picked her way over Jacob's things. Despite the mess, the apartment was clean; she'd give him that. It hadn't surprised her to find out Fletcher had gone to Jake. The two were so much alike it was almost funny. Alex couldn't see them sleeping together, but she hadn't seen a lot of things lately.

She resisted the urge to rub her eyes. She had arrived in town late last night and, figuring it would take at least a couple days to get Fletcher to listen to reason, had checked into hotel. And, yes, maybe she had been putting off the inevitable by lingering over her breakfast this morning, but she was here, wasn't she? Doing what she'd promised? Indeed.

"Jacob?" Alex paused until he came into the kitchen. God, why couldn't he be more like his brother? Ryan was a prince among men, a—

"What?" Jacob growled. "I thought you were helping me. You're not worried you'll get mussed up, are you?"

"It's occurred to me…" She waited until he was actually paying attention. "The only things destroyed are *your* things. And Fletcher stopped to write a note. Would she be able to leave a note if she were being kidnapped?"

His gaze traveled around the room. "You have a point, princess. What are you thinking?"

"It seems to me, Fletcher knew the intruder and went along willingly or pretended to." Alex pinched the bridge of her nose. "Did she leave anything behind?"

"Yeah. Her clothes, tablet, her phone"—he jiggled the cellphone in his hand—"oh, and that locket thingy she always wears."

The color drained from her face.

Chapter Two

"Would you mind sharing what this means?" Jake gestured around the room with his hand. The princess had been sitting there staring into space for a few minutes, and the hairs on the back of his neck were prickling.

Alex sighed. "Trouble."

"No shit. What kind?"

"First of all, Fletcher doesn't leave that tablet anywhere. She needs her show to sleep."

"Yeah, she's crazy about that damn show!" Jake hadn't been a fan of *Murder, She Wrote* until he'd had to watch every episode. That was one canny old broad.

Alex shook her head. "You don't get it, do you?"

He controlled his temper at her exasperated tone. He wasn't an idiot, but women were peculiar creatures, and Fletcher more so than most.

"Fletcher's birth name was Jamie, but she loathed the name and begged Dad to change it for her…what's the main character's name in the show?"

A slow smile spread on Jake's face. "The kid is too damn much! Imagine naming yourself after a cagey broad—sorry," he said when she glared at him. What? That shit was funny.

"But this"—she held up the white-gold locket—"is much more important. This has left Fletcher's neck only three times since our mother gave it to her for Christmas years ago. Twice it was stolen by people who wanted to harm our family, and twice we didn't believe her. Its significance cannot be ignored."

"Gotcha!" He took a seat on the carpeted floor and rested his hands between his knees. "Fletcher's told me lots of things, but I would've remembered if she'd said something about the locket."

Like him and his brother, the McKay sisters had been orphans, but unlike the Keller twins, who were raised by their grandparents, the girls had been adopted by strangers. They'd had a rough start from what Jake had heard, but you would never know it now; they were Emmit and Savannah McKay's children through and through. Even their younger brother Jebb had the same fight in him that the sisters did. Jake had never met a family who fought or loved as hard as the McKays. Some of the kid's stories were—

"And what did she tell you?"

Wouldn't you love to know? "All kinds of things. Like why she left Blue Creek. That was fucked up, by the way. Jasper Hart is a good and honorable man; I met him at Ryan and Casey's wedding and I knew immediately. And even if things hadn't added up where he was concerned, you know how important he is to your sister—"

Her cheeks reddened. "How dare you lecture me about my sister when you treat your brother like he's an imposition rather than your twin!"

He jumped to his feet. "Don't you lecture *me* on how I treat my brother, sweetheart. You don't know a damn thing about me or our relationship. I've never betrayed *my* brother." He was in her face, so he should have seen the slap coming—hell, all the McKay women got physical—but he didn't see it until the palm of her hand stung his cheek.

"Let me put this in a way you'll understand: Fuck you!" she shouted before she walked away.

Jake glared at her retreating form. "Women!"

****

Alex was combing her wet hair when she came out of the bathroom in her robe. The door of the hotel room had opened when she was in the shower, which would have alarmed her if Jacob's unmistakable grunt hadn't followed. So she didn't acknowledge him in any way as she collected the dress she'd laid out on the bed. She turned on her heel and went back into the bathroom to get ready.

"You aren't surprised to see me?" he asked the minute she came back into the room.

She slipped on her leather boots without looking at him. "No."

He grumbled something unintelligible and began to pace. "Do you own anything other than dresses?"

"No." She went to the mirror and applied her lipstick.

He stopped pacing and stood behind her. "Are you ignoring me?"

Alex turned around and stared at his collarbone, then met his steely green gaze. "It's hard to ignore the man who broke into my hotel room." She passed him to gather her things.

"Where are you going now? What about finding Fletch?" He followed her out of the room.

She looked over her shoulder. "I'm going home to tell my family what's happened. Do you have a problem with that?"

"Yes," he snapped and swung his keys around his finger. "Casey's pregnant!"

She hit the down button for the elevator. "I'm well

aware of that, thank you very much." It was another reason she'd given in to finding Fletcher. Her big sister was having a baby. Looking back, it wasn't hard to imagine Casey being a mother. She had taken care of Alexandra from the moment they met at the home for orphaned and abandoned children, and when Fletcher was put in their care, Casey hadn't hesitated; she was a natural protector.

The elevator dinged, and she stepped inside. Jacob crowded in next to her, even though they were the only two occupants. His woodsy, masculine scent filled the small compartment, and Alex closed her eyes. Did he have to smell so enticing? Not that she would *ever* be tempted by the likes of Jacob Keller, but—

He nudged her with his elbow. "*And* Charlie's pregnant."

She looked him up and down and stepped off the elevator. "Aren't we a fount of information." Charlie's pregnancy had been the tipping factor in her decision to take on this manhunt, or sister hunt, as it were. She was thrilled at the idea of becoming an aunt to two more children. With both her sisters pregnant—

"What I'm trying to say is, Fletcher being taken, or whatever in the hell is going on, might add a lot of undue stress on your sisters."

She paused for a moment, then headed to her SUV. "What *is* your point?"

"Why add stress? Listen," he began, shifting from booted foot to booted foot. "I'm sorry for what I said, okay? I was out of line. I just want to find the kid."

"Why? What makes you so gung-ho to find my sister?" She stored her suitcase in the back seat and waited while he squirmed.

"She's my friend."

Alex rose a brow.

"I swear on my dick, there's nothing sexual going on. I'm almost ten years older than her for one. And the other—"

"There's no need for you to swear on your anatomy; I believe you."

He scratched his bearded jaw. "You do?"

"Yes." She sighed. "Fletcher has this annoying habit of drawing the white knight out of men. Your ilk seem burdened with an incessant need to protect her, which is ridiculous considering she's more than capable of taking care of herself. I mean, even the people who want to protect her are intimidated by her." That made Alex smile, on the inside at least. Her sister was a force to be reckoned with.

"Yeah, I know," Jake grumbled, then snapped his fingers. "Noah Reed! If anyone hates the kid, it's him."

Noah had lived in their hometown of Blue Creek for several years. He had taken over as sheriff and had been a homicide detective before that. "True, which is why he wouldn't want to be stuck with her. So, no, it's not Noah."

"You're right. Damn!" He shoved his hands into his back pockets. "It sounded good. What with him dating the McKays' worst enemy."

Alex cocked her head to the side. "You *are* well informed." Noah was dating Marylou Thomas, the wicked bitch of the west side of the creek. Marylou was, and would always be, the McKay sisters' worst enemy. And the airhead had some misguided notion that Alexandra was her best friend. Go figure.

"Yeah, Ryan told me all about the rift between your family and the Thomases."

She shivered and pulled the sleeves of her sweater

over her cold fingers. “It’s not been as bad since Mr. Thomas died.”

“That’s the guy Casey calls the Prince of Darkness, right?”

“The very same.” The McKays and Thomases had both been founders of Blue Creek, but challenges of the depression revealed the true character of the Thomas family. Like many of his predecessors, Ian Thomas had been both vile and cruel.

Jacob made a production of stretching. “Maybe we should go back to Blue Creek and see if the kid left any leads in her cabin.”

She crossed her arms over her chest. “*We?*”

He nodded. “But we have to figure out a way to keep Casey and Charlie out of the loop.”

“Do you realize when they find out we’ve kept things from them they’re going to go ballistic and it’s going to be on your head?” Truth be told, she liked the idea, especially the part where it wouldn’t be her fault. Because when Casey found out she’d kill him.

He tapped at the pavement with the toe of his boot. “Casey can’t stand me anyway.”

She eyed him. “If you’re sure. I’ll meet you there,” she said and got in her vehicle.

****

It was a five hour drive southwest from Jake’s condo, so it was late evening by the time he pulled into the small parking lot at Granny Vaughn’s. The princess had turned her grandmother’s old estate into a picturesque B and B. Ryan had told him Alex used a good chunk of the inheritance her grandparents left her to renovate the house; a damn good investment if you asked him. He loved the place, though he’d never admit it to *her*. It was warm and welcoming, which threw Jake because Alexandra was an ice princess…or at least she was to him. Though, sometimes he had a feeling—

His phone beeped. His brother texted he was on his way. Ryan had not been happy, and Jake couldn't blame him. He'd promised his brother he would look after the kid. Hell, he'd been gone when the shit hit the fan, so there hadn't been much he could do.

He grabbed his duffel bag out of the back seat, along with the bag he'd stuck Fletcher's things in, and climbed the back-porch steps. He needed a shower and a change of clothes.

His gaze landed on her highness the minute the door closed behind him. She was wearing a long skirt and a pink sweater. Her dark red hair was in some sort of twist thing, and she didn't look pissed to see him. He almost smiled.

She looked up from preparing coffee. "How was your drive?"

"Long. Ryan's on his way; do you think I have time to shower?"

She wrinkled her nose. "Yes. Pick whichever room you'd like; they're all available."

He paused midstep. "Is business bad?"

"No, I can't have guests when I'm not here. So until Fletcher's found, I'm closed."

When she didn't go into further detail, he nodded and raced up the steps.

Ten minutes later, Jake was showered and back downstairs. His brother sat across from Alexandra at the kitchen table and was drinking coffee. Jake nodded at Ryan, then fixed his own cup and took a seat next to his brother. He sipped from his mug, savoring the hot liquid; Alex made the best coffee.

"So," Ryan began, "you said you fucked up. What

exactly did you do?"

Jake took a breath—

"We need to wait for the others," Alex said.

Jake glared at her. "What others?"

"Just because we aren't telling Casey and Charlie, doesn't mean we're *only* telling Ryan."

His rebuttal died on his lips when the door opened and in walked Craig Sutton, Emmit McKay, and Jasper Hart. Jake shook Craig's hand as the others got coffee. He had liked Craig from the moment they'd met. The guy was a couple of inches shorter than Jake and Ryan, but he was built like a tank. A former member of SWAT, Craig had been a renowned security expert before selling his business and moving to BFE to run a bar.

Emmit was in his mid-fifties with black hair that was grayer than the last time Jake had seen him, but his blue-gray eyes were keen. This father of five had once been an FBI sharpshooter, and Jake deemed him a forced to be reckoned with both inside and outside of this small-ass town.

Jake shook hands with Jasper last. The man was somewhere in his sixties, and he looked it. His military short hair was white, and his green-blue eyes were weary. He'd been sheriff of this place for thirty-some years until the ice princess had made him feel unworthy of the title. Jake had a fondness for the man because the kid did. Despite his short, wiry stature, Jasper Hart was one tough SOB.

"All right, Alexandra, we're all here. Tell us what's happening now," Emmit said.

Jake looked at Alex. "I'll go first, if that's okay with you?"

"Go ahead." Alexandra sipped her coffee while

Jake filled in the others. It wasn't much, but hopefully someone would see a clue they hadn't.

She glanced at Ryan; Alex always got a kick from the Keller twins being together. They were identical, tall and handsome, with dark brown hair and steely green eyes, but where Jacob was all caveman, Ryan was all class. He didn't wear Armani as much since marrying Alex's sister, but the polish hadn't worn off. He was a prince among men.

Craig patted her arm; it was his way of showing support and a show of affection she was still getting used to. It didn't feel like it, but a few months ago she hadn't known Craig existed. Now, not only was he engaged to Charlie, but he had also given Alexandra something she never thought she'd have. A blood connection. From the moment she'd been adopted, being a part of the McKay family meant everything to her, but then Craig had revealed he was her brother, and that mattered a great deal too.

The charms on her bracelet jingled when she fiddled with it to avoid making eye contact with Jasper. Even if she never admitted it out loud, she was ashamed of how she'd treated him. He had retired from the job he loved and now tended bar for Craig. Though he had said many times he enjoyed being a barkeep, there was a sorrow on his wrinkled face that she'd help put there.

Her father kept glancing her way like he had when she was a child and had used one of his ties as a hair bow. Obviously he was disappointed in her; both her parents were. Again.

"I swear that girl is a magnet for craziness," Jasper said once Jake had finished.

"I second that," Emmit said. "And we don't have a damn thing to go on but speculation and what she left behind."

Ryan shook his head. "That's not completely true, Emmit. We know *she* knows who she's with, or at least they know her, and she doesn't want to be there. I think I should say something to Casey."

Jake frowned. "We—"

"What good would it do, Ryan?" Jasper began. "Besides, she doesn't need all the added worry in her condition. And don't you get any ideas, Craig—Charlie doesn't need any more on her plate either."

"I don't want to go behind anyone's back, but Jasper's right," Jake said. "What we need to do is go to the kid's cabin and see if we can find anything useful."

"Charlie already searched Fletcher's cabin, Jacob," Alex said. "All she found were files on Rick Randle's murder. And we know who did that, but that's a dead end too." She shook her head, then got up to top off everyone's coffee.

A few years ago, Charlie had gotten pregnant, but she hadn't told anyone who the father was. Fletcher, being Fletcher and unable to keep her nose out of Charlie's business, started looking into who it could have been—setting off a deadly chain of events in the process. It was discovered that Rick Randle, who had married and divorced Marylou Thomas to get the Thomases' fortune, was the father of Charlie's daughter Mackenzie. Rick never met or claimed his daughter; he'd been murdered during a robbery—or so everyone thought—but, once again, Fletcher kept digging.

"Jake, did Fletcher happen to mention anything about her relationship with Rick's brother Daemon?" Craig asked.

Her gaze shot to Jacob, who squirmed. Daemon Randle had been a smart, devilishly handsome man, who was well liked by the community. Unfortunately, like his brother, he'd not been the person he portrayed.

Her father motioned with his mug. "If you have any information, it may help."

"We know she was investigating him, but he found out, so she flipped the script and started seeing him. He asked her to marry him, then a week or so later he killed himself," Alex said.

Jacob stretched his neck. "All I know is what she *didn't* say."

"What the hell does that mean?" her father asked.

Ryan patted Jacob's shoulder. "I realize you hate to break a confidence, but we need to know."

"She told me about her investigating him and blah, blah, blah. But when she talked about the guy, she got this strange look on her face, and she never said how she felt about him. Talked about the man like he was a character on that TV show of hers. And that's only when she talked about it."

"His death was ruled a suicide, but she claimed it was murder," Jasper mumbled.

"She said something like that to me too, but that's a dead end."

"I agree, Jacob," Alex said with a sigh. "There's no need to unearth the past."

Ryan picked at the floral placemat in front of him. "Where do we go from here?"

"I have no idea." And she didn't. "I would like to point out that whoever she's with knew where she was. Which means they had to have been following her."

"Fletch is a trained deputy and an expert tracker, dagnabbit," Jasper began. "She would've known if someone was following her. She had a sixth sense about things like that."

Jacob sat up straighter. "Exactly! If she knew she was being followed, why didn't she do something about it?"

"That's the million-dollar question," Alex said.

Emmit stood. "Maybe we should sleep on it."

"Probably best," Jasper said.

Alex walked her father to his vehicle, hugged him good-bye, then waved until he pulled out of sight. She turned when the door of Jasper's beat-up old pickup truck screeched open. "Jasper?"

He shifted from foot to foot. "What can I do for yah, Alexandra?"

She moved next to him. "I want to apologize." She probably wouldn't have voiced her sorrow if Craig hadn't encouraged her to.

He patted her shoulder. "I don't think there's any cause for that."

"I do…I *am* sorry. If I hadn't accused you of being involved, none of this would be happening."

"That ain't necessarily true." He crossed his arms over his chest. "I was gonna retire anyway; after that mild heart attack, I realized I needed to take a step back. And you said it yourself, whoever's with Fletch has been following her. More than likely it would've happened either way. As for the accusations, I'll admit I was hurt. Mrs. Hart—God rest her soul—and I couldn't have kids, and you girls were the closest thing to that for us. So, yes, I was hurt, but I may have come to the same conclusions in your shoes."

"Thank you." She hadn't expected him to let her off the hook so easily, but she was grateful.

He nodded and got into his truck.

She put her hand on the door before he could close it. "I know you love Fletcher." She didn't know why she said it, and by the blanch on his face he wished she hadn't as well.

He nodded. "She's been my right hand a lot of years now. But it's more than that, Alexandra, it's your family. I wouldn't ever do anything to hurt or hinder you McKays. I've known your dad all his life, and we've been good friends for years; there ain't a man I respect more. Look, we all do what it is we can in this life. Our choices aren't always good, but they aren't always bad neither—we're human." He started the engine. "And despite popular belief, so are you."

Alex rubbed her arms to ward off the chill and waited until the truck's taillights faded before she headed in. She ran into Craig on the porch steps and accepted his hug.

"Feel better now?"

"I guess. He doesn't blame me—"

"And that surprises you?"

She nodded. "It does. You and he are the only ones who don't." She let go of her brother and glanced into the kitchen. The Kellers had their heads together.

"Charlie doesn't blame you, Alex. She wants you to resolve this rift with Fletcher. You know Charlie." Craig smiled.

"Yes, always the peacekeeper." Alex followed him inside. She narrowed her eyes when Ryan and Jake stopped talking.

"Did Jasper leave?" Ryan asked.

Alex nodded. "He's closing the bar tonight."

"Hard to believe the old man's running a bar." Jake shook his head and sipped his coffee.

"Surprisingly, he's the best bartender I've ever seen. Even better than my old man was," Craig said. He handed his empty cup to Alex, who began loading the dishwasher.

"Your father owned his own place, right?" Jacob asked.

"Yep, that's how I learned about the business." Craig shrugged. "I grew up above his bar."

Alex closed the machine and started to clear the table while the men talked.

Jacob grinned. "Our grandfather liked his bourbon, remember, Ryan?"

"Yeah," Ryan said and handed Alex the placemat in front of him. "He'd go into his study after dinner and pour two fingers. It drove Grandmother bonkers." Ryan laughed. "Of course, Granddad always said if an issue couldn't be settled over a bottle of bourbon, then it couldn't be settled."

Alex dropped the placemats in the kitchen laundry basket and smiled to herself. Her own grandfather had preferred whiskey; though, after a horrid little fiasco, he had limited his intake. Her father, on the other hand, was a beer man through and through. She reached under the sink for the multipurpose spray and a rag.

Craig scooted back in his chair, so she could wipe down the table, and asked the Kellers, "You two were raised by your grandparents?"

"Our folks died when we were kids, and Granddad and Grandmother took us in…raised us. They've been gone…what, Ryan, ten years now?"

"About that." Ryan looked at his watch. "I need to get going."

Alexandra set her cleaning supplies on the counter, turning in time to wave at Ryan before he closed the door.

Craig stood. "I guess I'll head on home too."

"You and Charlie's house finished?" Jacob asked

standing.

Craig smirked. “Just.”

“It turned out even more lovely than the original,” Alex said. Charlie’s first home had been destroyed by fire, so she’d had to rebuild. Alex loved the new house.

“Yeah, we’re happy with it…and with the baby coming—”

“The timing’s perfect.” Alex smiled. “Otherwise you’d all be stuck in the apartment above my garage.”

“Hey,” Craig began, “don’t knock the apartment. Some pivotal moments happened for me there.” He kissed her cheek, shook Jake’s hand, and left with a wave.

Alex turned to Jacob the second they were alone. “You told Ryan to talk to Casey, didn’t you?”

“First, if we tell her now, she can’t be too pissed, and second, she might see something we don’t. There were six of us here, and we got zilch.”

“Oh, and you think Casey won’t—never mind.” Usually, Alex enjoyed a good argument, but there’d be plenty of that tomorrow. She pushed the chairs in around the table. Maybe she should go to bed; it was still early, but she didn’t know what else she could do.

Jake rubbed his abdomen. “You got any food here? I’m starving.”

“No, I hadn’t planned on being home so soon. I mean, there are eggs in the refrigerator and the freezer’s stocked, but I don’t cook.” She shrugged a shoulder. “Charlie prepares meals for my guests.”

“I can whip something up,” he said, pulling things out of her freezer.

She stared at him. Hadn’t he seen her cleaning the kitchen? Everything was put away and in its place.

His gaze me hers. “You hungry?”

Her stomach rumbled. “I guess.”

Chapter Three

The next morning Alexandra found Casey waiting in the kitchen. Casey had always been more exotic in looks than the rest of them. Her wavy black hair touched her lower back, her skin had a dusky hue, and her eyes were a strange shade of violet. Her coveralls were a lovely berry color, which matched the tinge in her cheeks. Wonderful.

Alex went to pour herself some coffee, thankful for remembering to set the automatic timer before she went to bed last night. "Good morning."

"I don't know what's so 'good' about it."

Alex drank from her mug and took a seat across from her sister. "Ryan told you what's happened."

Casey snorted. "Did you really think he wouldn't?"

Alex pretended to study her manicure. "Should I be expecting Charlie soon?"

"She's already at the diner."

"I should probably make a trip out to see her then."

Casey pursed her lips. "Probably."

"Will you please get to the yelling already?" Alex drummed her nails against the table in a small tattoo. "I can't handle the suspense."

"I'm not gonna yell—"

Alexandra widened her eyes with dramatic flair. "Really?"

Casey rolled her shoulders. "No, though I have every right to be royally pissed. Fletcher's been taken, and you weren't even gonna tell me. If Ryan wasn't worried about what the added stress could do, I'd find—"

"We don't even know if there *is* a threat. Think about it; Fletcher could have written the note to throw us off her trail."

Casey took a hair tie off her wrist and twisted her locks into a sloppy bun. "If she wanted to take off, she could have with no one the wiser. She wouldn't leave a note or her things—especially that damn locket."

"A mere suggestion." The locket is what worried Alex the most, but she wouldn't say so.

"Yeah, well, it sucked!"

Alex refused to be amused. "Thank you ever so much. If you had told me where she was in the first place, maybe this could have been prevented."

Her sister squirmed. "I didn't know exactly where she was, Miss Priss. Ryan only knew that she was staying with Jake, but he wasn't sure where that was. So I knew as much as—"

They both looked up as Jacob came in.

"Peachy," Casey grumbled. "Now my morning's complete."

"Ladies," Jake drawled and walked bare-chested to the coffeepot.

Alex stared at him as he poured himself a cup. Heat spread through her body. His chest was…umm—

"What?"

She gave herself a hard shake. "In this house, it is not appropriate to come downstairs without being fully attired," she said in the haughtiest tone she could muster, knowing it would amuse her sister.

"Excuse the fuck outta me, princess. I didn't get a copy of the rules!" He stomped off, then came back wearing a T-shirt.

Casey chuckled.

"Thank you," Alex said.

Jacob opened the fridge. "What's for breakfast?"

"Is that all you think about?"

"A man's gotta eat…I'll make something," Jake said pulling out eggs. "You hungry?"

"Yes, actually. Have you eaten, Casey?" Her sister looked suspicious, so Alex assured her sister that Jacob was a good cook. Surprisingly so.

Casey shifted in her seat. "I'm always hungry lately." The topic turned to the impending birth until they'd finished their pancakes, then Casey asked, "What's the plan?"

"I don't have a plan yet," Alex said, loading the dishwasher.

"I say we search Fletcher's cabin. I know you said Charlie had already been there, but she might have missed something. It's worth a try," he added when Alex shook her head.

"That sounds like a place to start," Casey said. The legs of the chair scraped the floor when she stood. "I need to get to the garage before my crew thinks they have full run of the place. And don't forget to go see Charlie, Alex."

"Pushy, ain't she?" Jake said once Casey was gone.

"You have no idea." Alex took her seat and asked Jacob why he was staring at her.

"You've got a little bit of syrup…" He touched the corner of his mouth.

Alexandra sucked in her bottom lip, savored the sweetness, then dabbed at it with a napkin. "Did I get it?"

He stared at her another moment, then cleared his

throat. “Yeah.”

Her cheeks heated, and she ran a hand over the soft skirt of her dress. “Do you need me to go to the cabin with you?”

“Nah, Ryan’s coming with me.”

“All right, I’ll go talk to Charlie before my phone starts ringing nonstop.”

“Sounds good. I’ll meet you back here later.” Jake gave her a mock salute and left the room.

She let out a breath and reminded herself of the plethora of reasons she couldn’t stand Jacob Keller.

****

Alex walked into the diner and waved at Charlie, who was waiting on a customer. Her sister and best friend was a petite woman with curly blonde hair and the friendliest brown eyes Alex had ever encountered. She was “the girl next door” to a T with her apple cheeks and sweet smile.

The diner had originally been called Ida Mae’s after the owner and town gossip Ida Mae. Their mother had bought the diner from the older woman years ago and renamed it McKay’s. Charlie owned and managed the place now, and it was better than ever.

The countertop was long and stainless steel. The stools and booths were topped with red vinyl, and the tables between the counter and booths were set for parties of two and four. Charlie always had fresh flowers on every table. It was the epitome of what a diner should be, and her sister made sure everyone felt right at home.

“Good morning, *Alexandra*,” Charlie said with exaggerated sweetness.

Alex took her customary seat at the counter and pretended she didn’t know her sister was trying to stay mad at her. "Good morning." Charlie set a cup of coffee in front of her, then went to take another customer their order.

"You have three weeks to find Fletcher before Craig and I go to the justice of the peace," Charlie began. "If I can't have all my sisters at my wedding, I won't have any. Understood?"

"I'm quite familiar with your conditions, Charlie, but circumstances have changed, as you well know, and I don't have the first clue as to where to find her."

Charlie patted her hand. "I know, Alex, but you need to mend your fences with Fletch."

"It's not that easy. We don't know where she is or what's happened—if anything." She told Charlie what she had suggested earlier to Casey.

"Sorry, but she's right, if Fletcher wanted to leave, she'd take off with none of us the wiser. And she never would've left her stuff." Charlie looked past Alex toward the window and jostled the coffee carafe.

Alex turned around and narrowed her eyes. Marylou Thomas was no longer welcome in the McKay diner. Which was fine with Alex; the woman was a parasite. "She can't come in here," Alex reminded her sister. "The restraining order will keep her out."

"Yeah. Noah had a real problem drawing that one up." Charlie smiled, then frowned. "What he sees in that woman is beyond me. Other than her blue eyes, perfect body, and blonde hair, I mean."

"I believe she's on her third boob job, and her hair isn't all hers."

"Really?" Charlie asked, leaning closer. "About the boobs?"

Alex laughed. "It's true. The twit told me all about it, then had the audacity to offer to give me her surgeon's name." Alex looked down at her chest. She was almost a C cup.

Charlie sighed. "You're perfect, and everyone in Blue Creek, including Marylou, knows it."

"Thank you…Where's Mackenzie?" Alex hadn't seen her niece in what felt like forever. She missed the little cherub.

"School, thank goodness. I swear, she has Craig wrapped around her finger." She shook her head.

"She's a McKay and *my* niece; it's only natural for her to have people eating out of the palm of her little hand."

"True, but she can't always have her way. I don't want her to turn into a snob. She already brags about Craig renaming his bar after her, and that's gotten her in plenty of trouble."

"She'll be fine. I'd say not to worry, but I know you too well." She put cream in her coffee and took a sip.

Charlie blushed, then rolled her eyes. "It's true. Now, what are you going to do about Fletcher?"

"Jacob and Ryan are at the cabin as we speak. The sooner we find Fletcher, the sooner that slob will be out of my home." She didn't care if he—

"Lighten up, Alex. Jake wants to find Fletcher as much as we do. He cares about her, and that's important," Charlie said.

Alex sighed. "I'm sure you're right."

Her sister cocked her head to the side, and her eyes widened. "Ohmygod, you like him!"

She almost choked on her coffee. "I do not."

"Yes, you do! You even had that sexy dream about him, remember?"

Heat seared her cheeks, and she shifted on the

stool. Oh, she remembered. It had been one of the most erotic dreams she'd ever had, but—"Remind me not to share my *nightmares* with you."

Her sister snorted. "Nightmare, shnightmare, you think he's hot, and it's making you extra catty."

"Excuse me?" She crossed her arms over her chest. Catty?

Charlie waved her hand in the air. "You know what I mean."

"I do not," she mumbled.

Charlie smirked and pulled out her order pad. "Deny it if you wish, but *I* know you, Alexandra McKay. Now, do you want something to eat?"

Alex shook her head, glad for the topic change, then eyed the order window. Tiny's large frame was at the grill. "I think I'll pass."

Charlie giggled. "He won't burn your food again, if that's what you're worried about."

"I'm not as sure of that as you seem to be. Besides, I'm not really hungry. Jacob fixed breakfast."

"He did?"

"Yeah." She wouldn't go into detail.

"That man is chock full of hidden talents, don'tcha think?" She bobbed her eyebrows and went to refill another customer's coffee.

Alex bit her tongue to stop the "catty" comment from leaving her lips. She wouldn't let what Charlie said bother her; she wasn't attracted to Jacob, she—The bell over the door rang, and Noah Reed walked in. Saved by the bell. She could shift her focus back to the situation at hand: her missing sister.

If there was anyone who didn't care about Fletcher, it was this man. The new sheriff was well over six feet and built like a professional football player. His hair was black, his eyes a peculiar shade of silver, and he had absolutely no love for her little sister.

"Alexandra," he said and took the seat next to her. Crowding her with his muscled bulk and body heat. "I heard you were back in town already. You found her fast."

Charlie put a cup of coffee in front of him.

"I'm back," Alex began with a shrug, "but without Fletcher. It appears she's been taken. Whether or not it was by force remains to be seen."

"Alex," Charlie hissed.

"It's the truth. Besides, Noah *is* the sheriff so he may be able to help."

Noah took a sip of coffee. "Abducted, huh? I find that hard to believe."

"Why do you say that?" Charlie asked in an almost unfriendly tone.

"I can't see your sister going quietly if she didn't want to." He turned when Alex took him through what they knew.

Charlie wiped up the counter. "Now do you get it?"

"I'm sorry to say this, ladies, but I don't give a shit about your sister's disappearance. In fact, I have my own missing person to worry about."

"What? Who?"

Noah glanced at the menu. "Larry Hines."

Alex looked at Charlie. "Did you know Larry Hines was missing?"

Charlie shook her head. "When did this happen?"

"A few days ago. He didn't show up for his retirement party, and people started getting suspicious."

"Do you have any leads?" Charlie wanted to know.

"No, we didn't find anything at his place, and his car's gone. Who knows, he could have finally taken that trip to Europe he's always talking about."

Charlie threw her hands in the air before heading for the kitchen. "Everyone's disappearing!"

Alex turned to Noah. "Do you have any advice on finding my sister, honestly?"

"I would suggest calling the feds, though I'm sure you know that—"

"Have you called the FBI about Larry yet?"

"No, but—"

Alexandra cocked her head to the side. "Why?"

"Because we'd like to handle the situation in house, if at all possible."

She smirked. "Exactly."

"Look, I don't personally care how you go about finding Fletcher. It didn't happen here, so it doesn't affect me." He shrugged his big shoulders. "Besides I have my own search to conduct."

"I know, Noah." She sighed. "I was hoping maybe you'd think of something I didn't."

"Maybe it's for the best she's gone," Noah said almost to himself.

She would never admit she didn't entirely disagree with him.

****

Jake was rummaging through Fletcher's things, hoping to find something to go on. He and Ryan had been searching the small cabin in the middle of the woods for over an hour, and had yet to find anything of importance. The place was nice, and Fletch had built it from the ground up, herself; it was another thing he admired about her. The kid had skills.

"I forgot to ask how things are going with Alex," Ryan said.

Jake looked up from the drawer he'd just opened.

"Fine," he mumbled. It was true, the princess wasn't giving him too much crap, which was a nice change.

"Just 'fine'?"

Jake slammed the drawer shut, making its contents rattle. "That's what I said." In truth, being around Alex was like playing with matches, sometimes there wasn't a spark, other times—whoosh—full flames burst, but in the end, you were always playing with fire. He glanced at Ryan, who was lifting up the cushions on the couch. "Why?"

His brother shrugged. "Just curious."

Jake crossed his arms over his chest. Ryan was never "just curious." There was more to this than his brother was letting on. He opened his mouth to ask what the issue was when Ryan said, "Maybe we should look in the bunker."

"What bunker?" Jake asked, forgetting everything else.

"Fletcher built a bunker for…I'm not sure why exactly. Let's see if I remember how to get into it." Ryan went over to the fireplace and pressed on the third brick from the left. He stepped back, next to Jake as the wall of the fireplace slid apart and a set of steps appeared.

"What the hell?" Jake followed his brother down the steps. The wall slid back in place, and small lights came on. It was warmer and drier than any tunnel he'd had the misfortune of being in; it was more a hallway than anything. He figured they were about seven feet underground, but he didn't feel like the walls were closing in around him.

Ryan punched in the code when they reached a door with a keypad. "It's the date their parents were married."

Inside was a small room with an empty desk and a cot, but that was it. "There isn't anything in here."

"I know, it's just…" Ryan circled around the room.

Jake followed suit. "What?"

"Why would she make the bunker so small? The first time Charlie showed us this place I thought the same thing. I mean, why go to all the trouble?"

"You think there's another door somewhere." Jake grinned. His brother was one smart son of a bitch.

"Exactly. The question is where?" Ryan sat down on the cot.

Jake continued to check out the room. "Okay, we have to think like her. If I were the kid, where would I put a secret entrance?" The small room was filled with pictures of American heroes, Benjamin Franklin, JFK, George Washington, honest Abe, and…Jake cocked his head and pointed to the picture. "Who's that?"

Ryan smirked. "You never paid attention in English class. That's Edgar Allen Poe."

Jake shrugged. "Do you think it's strange that all the other pictures are of presidents except this one?"

The cot creaked. "You do know Benjamin Franklin wasn't a president, right?"

"I know that, fuckface. How dumb do you think I am?" Jake pointed at his brother. "Don't answer that. What I'm saying is all the other pictures are of political figures…all except this guy."

"Yeah," Ryan mumbled. He got to his feet and lifted the picture from the nail. "Nothing."

"No, it's a clue." He took the picture from his brother and started removing the backing.

"Did you find something?"

Jake flipped the small piece of plastic in his hand. "Key card." He set the picture against the wall and began searching for a keypad.

"Let's take a moment to consider this?"

"What for?"

"Fletcher put the key in *that* picture for a reason. And we have to figure out what that reason is."

"Fine, how?"

"I don't need the attitude, Jake!"

He grinned. "I don't get attitudinal."

"Don't be an asshole, then."

Jake snorted. "Poe was a writer, right?"

"Yes, an important writer."

He rubbed his beard. "He wrote creepy shit."

His brother shrugged. "I don't think anyone would disagree with you."

"Yeah, something about a body under the floorboards." Jake shuddered. Creepy shit.

Ryan lifted up first one foot, then the other. " 'The Tell-Tale Heart.' "

"No way it's that easy."

"Think about it. This room is underground and is bound to get cold. Why not put down carpeting to insulate it?" Ryan squatted down on the floor.

"Good point." Jake got down on his knees. "If there is a door here, it would have to be easily accessible," he said annoyed. All the panels looked the same to him.

"True." Ryan sat up. "Do you see anything out of place?"

Jake crawled over the smooth wood floor. "There are two holes here; about a foot away from the desk." He tried using his index finger, but it didn't work. "Nada."

"No, there has to be a way!" Ryan leaned back and knocked into a folded metal chair.

Jake's ears rang from the resounding crash. "Watch what you're doing!"

Ryan massaged his shoulder. "Yeah, yeah."

Jake glared at the offending object. Why was the chair folded at all? He stood. "That's it!"

"What?"

Jake got the chair and stuck two of the legs into the holes. "I'll be damned."

The wood gave a groan of protest, then eight joined planks came up. Ryan helped him remove the slab, setting it aside and out of the way. They both hunched over to see what they had uncovered.

They'd found the door. Bending down, Jake inserted the key card and stood back as the latch unlocked. "She couldn't have built much deeper in the ground, could she?" Jake asked before he took the couple of steps down into the passageway. Christmas lights began to twinkle on. It was cooler in this tunnel than the other had been, and the damp air slithered over his skin; he shivered.

"We're in the mountains and a good deal above sea level, so your guess is as good as mine." Ryan climbed down and stood behind him.

They followed the small corridor until they reached another set of steps. "She must have dug underneath the bunker and then added another space right beside it," Jake mused aloud.

"But why go to all that trouble?"

Jake shrugged and opened the hatch. "Who the hell knows what goes on in that kid's brain." He climbed up into the space, felt around for a switch, and turned on the light. "Now this is a bunker," Jake said and grinned at Ryan.

There was a tiny kitchenette, a bathroom, a cot, and

a decent-sized workspace. The place was fully stocked and functional. He spotted the fridge and took a look inside. “Want a beer?”

Ryan nodded and took one. “Now this”—he swept his hand around the room—“falls under the category of creepy shit.”

“Nah, this falls under para-fucking-noia.”

“Agreed.” They clinked bottles.

Jake pointed to the pictures lining the wall next to the desk. They were of a man with blond hair and hazel eyes. The guy had more of Ryan’s style than his own; he was wearing a suit and his “do” was perfectly styled. “Who’s the douche bag?”

“Daemon Randle.” Ryan shook his head. “You’d think she’d take them down.”

“Maybe she was in mourning or some shit like that.”

“Could be. We don’t know what her feelings were for the man—her real feelings anyway.”

Jake nodded. “True.”

Ryan sat down at the desk and booted up the computer. A picture popped up on the screen.

Jake stood behind his brother and grinned. “That’s the sisters when they were kids, right?”

“Yes. But I’ve never seen this place before.” Ryan pointed to the house behind the girls.

Jake shrugged and sat on the arm of the chair. “What are you waiting for? Let’s see what she’s got in that thing.”

Chapter Four

"Did you find anything?" Alexandra asked Jacob the second he walked through the door. He'd been gone all day, and she'd sat waiting. Well, okay, she'd worked most the time, freshening up some of the rooms, but he didn't need to know that.

"The kid's fucked up." Jake shook his head, went to the fridge, and pulled out one of the beers he'd asked her to buy.

Alex fixed herself an iced tea. "Why do you say that?"

"We went to her cabin and found her bunker—"

"I told you Charlie's been there and didn't find anything important." She got a lemon wedge from the fridge and put it in her tea.

"She didn't find the other room, though, did she?"

She ignored his tone. "What other room?"

Jake explained what he and Ryan had found.

"How does that make her 'fucked up'?" Clever? Sure, Alex admired that.

"The office was covered with pictures of Daemon Randle." Jake shook his head.

She took a sip of tea, then said, "And?"

"He was shady as fuck," Casey said.

Alex turned as her sister and brother-in-law came into the kitchen. "How did you get here so fast?" Alex looked at Jake.

"I stopped by the store first. Let me go get the

groceries, and then we'll talk," Jake said, grabbing his brother's arm as he went.

"Do you know what's going on?" Alex asked her sister. Casey looked like she was going to throw up, which was nothing new lately, but still.

"No, Ryan said Daemon did shit to Fletcher's head. I called Charlie, and she's headed over. Craig's at the bar, so she's leaving Mack with Ma."

"Is Dad coming?"

"What do you think?" Casey sneered, then sighed. "Sorry, I'm in a piss-poor mood."

"Okay." Alex pulled out a chair and motioned for her sister to sit. Casey wasn't known to apologize, so she must not be feeling well. "Should I make some coffee or something?"

"I'll do it," Jake said, coming back in. Both his and his brother's arms were loaded down with bags.

Alex's brow pinched. "All right." What in the world was going on?

Half an hour later, Emmit and Charlie arrived with Jasper coming in behind them. Jake had the table loaded down with mac 'n' cheese bites, potato skins, vegetable truffles, and some kind of chicken dip, all of which he'd made from scratch. Once everyone had taken a seat and Alex had given them a drink, Jake suggested they eat first. No one argued.

Charlie popped a pimento puff in her mouth. "Jake, if you ever need a job…please, please, come see me at the diner."

"She's right, Jake. You have a talent for food," Emmit said.

Alex stood and began clearing plates. Jake didn't understand her. Couldn't she sit and chill for a couple minutes? They'd only just finished eating, and people were still picking at the food. He swatted at her hand when she moved to take his plate. She narrowed her eyes at him, but he only grinned.

"Now that our bellies are full, tell us what you boys found," Jasper prodded and handed his plate to Alex.

"Ryan, you start," Jake suggested. Should he help Alex? Maybe put the leftovers away? He caught her eye, and she glared at him. Fine, let her do it. He sat back while his brother explained finding the bunker within the bunker.

"We hit pay dirt once we booted up her computer," Ryan said.

Jake picked at the label on his beer. "I'll warn you, there was some crazy shit in her files."

Jasper's coffee sloshed out of his mug when he sat up. "What do you mean by 'crazy'?"

Jake threw his cloth napkin on the spill, winning him another glare from her highness. "She kept video surveillance of Daemon Randle." He got up and got another beer and let that bit of information sink in. He wouldn't tell them everything; hell, he wished he hadn't seen it himself.

"But Daemon's dead, so does that matter?" Charlie asked.

Jake reclaimed his seat. "No, but on the footage we saw another man—"

"We couldn't make out his face, but the video surveillance caught him lurking around both Daemon and Fletcher's places," Ryan said.

Jake nodded. "We also found emails she'd saved from someone named Dan. The emails began the day of Daemon's death and claimed that it was murder, not suicide. Fletch had made a note that Dan was possibly the man in the video."

Emmit handed his empty plate to Alex. "What good does that do us?"

"Noah and I both looked at Daemon's autopsy," Jasper began, "and it seemed like a textbook case of suicide. So if murder was the real cause of death, the only person who could know that would be the murderer."

"Dan," the sisters said in unison.

"They sound like us, bro." Jake grinned at his brother, then moved on. "We called a friend to get us information on Dan."

"Uncle Marty?" Casey guessed.

"Who's Uncle Marty?"

"You remember, Jasper," Alex began from where she was loading the dishwasher, "you met him at Casey and Ryan's wedding. Big Scottish gentleman."

Charlie giggled. "The one wearing the kilt."

"Oh, yeah," Jasper said.

"Yep, Uncle Marty." Jake nodded. Marty, was their self-appointed uncle, who would do anything for them, and had.

"He may seem loony, but Uncle Marty has killer connections. Don't ask how; he won't even share that information with us," Ryan said.

"We should know who this guy is by breakfast." Jake got up and handed the princess his plate, then got a beer for Ryan when he asked.

"And you two think this is the man who has Fletcher?"

Jake reclaimed his seat next to his brother and handed him the bottle. Ryan said, "What we do know, Emmit, is that she saved the emails she wrote to him, and she always signed Jamie at the end."

"So," Emmit grumbled, "we wait."

"Yeah."

"All right, we wait. Now what else did you find? And don't even try to deny you found more than you're saying, Ryan Keller, because I won't believe it. You looked sick when you picked me up. Now spill your guts!" Casey said.

"Honey, please calm down. I was going to tell you later…" Ryan whispered, then winced.

"Tell her what?" Alex closed the dishwasher and stepped back to the table. She pointed at Jake. "You, spill."

"It's not my place—"

"Tell us what's going on," Emmit demanded.

"It's the kid's business," Jake said shifting in his seat.

Jasper pointed to Ryan. "You tell us."

Charlie pulled Alex down in the chair next to her. "Please."

"I'm sorry, Jake," Ryan said.

Jake grunted, then decided putting away the leftovers was a good idea.

"We figure Fletcher must have confiscated the video surveillance we found on her computer from Daemon Randle. Apparently, the man had been watching her for months. He, ah, taped the two of them—" Ryan cleared his throat. "That is, Daemon taped Fletcher and himself during intimate moments…"

"The man was one sick son of a bitch!" Jake said, slinging food into the containers for emphasis.

"What do you mean by that?" Casey asked.

"What he means is…well, what we saw…" Ryan stumbled over his words.

Emmit shifted in his seat. "What do you consider 'sick'?"

"It wasn't right," Jake said.

"People have different sexual preferences," Charlie said, her cheeks turning bright red.

"That may be true, Charlie, but I don't think it normal for someone to give their partner a drug before the fact," Ryan said.

Casey jumped. "What do you mean 'drug'?"

Alex shook her head. "No, Fletcher told Charlie she was—"

"That's right! I asked Fletch if she was intimate with Daemon and she said yes," Charlie told the table.

Ryan took his wife's hand. "What Jake means is Daemon slipped something into her drink and he taped the entire thing."

"Okay, so maybe she didn't know he slipped her drugs until she got the tapes," Alex suggested. "But when did she get them? And what did she do when she found out?"

Charlie sucked in a breath. "Oh, God!"

"It would make some kind of sense." Alex didn't know what to think.

"The kid didn't kill anyone," Jake shouted. "She would cut out her heart and give it to any one of you if you fucking asked her to. All she talked about is my family this and my sisters that. And you people think she's capable of murdering someone in cold blood. Well, fuck you. I'll find her my own damn self and keep her the hell away from here." Jake slammed out of the room.

"I think we all need to calm down."

Casey stood up. "You calm down, Alexandra. I'm with Jake on this. Fletcher didn't kill that psycho, no way in hell. I'm pretty sure she thought she was in love with the sick bastard; she wouldn't have killed him."

Ryan got to his feet. "I don't think so either."

"Pops?"

Emmit rubbed his hands over his face.

Casey turned. "Jasper?"

"I don't know what to think right this second. I…I don't feel too good. I'm gonna head on home."

"Charlie?" Casey asked after Jasper left.

"I don't want to think she killed him, but we all know she's capable." Charlie winced.

"I won't even ask you, Alex. We all know what you think. But who are you to judge? You've killed two people. Self-defense or not, we all know it."

Alexandra's stomach rolled, but she didn't say anything when Casey took Ryan by the sleeve and went out the door.

"Well…" Charlie cleared her throat. "That sure took a turn, didn't it?" Standing up, she hugged her father and kissed Alex's cheek. "I need to go talk to Craig." She gave a small sigh and left.

"It's just you and me now." Alex smiled at her father. Casey's words had hurt, but Alexandra McKay would not give that away.

"I don't believe she killed that man," her father mumbled.

"Then why didn't you say so?" She should have known. Her father wouldn't think such a thing. And why the hell hadn't he defended her? Did he feel the sa—

"This might have gone beyond your notice, but I'm having trouble absorbing all this." Emmit's tone was rough. "I don't know how the hell I'm going to tell your mother."

Alex was about to say something, when Ryan came running inside.

"Jasper's collapsed!"

****

Jacob couldn't seem to stop fidgeting. First, he picked up a magazine, then put it down for another; he got up, paced around, then finally took another seat. What in the world was his problem? Why did it matter? Alex sighed and pinched the bridge of her nose hoping to ward off the headache forming behind her eyes.

She sent Jacob a glare when he switched seats yet again; he returned her look then made a point of staring at her parents, who were deep in discussion. Jacob Keller couldn't possibly understand their family. The McKays were a group of misfits. Orphans. All except their father and little brother Jebbediah.

Alex smiled on the inside. She loved her family. She was glad Ryan had taken Casey home; the last thing they needed was to make some big scene in the hospital. Charlie was with Jebb and her daughter; Craig was still at work. So here she was sitting with her parents and Jacob. Oh, goody.

"Are any of you here for Jasper Hart?" a doctor asked.

"We are!" Her father and mother stood.

"Family?"

"Yes, we're his family!" her mother's tone dared anyone to say different. Savannah McKay was lovely woman; small in stature, with honey blonde hair, and beautiful sapphire eyes. But it was her fire—her fierceness—that Alexandra admired. Both of which her mother was presenting now. No one messed with their family.

The doctor nodded. "Mr. Hart had another heart attack; this one was worse than the previous one, and he needs surgery. We're preparing him for an angioplasty now."

"Angioplasty?" her father asked.

"Yes," the doctor began, "there are blockages in his arteries and we need to restore blood flow to his heart."

Her mother paled. "Open heart surgery?"

"No," the doctor assured her. "We can fix the blockages without opening his chest. We'll go in with a catheter through a blood vessel…"

"That's a common procedure, isn't it?" Alex asked after the doctor finished explaining the process.

"Yes," the doctor said. "He'll be in the hospital for a couple days at least, but he'll be in much better shape over all."

Emmit put his arm around his wife. "That's good news then."

"It is." The doctor turned toward Alex. "I know you from somewhere, don't I?"

"You helped my sister a while ago."

The doctor's eyes widened, and his cheeks reddened. "Yes," he said and cleared his throat. "Well, ah, the procedure takes several hours, so you should all go home and get some sleep. You can visit Mr. Hart in the morning."

"Thank you," Emmit said as the doctor made a hasty retreat. He looked at Alex. "What was all that about?"

"He's the doctor who treated Fletcher after she'd been drugged."

"I don't remember him," Savannah said.

"He's an ER doctor, so your guess is as good as mine. Now I'm going to take his advice and go home. Are you two coming?" she asked, getting her purse.

"I want to ask the nurse a few questions and then

we'll leave," Savannah said.

Her father kissed her temple. "We'll talk in the morning."

"All right. Bye."

Alex wasn't surprised when Jake followed her into the elevator. Annoyed, but not surprised.

The elevator doors slid closed, and he turned toward her. "What was the thing with the doc really about?"

She sighed. "While I was visiting Fletcher, he made me a proposition and I turned him down."

"Oh," Jake said, shifting from foot to foot. "So, princess, tell me why you're such a—"

"Don't you dare!" Alex hissed.

"Oh, come on, Alexandra. You get off on messing with people's heads—like that doc. Admit it. You like to fuck with people." Jake caged her in.

His woodsy scent filled her nostrils, and his body heat embraced her, but she ignored both. The nerve! "I'll admit no such thing."

"Tell me the truth. Why do you hate the kid?"

She seethed. "I do not hate my sister."

"Oh…now you're lying to me, sweetheart."

She glared at him, then her eyes widened at the heat in his gaze. A different kind of heat... He moved a loose tendril of hair behind her ear and she froze.

"Here I go, playing with matches," he murmured, then kissed her.

Alex sucked in a startled breath, then opened her mouth to his. Accepted his tongue as he thrust it inside. Jacob's beard caressed her skin like a cashmere scarf, more seductive than Alexandra could have imagined. He tasted like beer and something else, but she didn't even care. She wrapped her arms around his head and kissed him back. She relished the solid feel of him; she couldn't help it, from the first time she'd seen him, to the erotic dream she'd had, Jacob was…she was kissing Jacob! *Oh, shit.* Alex opened her eyes and looked right into his. Realizing her mistake, she took hold of his shoulders and lifted her knee right into his crotch.

He grunted and grabbed himself. "What in the hell did you do that for?"

"I wanted to knock some sense into you and figured your brain was the best place." The look on his face was priceless. She hopped out of the elevator as soon as the doors opened. And didn't fan herself until she was out of sight. Whew.

Chapter Five

Kissing Alex had been a mistake, stimulating, but stupid nonetheless. Hospitals made him edgy, and he'd needed an outlet—wrong move. Jake shook his head and took his duffel bag out of the back of his luxury SUV.

He wasn't about to stay in the same house with *Ms. Alexandra McKay*. Nope, he decided staying at the kid's cabin was a better idea. Besides, he'd let her stay at his place—fair was fair. Hopefully, Uncle Marty would have something for him tomorrow, and Jake could get the hell out of here.

He unlocked the door, dropped his bag, and hit the light. He figured he could go through the bunker and her computer again to see if they'd missed anything. If Daemon Randle wasn't already dead, Jake would kill the bastard. Slowly.

When he finally made it down to the second level, he turned on the computer and took a beer from the kid's fridge. He sat down and checked his personal email to see if Uncle Marty had found anything yet.

He choked on his beer. The kid had emailed him.

Jake,

I hope you and your fiancée are speaking again. I told you keeping secrets hidden from those you love is a load of bunk. Buy her a present, a book by Edgar Allan Poe, maybe? I know how you feel about Summer, but don't judge her too harshly or let guilt lodge itself in your heart. Maybe you should take her on a treasure hunt. Oftentimes the key to finding truth is to figure out where your heart lies. Nothing new here. I'm well if not a little antsy.

Jamie

"Okay, kid, what the fuck are you trying to tell me?" Jake glanced at the clock on the monitor and swore. He knew better than to call Ryan this late. He printed out the email and reread it.

He smiled. Jake couldn't deny the kid's wily mind. Using "hidden secrets," "bunk," and "Edgar Allan Poe." She was leading him to the hidden room. *We're one step ahead of you there, kid.*

He didn't have a fiancée and didn't know anyone named Summer either; maybe her sisters did. Jake wondered if he should march right over to Alexandra's and wake Sleeping Beauty? Squeezing his thighs at the memory of their last meeting, he decided against it. The kid said she was doing "well," which was a relief.

Jake clicked back to his inbox; no one else had emailed him. Wait! If she was able to send out an email, maybe she could receive one as well. What could he write? He needed to be smart about it. Jake killed his beer and began to type.

Jamie,

Poe is a great idea. I remember reading "The Tell-Tale Heart" in high school; that was some story. As for Summer, I feel like I don't know who she is anymore. Which worries me. But I'll talk to Ryan and see if he has any ideas. Hope to see you soon.

Jake

He hit the send button and sent up a prayer that she'd get his message. He didn't know if she was being watched or whatever. In fact, he didn't know what the hell was going on. He kicked off his boots, lay on the cot, and went over the email again.

The incessant ringing of his phone woke him the next morning. Grunting, Jake reached into his pocket; a picture of his uncle filled the screen.

He sat up and rubbed his face. “Marty, you find anything?”

“Good morning to you too, boyo. I’m sorry to say, but no.”

“Seriously?” Jake jumped to his feet. He’d been so sure Uncle Marty would find something. Anything.

“I’m not sure what you boys have stumbled onto this time, but I couldn’t find a damn thing. Whoever this ‘Dan’ is, his email is a dummy account; it can’t be directly traced to an IP address, and the only person he ever emailed was Fletcher.”

“Damn!” Marty had amazing connections. If he couldn’t find anything…

“I’m sorry, boyo. Maybe if I had more to go on.”

“Yeah, I know you tried.” Jake paced between the cot and the office, then stopped. “Do you think you could trace where an email was sent from?” Jake smiled at Marty’s deep laugh.

“I can surely try; just forward it to me, and I’ll do the rest,” he said, and the line went dead.

Jake forwarded the kid’s email to his uncle, then glanced at his watch. Breakfast time.

He parked his vehicle right beside the screened-in porch of the B and B—more to annoy the princess than for convenience. Jake walked inside and stopped on a dime. “Good morning.”

Savannah McKay turned from where she stood at the counter. “Good morning, Jake. Alexandra is still asleep, so I figured I would go ahead and make some coffee. Would you like some?"

Jake smiled. "I wouldn't say no."

She motioned for him to sit, poured them both a mug, then took a seat across from him.

He took the coffee. "Thanks."

"You're welcome."

They sipped in silence for a while; then he asked, "You knew Fletcher was staying with me, right?"

Savannah nodded. "She messaged me at least once a week. I didn't know where she was, just that she was with you."

Jake usually didn't feel like he needed to explain himself, but for some reason he was compelled to now. "She and I weren't a couple or anything."

A small smile played at Savannah's lips. "She told me you weren't."

"I figured as much." Jake shook his head and contemplated making breakfast. Deciding it was a great idea, he got up to gather ingredients.

"How was she? I mean, she wrote to me, but it's hard to get a sense of how someone is through an email or text. Especially someone as good at keeping things to herself as Fletcher is."

"She was fine before I left on my last case. You know, Ryan gave up his share of the business, and Fletcher was thinking about taking over as my partner. We'd talked about it but hadn't made any decisions."

"That doesn't surprise me one bit. My daughter loved being a deputy, and she's very skilled at tracking people down."

He snorted and turned on the oven. "That's putting it mildly." He got out the dough he'd stored in the fridge the day before and grabbed a rolling pin. "If she didn't go into business with me, she was thinking about going out on her own."

"You know my daughter pretty well."

"I know what she told me," Jake said. He got a glass from the cupboard and began cutting biscuits. Her gaze was burning a hole in his back, but he ignored it.

"What *did* she tell you, Jake?"

"Lots of things. Listen, she's my friend, and we were roommates—we talked. But nothing she said has to do with what's going on now."

"I'm not asking you to divulge secrets, but my daughter only has two friends outside of this family and one of them is lying in a hospital bed. So…I'd like to know—"

He rinsed his flour-coated hands in the sink, then dried them on a fancy towel. "And I want to know what you and your husband know about Daemon Randle?"

"Yes, Mama, please do tell."

Jake's eyes shot to Alexandra's as she entered the room. Had she been listening the entire time? Did it matter?

"Morning, sweetheart," Savannah said, and stood to hug her daughter.

"Good morning." Alexandra returned her mother's embrace, then maneuvered around Jacob to pour herself a cup of coffee. He didn't say anything to her, which was probably a good thing. She still couldn't believe he'd kissed her. Some men never evolved beyond Cro-Magnon. She took a seat and looked at her mother. "So are you going to tell us what you know or not?"

"Why do you think I know more about Daemon than you do?"

"But you *do* know something." Alex narrowed her eyes. "You're avoiding the question."

"You may have forgotten, but I *am* your mother,

Alexandra, and I don't like your tone."

"And I don't like having to put my life on hold, but I'm doing it, aren't I?" Alex didn't talk back to her mother, but she was sick and tired of everyone bitching at her. She had responsibilities too.

"What has gotten into you lately, Alexandra? Don't you care that your sister's been taken?"

And Alex was sick of this. "I'm sorry, Mama, but we don't even know for sure what's going on. Things aren't adding up, if you ask me. But *no one* asked me. Everyone blames me though," she said. "Fletcher's an adult and makes her own decisions. She could have stayed here and let us explain—let *me* explain—but she didn't. And why has no one brought up the fact that she could have seriously hurt or even killed Craig. Why? Because this entire family revolves around Fletcher, and I—"

"Alexandra!"

Alex bit her tongue, embarrassed her emotions had overwhelmed her good sense. "For the record, I don't want any part of this manhunt."

"But you'll do it," Jacob said pointing his wooden spoon at her.

She didn't care that whatever he was cooking smelled amazing, she glared at him anyway. "Yes, I'll do it." She didn't like the smug look on his face, but she ignored him and sipped her coffee.

"I—"

Alexandra shook her head. "Don't worry about it, Mama."

"I *am* worried. I didn't realize how unhappy this was making you."

She picked at her bracelet. "I'm not unhappy."

Before her mother could respond, Jacob asked,

"Any news on Jasper?"

"The doctor said that the procedure went well, and Jasper's resting," Savannah said and filled them in on the details, until Jacob set plates of biscuits and gravy in front of them.

"Let's eat," he said, and for once Alex was grateful for his presence.

Other than "oohing" and "ahhing" over Jacob's culinary skill, and a bit of small talk, they ate in silence. Alex helped her mother clear the table, while Jacob put away leftovers.

Once the kitchen was back in order, her mother went to put on her jacket.

"Mrs. McKay?"

She looked over at Jake. "I told you to call me Savannah."

"Savannah, then."

"Yes?"

"About Randle?"

Alex turned toward her mother. "Mama?"

Savannah sighed. "Emmit said you found video, but Daemon didn't hurt Fletcher—not the way you—"

"I watched all of it, Savannah, and my eyes weren't deceiving me," Jake said.

"I know what you think you saw." She shifted on her feet. "Fletcher knew what was going on…"

Jake crossed his arms over his chest. "She knew he was drugging her?"

"She knew she was being recorded. She had no illusions about who Daemon was."

"If that's true, then why was she thinking about marrying the man?" Alex asked.

"She wasn't." Her mother rummaged through her purse until she pulled out four small books and handed them to Alex. "The letter Fletcher wrote me before she left town told me where to find these if anything should happen."

Alex took the journals from her mother. "And you're only *now* showing them to me?"

"I didn't go in search of them until a couple days ago." She motioned to the books. "The things in there are private, and I'm only giving them to you in hope they might help. I realize this isn't easy for you, Alexandra, and I'd find Fletcher myself if I thought I stood a chance."

"Mama, I—"

"Just read those and try to find your answers. Jake, you take a look too, but this isn't for the others."

That got Alex's attention. She glanced at Jacob, who looked like someone had asked him to purchase feminine hygiene products. "What do you mean?"

Savannah sighed. "Read them," she said, then left.

Alex stared out the window until her mother's vehicle was out of sight. She took a seat at the table. "I assume we should start reading."

Jake topped off their coffees and sat down. She grabbed the top book and handed the next one to him.

"Here goes…" Jake mumbled.

Alex shrugged and opened the book to the first page, surprised to find it had been written when they were children. How could this possibly help them now?

This ain't a damn diary—I don't do diaries—I ain't no sissy. This here is the journal of Fletcher J. McKay. Not that I wanted to write the stupid thing, but Pops caught me picking locks again and said I needed a new outlet.

Alex shook her head and took up another journal. She flipped through the pages and stopped when her own name stood out in the ink. She looked at the date; it was right after Casey had left.

Alexandra's taking most of the blame for all this, though it wasn't her fault. I kept the secret too, and goodness knows I'd do it again. People 'round here think Alex is cold and selfish, someone who doesn't care about anyone but herself, but I don't believe it. Is she a prissy pants? Hell, yeah, but she ain't a sissy and she ain't a liar. We all have problems and even though she wants us to think she's perfect, she's not. She's human and my sister...

"I think I found it," Jake said.

Alex closed the book. It wouldn't do her any good to read about things from the past. This was the here and now, and that was what she needed to focus on. "What does it say?"

Jacob cleared his throat.

Last night I slept with the subject. Knowing it was my first time, he offered me something to help me relax. I knew from a previous visit that he had cameras in every room, so I took what he offered in order to get the job done. Sometimes a body has to do things to find out the truth, things they wouldn't normally do. I'm trying not to let my emotions into this investigation, but it's hard...

"So he was slipping her something, but not without her knowledge," Alex said after Jake had stopped reading.

He fisted his hands on the table. "Seems that way."

"Was that all?"

"There's more, but it's the last entry we need to concentrate on," Jake said flipping to the last page.

Subject appeared to have taken his own life, but it's a cover-up. A man named Dan emailed me and said it was murder. I had previously disabled the cameras in the subject's home, so there is no proof. Personally, I don't believe it was suicide.

"It stops there, but"—he turned the book so she could read—"she noted she had a meeting with Dan."

"She left town the day before that," Alex told him. She wouldn't forget the night Fletcher had left, the argument they'd had, or the words said. Her gaze landed on the pictures hanging on the wall, now still, but that night...

Fletcher swiveled toward Alex, quick as a snake. "Fuck you, Alex! You really think the world revolves around you, don't you?" There was no humor in Fletcher's laugh. "Jasper's been covering for your ass since we were kids."

"I—"

"What, Alexandra? Cat got your tongue? Well, stick this in your craw...Jasper cashed in just about every favor he was owed to make sure you could open Granny Vaughn's, despite the fact it was tied up in Granny's estate until one of us got married."

"Fletcher—"

"No, Charlie, she needs to hear this. All this because you got it in your thick skull that Jasper was keeping secrets." Fletcher shook her head. "He damn well is keeping secrets—yours, mine, and Charlie's—but he does it to protect us. So you can have your brother, this town, and whatever else your cold heart desires; just make sure you take it back to hell with you when you go." The door slammed so hard behind her it shook the pictures on the wall.

Alex shuddered. She hadn't known then, never would have guessed Jasper had done those things for her, that he—

Jacob waved a hand in her face.

She swallowed the memory. "Sorry, what?"

His expression was pained. "I said, should we assume she never made it to see him?"

"I think that's a safe bet." She got up and put her mug in the sink. "Do you think she's with this Dan?"

"That's what we have to figure out," Jake said and began leafing through another journal. "If Uncle Marty can track where she emailed me from—"

"What email?"

"Oh, shit. I forgot!" Jake stood up and pulled a piece of paper from his pocket. "I got it last night and printed it out," he said, then explained.

Alexandra read the email and closed her eyes for a second. "Okay, what is she trying to tell us?"

"I have no idea," Jake grumbled. "I don't know anyone named Summer. Do you?"

"No one in Blue Creek is named Summer." Alex cocked her head to the side, then put her finger to her lips.

Jake raised his brows.

She slipped off her shoes, walked in stocking feet to the pantry, then pulled open the door. "Jebbediah McKay! What are you doing?"

Alex stepped back as Jebb slunk out of the pantry closet. She seriously thought about smacking him, but he was already bigger than her and they had an audience. "How many times do I have to tell you not to hide in the passageways?"

"What passageways?" Jake asked, grinning.

"Granny Vaughn's first husband was paranoid and built passageways throughout the house. They come in handy, but they are not to be used except during emergencies."

"That's cool," Jake said and winked at Jebb.

Alex rolled her eyes. "Please don't condone his behavior, Jacob."

Jake shrugged.

"Sit down, Jebb." Alex pointed to the table and tucked Fletcher's notebooks into a drawer.

Jebb motioned toward the window. "I see you got an SUV like Ryan's."

"Yep."

"Now that we have that out of the way…I'd like to know why you aren't at school." Alex didn't want her brother getting into trouble. It was bad enough that when she and her sisters had been children they'd been labeled "heathens." Imagine her, Alexandra McKay, a heathen.

Now, however, Jebb was called a wild child. He was a perfectly respectable young man if you asked her. Sure his black hair was shaggy, and his blue eyes were mischievous, but he was a good young man with an even better heart.

"It's a teacher conference day, and we don't have school," Jebb said, then changed the subject. "Pops is still at the hospital with Jasper—"

"Your mom said the procedure went well?" Jake shifted in his chair.

"It did! Jasper should be out of the hospital soon. The doctor said he has to recuperate for a few weeks before going back to work. Oh, and he shouldn't do anything strenuous." Jebb smirked. "You know *that'll* drive him plum crazy."

Alex narrowed her eyes. "That still doesn't explain why you were hiding in the passageways."

"I want to find Fletcher too!" Jebb thumped the table with his fist, making the centerpiece bounce. "I'm not a baby, Alex; Charlie let me help last time."

She rose a brow. "How stimulating for you."

"And Fletch trusts me!"

Alex pursed her lips. "She also calls you Bullfrog." It was the nickname Fletcher and Casey had given their brother when he was born—Jebbediah sounded so much like Jeremiah that they hadn't been able to resist. It was somewhat ridiculous, but amusing nonetheless.

Jebb blushed. "Yeah, but—"

"Take a look at this," Jake said handing Jebb the copy of the email.

"Thanks." Jebb pulled a pen out of his pocket, clicked it, and started to mark the page. He grinned. "I've got it."

Alex stared at her brother. "What? What do you mean you've got it?"

Jebb laid the paper flat on the table so they could see. "Jake doesn't have a fiancée, so the name Summer is important. The words 'judge' and 'lodge' are things that pertain to how she makes you feel or shouldn't. Whatever." Jebb shook his head and pointed to the other words he circled. "Because this person doesn't exist. She's telling you about a 'treasure hunt' and 'the key to finding truth' is where 'the heart lies.' "

"But how does that tell us where she is?" Jake asked, annoyed when the boy rolled his eyes. He glanced at Alexandra who didn't seem to be getting it either.

"Okay, Summer isn't a person—"

"We understand that, Jebb." Alex sat up. "Summer is a season though!" She jumped to her feet and gave her brother a big kiss. "You *do* think like Fletcher."

"Still not getting it," Jake complained.

"Our granddaddy, *Judge* J.T. Vaughn, owned a

hunting *lodge*," Alex told him her eyes shining. "We usually went there in the summer."

"That he did!"

"Damn, Jebb." Jake shook his head. Then started getting his stuff together. "Where's this lodge?"

Chapter Six

"The lodge is an hour or so up the mountain," Alexandra told Jake, then paused. "What about the other things? A treasure hunt, the key, and where the heart lies. What does that have to do with the hunting lodge?"

Jebb squirmed. "I gave you the location; what else do you want?"

"Maybe it was just filler," Jake suggested.

Jebb scratched his chin. "Could be."

"Wait a minute. Granddaddy sold the lodge years ago." Alexandra sat down and rubbed her temples.

"Maybe Fletcher bought it back," Jebb said. "It's what I would have done."

"Why would she? Never mind. Our sister never does anything normal."

"Are we going or not?" Jake asked. He'd go by himself if need be. He always checked a lead.

"I don't think we have a choice," Alex said. "I need to run to the store."

"What the hell for?" Jake wanted to know.

"Because I don't have anything to wear," Alex told him and smacked Jebb when he laughed.

"You've got to be kidding me," Jake growled.

She crossed her arms over her chest. "If you must know, I don't own a pair of jeans or the appropriate boots for hiking, and I'll need them."

"We have to hike?" Jake looked at Jebb, who was

still rubbing his head.

"What part of it's *up* the mountain didn't you understand?" She smirked, then sighed. "In all honesty, there usually is an access road, but it got washed out last summer when we had some torrential storms."

Jake grumbled.

Alex grabbed her purse. "I'll be back in a bit."

"We don't have time to waste, princess."

"I'm well aware of that fact, Jacob. You can wait here," she said and went out the door.

"I should just go without her," Jake griped and sat back down.

"The only problem is that she knows the way and you don't," Jebb pointed out. "And before you ask, no, I don't know how to get there."

"I hate waiting."

"You get used to it." Jebb squirmed in his chair. "Look, I know you don't particularly care for Alex."

Jake crossed his arms over his chest. "What gave it away?"

"People don't understand her 'sall. She's on the other end of the spectrum from Fletcher as far as most things go, but she's smart."

"I know." Jake sighed. Jebb was protecting Alex's honor or something.

"So are you and Fletcher…you know?"

Jake laughed. Hard. "No. It's not like that, Jebb. She's like the kid sister I never had. We're friends, that's it. So don't worry."

"I wasn't worried. Just curious." Jebb grinned, then pointed toward the counter. "Is there any food left?"

****

"Not the outdoors type are you, princess?" Jake asked to annoy her.

Alex glared at him over her shoulder. "You know very well I'm not."

Jake walked behind her in silence and took in lungsful of fresh mountain air. He ignored his cold nose and focused on the forest around him; he'd forgotten how much he loved the outdoors. There was still snow on the ground in the higher elevations, and from the graying of the sky, it looked like they might get some more. "Tell me again why you didn't want to bring your brother?"

She mumbled.

Jake grinned. "Sorry, princess, I didn't catch that."

"I didn't want Jebb to get in the middle of whatever happens. And, yes, I'm sure there *will* be something; there usually is when Fletcher's involved."

"Fair enough." He continued walking behind her. Despite what had led them here, he couldn't help enjoying the hike; being out in nature did a body good. What didn't do any good was the fact that Alexandra McKay was fucking hot in a pair of tight jeans. Her ass was spectacular. Go figure. *Don't play with matches, pal.*

"It's not much farther."

He moved a branch out of his way. "Do you think she'll be there?"

"It's a possibility. When I called my father, he confirmed Fletcher had bought the place, so your guess is as good as mine."

"I'm surprised he didn't come with us." Emmit McKay was a first-man-out-the-door kind of guy.

"He wanted to, but time is of the essence."

He shook his head. "And you want to get this over with so you can get back to you."

"Rude, but accurate."

"That's good to know." Jake stopped when she did. "What is it?"

Alex inhaled deeply. "Nothing. Just a memory of coming out here with my grandfather."

"That must have been nice. Granddad took me and Ryan hunting every year." Jake smiled. Those had been the best times of his life.

"My sisters always enjoyed coming to the lodge. Fletcher and Casey especially."

"Not you though?" That didn't surprise him.

"I liked spending time with Granddaddy and my sisters, but coming out here was not my idea of fun. Granddaddy always made it up to me though."

"The kid told me J.T. Vaughn was a good man, but he sired the spawn of Satan."

Alex whirled around. "She told you about Gracie?"

"No…you forget, my brother's married to Casey. Ryan likes to talk about things that bother him." His brother was soft-hearted and, boy, could the guy talk.

She crossed her arms over her chest. "Oh, please. Casey wouldn't talk about that woman with Ryan or anyone."

"You don't have to believe me, princess, but Casey talks to Ryan and he talks to me. All Fletcher said was that the first Mrs. McKay was the genuine-article bitch, so I asked Ryan what he knew." His brother was very pliable if you knew how to angle him.

"Fine," she said through clenched teeth.

"I also know about the place you guys lived in before you were adopted." He didn't know why he was pushing her buttons, but he wished he hadn't when she spun around again and tried to smack him. He grabbed onto a nearby tree for purchase. "Watch it."

"You watch it! I don't care what you think you

know, Jacob Keller, but you have no idea what that place was like. You—oh, never mind."

"I can relate, okay? Our parents died when Ryan and I were—"

"You still had parents. You went to live with your grandparents right away. You didn't have to sleep on a rickety cot with threadbare blankets and cold concrete floors. And the rats…" Alexandra shivered.

"I know about that too," Jake said softly. Ryan had told him all about it, and it had sickened Jake.

"Yeah?" She sneered at him. "Try living it."

"Is that why you're such a bitch? Because you were poor little orphan Alex? So were your sisters and they're not as cold as you." Okay, that was low, but damn it, he wanted to understand.

"How dare you," Alex hissed.

"Then explain it to me; I'm dying to know what makes you tick. And why you hate your sister."

"For the last time, I do not hate my sister! I'm here on this godforsaken mountain with you looking for her."

He blew a hot breath into his numb hands. "Not because you want to be."

"What about you? What about the fact that you've only come to visit *your* brother a couple times in almost two years? How about you tell me why you treat Ryan the way you do? What? Oh, I see, you don't have to answer any of my questions, but I have to answer yours. Sorry, I don't work that way!"

"You wouldn't understand."

"Nor would you."

"Fine," he said, then bumped into her when she stopped suddenly. "What now?"

"We're here." She pointed to the two-story house

nestled in the side of the mountain.

"That's not a lodge." Sure, the house was in the middle of nowhere and had log siding, but it was not what he considered a hunting lodge. His grandfather had taken him to one and this was nothing like it.

"No. But that's what Granddaddy called it. Do you hear that?"

He nodded. The hum of an engine echoed in the silence. "Generator?"

"Exactly."

He cocked his head to the side when they got closer. "Wait…"

"What?"

"This is the place on her computer in the bunker."

"What are you going on about?"

Jake controlled his growl and pointed to the lodge. "The screensaver on the kid's computer—it's this place."

Alex looked over her shoulder, then back at him. "That's why she led you to find the second bunker."

He nodded. "She hoped the picture would lead us here, but she left the clues just in case."

It was her turn to nod. "Smart." She knelt on the ground and opened her pack.

Jake's eyes widened when she pulled out a revolver. "Where the hell did that come from?"

"Did you honestly think I'd go into something blind? You brought a gun, didn't you?"

"Yeah, but"—he waved his hand in the air—"what the hell are you going to do with that thing?"

"Hopefully nothing," she said and started for the lodge. She went a couple of yards, then bent down and swept leaves out of her way. "Someone's been covering their tracks," she whispered, turning to find herself nose to nose with Jake.

"Seems that way," he whispered back.

Alex ignored the look in his eyes and stood up. She didn't need to get involved with Jacob Keller. What she needed to do was get the hell away from him. She pointed to the smoke coming out of the chimney. "Should we go in guns blazing?"

He shook his head. "Quiet and careful. I'll take the front if you take the back."

"Fine," she said and crept up to the back window to peek inside. She couldn't see anyone. Taking off her gloves, she slowly removed the screen and tried to open the window, but it wouldn't budge. Didn't it just figure. She hadn't wanted to try the back door, but she hadn't really wanted to be here either.

Alex opened the screen door and tried the knob, surprised when it moved. She stepped back and drew her revolver up. The revolting smell hit her first—an unmistakable odor.

With practiced care, she moved into the den. Though it was overcast, there was enough sunlight for Alex to navigate the room. The only occupants were the leather sofas, brick hearth, and small oak coffee table. She tiptoed through the doorway into the hall. The front door was open, so she assumed Jake had gone to check out the upstairs rooms.

She went into the kitchen next. No one was in there either. Slipping the gun into the waistband of her jeans, she opened the fridge, surprised to find it fully stocked. "Someone's been here," she said to herself.

"They're not here now," Jake said, making Alex jump.

"No sign at all?" she asked once her heart stopped racing.

"Fresh sheets on the beds, and the bathrooms are stocked, which tells me someone was here recently."

"The fire is smoldering too. If Fletcher was here, we missed her by hours," she said annoyed. It still didn't explain… "Did you smell—"

"Something rank? Yeah, you think the septic tank backed up?" Jake asked. He opened the fridge and pulled out a bottle. "Will you look at that!"

"You don't know what it is?"

"It's a beer."

She closed her eyes and refused to smile. He was too much sometimes, but she wouldn't encourage him. "The smell."

He opened the beer and shrugged.

"Death," she said and hit the light switch, cringing when the electricity crackled.

Jake coughed and set his drink down with a thunk. "Excuse me?"

"When a person dies, the body oftentimes releases its bowels," she explained. One would think he would know that.

"And that's what the smell is."

She eyed him. "Well, that and the coppery—"

"I'm aware of the decomp process, but it sounds like you have first-hand experience with this?"

"I'm sure you know the answer to that. You know *everything,* don't you?"

"I'm not trying to start an argument, princess, but I don't particularly want to find a dead body either. And that's what you're saying that smell is."

"More than likely, but I didn't say it was human."

"That's a relief."

She opened the pantry door; it was stocked too. "The smell isn't as harsh in the kitchen."

"There weren't any bodies upstairs," Jake told her.

"No, the smell is strongest in the den," Alex said and headed that way. "It has to be here somewhere." What would she do if it was Fletcher's body? She shoved the thought away.

"Uh, Alex?" Jake said from the door at the far side of the den. "What's down here?"

"Granddaddy's game room, or at least it used to be." She walked in front of him hiding her irritation. How could she have forgotten? Basements usually held secrets when one of her sisters was involved. She found the switch and waited for the lights to come on; it had always taken forever. Once she could see, Alexandra headed down the stairs.

"Jesus!" Jake pulled the collar of his shirt up over his nose.

Alex glanced at him over her shoulder. "You want to go first?"

He glared at her, then walked past her and down the steps, which groaned under his booted feet. He got to the bottom and said, "Oh, for fuck's sake!"

Alex passed him and caught sight of the body on the floor. "If you need to throw up, please go and use the bathroom."

He rushed up the stairs.

Once he was gone, Alex let out a shuddering breath and sat on the wooden steps. Though it shamed her, she was entirely glad it was a man and not her sister. But the more damning thought was that it could have been her sister who killed him.

She took several seconds to collect herself, then stood up on shaky legs and went to the body. Careful not to walk in the drying puddle of blood that surrounded the upper torso, she bent down to take a closer look and sucked in a breath. She knew him.

"We need to get the police up here," Jake said coming back down the stairs.

"His throat's been slit." Knives *were* Fletcher's weapon of choice.

"I figured that out. We need to get the police out here," he said again.

She took in the rest of the room, then glanced at Jacob. "I know him. Or knew him."

Jacob threw his hands in the air. "What is your fucking deal?"

What in the world? She stood. "Excuse me?"

"You're standing next to a corpse, and you're acting like you're picking out furniture. What the fuck is wrong with you? How the hell are you so detached?"

"What would you have me do, Jacob? Faint?" She pinched the bridge of her nose. "What do you want from me?"

"I don't want a damn thing from you, sweetheart. What *I* want is to find your sister and get answers."

"And you don't think I want the same?" She marched past him and up the stairs. His boots thudded behind her.

"That's the problem, I don't know what the fuck you want." He grabbed her arm and whirled her around when they reached the den. "Talk to me, goddamn it!"

"What?" Alex shouted around the lump in her throat. Tears glazed her eyes.

He reached up toward her cheek. "Why are you like this?"

She pulled out of his grasp before he could touch her face. She needed to be alone, to get control of herself.

He stared at her a moment, then asked, "So who is

he?”

“Larry Hines. He’s a retired police officer.” She closed her eyes for a second. “He’s missing.”

Jake paced in front of the dying embers in the fireplace. “Yah think?”

“No, I mean, Noah’s looking for him.”

Jake mumbled something about Noah under his breath, then said, “Since when?”

“A few days, according to Noah. Larry never showed up for his retirement party.” She glanced at the door leading to the basement and shivered. “And he never will.”

“Who the hell is he anyway?” Jake wanted to know. “I mean, other than the dead guy in the basement.”

Alex sighed. “He worked for the sheriff’s office for a while; then he was a beat cop for the city. A native of Blue Creek, but he never married or had children. Most people liked him; in fact, I think everyone did except Fletcher.” She sat down on the leather sofa and crossed her ankles.

“You’re saying Fletcher murdered him?”

“I didn’t say that, Jacob.”

“No, but you’re implying it.”

“His throat was slit. You’ve seen Fletcher’s knife. She loves the thing. And she knows how to use it.” Alex glanced out the dirty window. They needed to call Noah. The sheriff should know about a murder in his town, even though technically the lodge didn’t have a designated jurisdiction. But Larry was Noah’s missing person.

“That doesn’t prove a damn thing!”

“Will you stop shouting at me? I know it doesn’t prove anything, but how do you think it looks, Jacob?

Seriously? Fletcher owns this place, and no one has seen her. Do you really think *Noah Reed* won't suspect Fletcher first thing?"

"Okay, you have a point. But you're awful quick to point your manicured finger in your sister's direction."

"Believe what you want." She stood. "What we need to do is call Noah." She glanced at her cell. "Does your phone have service?"

"Yes, your highness, it does." He handed her the phone. "I'm going to go finish that beer."

"Oh, by all means," she hissed.

Chapter Seven

"Thanks, Noah. Yes, I know. Good-bye."

Jake peeled the label off his beer. "What'd Noah say?"

Alex sighed. "He's heading up to the lodge."

"Now?"

"No, tomorrow. Yes, now." She shook her head.

"Don't act like it was a stupid question, princess. You said the road's washed out, and it's a long-ass hike up here. In fact, we should start heading back." He downed the rest of his beer, then threw the bottle into the trash.

"Noah wants us to stay put."

"They'll take forever getting up here."

"Unlike you and me, Noah has connections with the city police department and they have these lovely things. Perhaps you've heard of them." She cocked her head to the side. "They're called helicopters."

"Lucky them." Was she being a smart ass?

"Yes, I think so."

"So we're just supposed to sit here with our thumbs up our asses and wait?" The sun was already beginning to recede. Great, just great.

"That's the idea."

"Fine. I'm going to search around some more then."

"You do realize this place is a crime scene, right? And you're compromising it."

Jake glared at her. "I'll just go compromise more of the fucking crime scene then!"

His boots thudded against the hardwood until he'd stalked out of sight. Alex sighed and concentrated on the embers glowing in the hearth. The fire had to have been going this morning, which meant someone had been here. Alex couldn't imagine it was anyone other than Fletcher, which meant her sister had to have known about Larry.

But why would Larry have come to the lodge in the first place? How had he even known it was here at all? Also, Noah said Larry had been missing for a couple of days, and she knew he hadn't been dead for very long. Had Larry been here the entire time he was thought to be missing?

Noah was going to have a field day with this. Larry was murdered on Fletcher's property, and Fletcher was unaccounted for. Not for the first time, Alex wished Jasper was still sheriff; he wouldn't condemn Fletcher as fast as Noah would. Or as fast as she herself had.

Alex jumped when Jake stormed back in the room.

He crossed his arms over his chest and glared at her. "What exactly did you say to Noah?"

"Let's see, I told him we came up to Granddaddy Vaughn's old lodge looking for Fletcher when lo and behold we came across a rotting corpse. And oh, you know how you're looking for Larry Hines? Well, you can stop because he's here with his throat slit!" She stood up and clenched her fists. "But the best part was when he asked if we'd found Fletcher too. And I told him that unfortunately *no* we hadn't."

"I wasn't imply—"

"Give me a break. You've been making asinine assumptions all along about things you know nothing about. The accusations are written all across your smug face!" She was too strong to let it hurt her feelings.

"Hey…I didn't mean to—"

"To what, Jacob? Be an asshole?"

"Now wait just a damn minute. All I asked was what you said to Noah; there's no need for you to blow up at me, for fuck's sake! It was a simple question, princess, so don't even try to blame me for your guilty conscience."

"I don't have a guilty conscience, Jacob. *I've* done nothing wrong."

"Now who's throwing around accusations?"

"I wasn't talking about you." And she hadn't been. No, she'd been trying to remind herself that she *wasn't* to blame for all this. She wasn't. She couldn't be.

"Can't prove it from where I'm standing," Jake said and took a seat.

"Sorry."

"Bullshit."

"You're right, I'm not sorry." She squeezed her eyes shut and tried to breathe. She was nearing the end of her rope. She didn't know if she could do this anymore. Any of it. Tired didn't even begin to describe how she felt.

"What is your—" Whatever Jacob was going to ask died on his lips as the "whoop, whoop" of a helicopter filled the room. "Finally!"

"My sentiments exactly," Alexandra said heading for the door to greet Noah.

****

By the time they reached the B and B, night had fully fallen. They'd hitched a ride back with the sheriff. Jake pinched the bridge of his nose. Noah Reed had made himself number two on Jake's shit list. Number one was whoever had the kid, but *Sheriff Reed* was definitely number two. A shit indeed.

The man strutted into the lodge with the tenacity of a bull. Ordering people around like he was royalty—king of dickheads, maybe. He certainly had it in for Fletch too. Oh, he didn't accuse the kid outright. No, he was too damn smart, but he'd implied it.

"Fletcher usually carries a knife, doesn't she, Alexandra?" he'd asked, then, "Sure does seem that someone's been staying here, and no forced entry would suggest the owner…"

It was all bullshit. Reed knew what he was about. Jake made certain to watch every move the good old sheriff made. There wouldn't be any planted evidence while Jake was around. He wouldn't put it past Reed; the man was one hateful SOB.

Jake took a seat at Alex's kitchen table; speaking of…The only words he and her highness had spoken on the way back had been the necessary ones. Not that he'd known what to say. She seemed to have already convicted the kid, so what could he do?

"Are you staying here?" Alexandra asked.

He stared at his hands. "Do you need me to?"

"I don't need anything from you," Alex said and started to leave the room.

"I got that," Jake began and waited until her blue eyes met his. Oh yeah, the battle was on. "You don't need anyone, right? Least of all me."

"Thank you for pointing out the obvious."

"What is it with you?"

"Stop asking me that! You're the one with the problem here."

Jake stood and got in her space. "How's that?" He was willing to risk getting slapped or worse if he could get a straight answer out of her.

"Don't you understand?"

"Nope."

"Why are you here, Jacob? Truly? Why are you searching for my sister? You hardly know her."

He opened his mouth, but she held up her hand. "I know you *think* you know her, but you have no inkling to who and what she is."

"You do, though, right? That's what you're getting at. You know everything about everyone, and you're superior to all of us. Especially Fletch."

"You have no idea what you're talking about. And I don't need to explain myself to you or anyone."

"I think you do. In fact—fuck it. What I think means exactly dick to you." Jake shook his head and moved toward the door. "You want to know why I'm searching for your sister?"

"Please enlighten me."

"She's the only other person I know in the world, besides my brother, who doesn't put themselves first. She's willing to risk everything, give anything, for the people she loves."

"Yourself included."

"I'm a selfish bastard, Alexandra. I know that, and *I* can admit it." He went to the door and grabbed the knob, then turned back to her and said, "As far as love goes, yeah, I love your sister. Not sexually or whatever. I love her for who she is. Because she loves me for who *I* am too. And that, Alexandra, is the rarity that is your sister. That's why I'm here, and that's why I'm going to find her."

Alex held herself perfectly still while Jacob slammed out of the house hard enough to make the pictures on the walls rattle. She stared at the door for a moment longer than necessary, then went to the drawer where she'd stuck Fletcher's journals. She took a seat and flipped through the pages again, stopping when she saw her name.

…I had a fight with Alexandra again today. Hell's bells, she pisses me off. Why can't she just let me be? I let her live her life, don't I? I sure as hell do! All I ask for is the same courtesy. But she treats me like I'm some dumb kid. Oh well, I'll never get her…

Alex closed the journal; she didn't want to read what her sister wrote about her. She wanted this to be over. She wanted her life back. She needed Jacob to go; having him here was becoming too risky, he made her want—no, she wouldn't go there.

When did things get this out of control? She sighed. Life had been chaotic since she met Casey all those years ago, not that she would change anything, or at least not much. *She* had changed. There was a time when Alex had been naïve and people had even called her sweet. But that was a long time ago. Another life—another Alexandra.

She rolled her eyes at her self-pity and pushed the journals away from her, sending one of the books to the floor. Annoyed, she got up and retrieved it, narrowing her gaze at the picture that fell out.

Her stomach turned at the sight before her. Shaking herself, she looked at the back to see the year the picture had been taken. She'd been seven then, Casey nine, and Fletcher six. Charlie hadn't even existed to them yet. They'd been so young, with more life experience than they should have had.

But it wasn't the faces of her sisters reaching out to choke her. It was the three adults behind them. Three people who had taught them what betrayal meant and had changed them forever. Three lives fated to twist Alexandra into who and what she was today, captured for all eternity in a single snapshot. Their two honorary uncles, Kyle Ruthie and Evan Jessup, stood next to the first Mrs. Emmit McKay, Gracie.

For a second, she was ten years old again, hiding in the closet with her sisters while her uncle was murdered. She shivered. That night had changed everything.

When they'd come out of the closet, Casey and Charlie had run for help, while she and Fletcher had stayed with their uncle. Sometimes she could still imagine his blood on her fingers, dried on her face—she could smell it. It had been during those crimson moments she and Fletcher had learned a secret; they'd kept it from everyone, hidden it away, until Casey found it and ran out of their lives.

Only years later did—no, she wouldn't think about it. Alex put the picture back in the book and closed it. She didn't know why Fletcher had kept it in the first place.

Some memories were better left to gather dust. She swiped at her heated cheeks, angered by the tears that had escaped. "Stupid," she muttered.

"Who?"

Alex sucked in a breath and turned to find her brother watching her. "When did you come in?"

Craig's gaze didn't leave hers. "A moment ago."

She smoothed a hand down her pantleg, cringed at the grime beneath her fingers, and took a seat.

Craig sat next to her. "Want to talk about it?"

"No," she said, patting his hand. Surprised when he took hold of hers. "Is something wrong?"

"Yeah, you're not talking to me. You're bottling

everything up, and one day you're going to explode or worse implode. Talk to me. Is there something I can do?"

She snatched her hand back. "Find Fletcher!"

"If I could—"

"Oh, please!" Alex shouted and got up to pace. "Don't you think that if *I* could find her I would have already. What do you people want from me? Damn it!"

"Calm down, and tell me what happened?"

Alex told him, rather loudly, about the lodge, Larry, and Noah. "And if I have to spend one more second with that Cro-Magnon, thinks he's God's gift to women, overbearing, egotistical oaf, I'll go insane!" Or worse.

Craig's brow puckered. "Noah?"

"No! Jacob Keller. I swear every five seconds he's accusing me of something. I can't take it anymore, Craig. I am seriously getting this close"—she put her index and thumb finger an inch apart—"to losing my composure." Or caving into the ludicrous desire to open up to—

"Maybe we need to call in some help."

Alex scoffed. "McKays take care of their own problems, as you well know!"

"Okay, have you spoken to your parents yet?

"No!" She stared at the ceiling for poise, then narrowed her eyes a bit, then a bit more. What the—? "Craig, this is going to sound rather rude—"

He rose a brow. "Okay…"

"I would like you to leave. And please inform my parents of the latest, all right?" She motioned him toward the door.

"Alexandra, if you need to talk some more…that's why I came."

She almost growled. “I don’t want to talk.”

“I think you need to—”

“Get out,” she practically shouted. Okay, she did shout, but she’d done so with some semblance of grace. Or at least she tried to.

“Alex,” he said holding up his callused palms. “You don’t really mean that.”

Her eyes narrowed. “Don’t I?” Why was everyone questioning her?

“Alexandra, honey, calm down.”

“Don’t you dare speak to me like I’m a child, Craig. I need some time to myself.” She glanced at the ceiling again. Hysteria was bubbling in her chest. She was sure she looked possessed. She was in hiking pants—of all things—dirty, and her hair was—she didn’t even want to think about it. Craig needed to go. “Just leave.”

“No, I don’t think so.” He planted his feet on the linoleum, and Alexandra was pretty sure her growl was audible this time.

Fine, he wouldn’t go on his own. She needed to break out the big guns. Literally. She went to the drawer, pulled out Granny’s trusty old revolver and pointed it at her brother.

“Alexandra? What are you doing?”

“What don’t you understand? I want you to go; I want everyone to leave me the hell alone. What’s so hard about that?” She knew she was acting crazy. She *was* a little off kilter, a tad shaky, and a whole hell of a lot frantic.

“Seems the lady wants you to leave,” Jake said from the other end of the room.

Oh, goody! “This doesn’t concern you, Jacob,” Alex hissed. What didn’t they understand about the word “alone”? A simple concept.

Jake shrugged and mouthed to Craig that he’d handle it. “It” no doubt, being her. The nerve!

“Okay.” Craig headed for the door. “I’m going. Alexandra, you get some sleep.”

Alex swung toward Jacob. “You can go too.” She pointed to the door.

“I don’t think so.”

He was in front of her before she could blink, and he had the gun out of her hand a second after that. Not that she cared.

Jake checked the revolver. “It’s not even loaded.”

“Of course not! Do you honestly think I’m stupid enough to point a loaded gun at someone I don’t *want* to harm?” Alex rolled her eyes and hurried up the stairs. Annoyed when he followed her. She went to her closet, pulled out her luggage, and grabbed the bag of toiletries she always kept packed.

“You had Craig believing it was loaded,” he said. “Where the hell do you think you’re going?”

“Wherever I want. I don’t have to answer to you or anyone.” The hooks of the hangers scraped against the metal rod as she yanked down clothes and shoved them in her suitcase.

He hovered in the doorway. “What about the kid?”

“You can find her.”

“Oh, I see you’re giving up, is that it? Things get a little rough and there goes the princess. What? You afraid you’ll break a damn nail?”

She got as close to his face as she dared. “I have never given up on anything in my entire life. But you probably know that because you know *everything*!” she shouted. “I. Just. Want. To. Be. Left. Alone.”

“I get that. But what about—”

"I don't give a rat's ass about *Jamie*, *okay*?" she practically screamed. She zipped up the suitcase and patted the keys in her pocket. "I'm fed up with the entire situation."

Jacob stepped in front of her. "Are you fucking serious?"

"Yes," she sneered. "I swear to God I don't give a damn about *Jamie*. Got it?"

Jake let out a humorless laugh. "I knew you were a cold piece of work, but I didn't know you were mercenary too. I mean, God, it feels good being right!" He went as far as to slap his thigh.

"Laugh it up, asshole."

She went down the steps as fast as her legs could take her. She'd been up and down the staircase a thousand times and knew every dip and curve. She wouldn't get upset now; she'd save useless tears for later when she was by herself.

"Alex! Wait!" Jake hollered from behind her.

"Go screw yourself!" She shut off all the lights and headed out the back door.

"Damn it, Alexandra, hold the hell on."

She motioned him out the door, then locked up. His gaze bored holes into her back, but she ignored it.

"You want to tell me what's going on, princess? 'Cause I'm fucking lost."

"Leave me alone, Jacob." She set the last lock, then swiveled around and started toward her vehicle, her suitcase banging on the steps behind her.

Jake grabbed her arm.

"*What?*"

"Talk to me."

"I have nothing to say."

"Bullshit! Something's going on here. Where's the

fucking fire?"

She stared into his steely green gaze, taken by the genuine concern. Then she did something that shocked them both; she pressed her lips to his.

She closed her eyes and went with the feeling. Not that she'd wanted to kiss Jacob again. She hadn't. And she definitely wasn't enjoying it. She wasn't. Maybe a little. That's probably why she opened her mouth when his tongue sought entrance, and his hands held her face. She let herself taste him again, for more than a moment, then broke her lips away. She kept her eyes shut, traced a path of kisses to his ear, and whispered.

He went rigid. "Damn it!"

She didn't give him another look, just hopped in her SUV, and turned on the ignition. He would follow her; of that she had no doubt.

Chapter Eight

Alexandra parked her SUV in the motel parking lot, walked into the dingy lobby, and paid the attendant for two rooms. She didn't usually stay in places like this; it was rundown and drab, but it was clean and discreet. And they took cash without batting an eye.

The neon sign changed from a green Vacancy to a pink No Vacancy, and she sighed. She unloaded her bag from the backseat and waited for Jacob to show up. It didn't take long.

He slammed his vehicle door shut and stalked over to her. "Now will you tell me what the hell's going on?"

"Here's this," she said and handed him a room key. "I need to freshen up first."

"Fine," he grumbled and turned on his heel.

Alex took her time in the shower. Letting the near scalding water warm her from the outside in. She washed her hair twice and scrubbed her skin until it was pink. She shut off the spray, dried off, then got into her comfy cotton nightgown. She wrapped her hair up in a towel, then began to apply her moisturizer.

There was a brisk knock on the door, and Alex rolled her eyes. She checked the peephole and stood back to let Jacob in. She set the security chain in place and turned to find him staring at her. His hair was wet and loose, hanging a bit past his shoulders, and his clothes were fresh. She hoped he hadn't cleaned up on her account.

She motioned for him to sit in one of the rickety chairs, but wasn't surprised when he chose the bed. Typical.

She took the towel off her head and shook out her wet hair. Her lavender-scented shampoo smothered the disinfectant odor that seemed to cling to the walls.

"All right, I followed you out here, as per your request. Now, will you explain—"

"Someone bugged my house."

"What?" Jake shot to his feet. "What do you mean someone 'bugged' your house?"

"Exactly what I said. Someone, no doubt for some nefarious reason, put at least one listening device in my home…and a camera too, if I'm not mistaken. One of those fiber-optic ones that signals right over the Wi-Fi." The bastards.

"I didn't notice anything." He paced the small confines of her room. "Where was it?"

"The ceiling fan," she said, glancing down at her nails and ignoring his enticing scent. "There was a new fixture on the fan pull."

He stopped short. "What the hell's a 'fan pull'?"

Alexandra rolled her eyes. "The little piece on the end of the fan chain that lets you adjust the fan's speed or the light?"

"Oh." Jake nodded. "The pulley thing. Okay, what about it?"

"Each room has its own unique pull; I had them all custom made."

"Why the hell do you need some special damn doohickey for the fan? Who even pays attention to that crap?"

"You'd be surprised."

He grunted.

"My guests always comment on them; people often appreciate the small details."

"That's good then."

"Yes." Her guests wouldn't be caught dead in a place like this.

He crossed his arm over his chest. "But what does this have to do with—"

"Like most ceiling fans, the one in the kitchen has two chains. One for speed and one for the light. The one for the light is on a shorter chain and is a figure of a porcelain teapot. The fixture on the fan speed is a porcelain teacup and saucer; its chain is longer."

Jake shook his head. "Who the hell thinks of this shit?"

Alex raised a brow.

"Fine," he grumbled. "What else?"

"Well, when we came home this evening the teapot was on the longer chain and the teacup and saucer was on the shorter chain."

"And…"

Her face heated. "I'll have you know, there was a small hole in the bottom of the teacup which was not there before."

"There had better be more to it than a different length of chain and a mystery hole in a fan doohickey. Over an hour's drive to some dive motel in the middle of no-man's-land had better not be for this stupid shit," Jake said sitting down on the bed again.

"Laugh all you want," Alex began with a touch of ice. "But the teacup and saucer I had made were colonial green with small flecks of butter yellow, and the teapot was butter yellow with colonial green flecks."

"And your point is?" he asked when he stopped laughing.

"The fixtures that were there were *pea green* with dandelion yellow flecks!" Ha! She crossed her arms over her chest when he burst into another fit of laughter.

"This is just too damn rich." He shook his head. "You mean to tell me all this drama was because of a stupid fan thingy? This has got to be the dumbest thing I've ever been a part of," Jake said standing. "I'm going to go get a few hours of shut eye, and then I'm going back to Blue Creek."

"Fine. I'm going to call Craig and ask him to check out my house," she said reaching for her cell phone.

"What?" He smirked. "You don't think the phone's bugged to?"

"For one thing, I've had it with me the entire time, and secondly I've already checked it."

He shook his head. "Do you really think Craig's going to want to talk to you after you pulled a gun on him?"

"It wasn't loaded," she said. Craig wouldn't mind. "Besides, once I explain to him about the bug, he'll understand why I acted the way I did."

"So it was all an act?"

"Naturally." Her brow pinched. "I've always been good at making people see what I want them to."

Jake headed for the door, shaking his head. This was the dumbest thing he'd ever heard. And who the hell had fan doohickeys custom-made? He turned when she started talking to Craig on her cell. This should be good.

"Yes, I'm fine. No, no seriously, I'm perfectly fine…It wasn't loaded. You should know me better than that. No, I'm not home…at a motel with Jacob. Don't be absurd; I got two rooms. I'm calling because I want you to clear my house. Yes, do a full sweep. Exactly. Tonight? No, it can wait until morning. Okay, give my love to Charlie and Mackenzie. I love you too. Bye now."

"He's going to check it out?" He wasn't so dense that he didn't understand the "don't be absurd" part. Craig had asked if Alexandra was sleeping in the same room as Jake. Well, actions speak louder than words, sweetheart, and that kiss spoke volumes to Jake. Maybe they were both playing with matches now.

"First thing tomorrow morning." She yawned. "I suggest we get some sleep."

"Fine," he grumbled. His cell rang.

"Jake, Uncle Marty here," came the gruff voice on the other end.

"Uncle Marty," Jake greeted. Alexandra stopped whatever she'd been doing to stare at him. "Did you get a lead on that email address?"

"I sure did, boyo. Seems to be up in the mountains an hour or two out from where you are."

"Let me guess…" Jake rattled off the location of the hunting lodge.

"Well, if yah already knew the damn thing, why'd yah bother to ask me?"

"I didn't know it until after I talked to you. And I haven't had a chance to call you back. Sorry, Marty." And Jake was; he'd been so busy he'd completely forgotten about his uncle.

"Did yah find her then?"

"No, it was a dead end." A really dead end with body included. "But this does help us, Marty. It proves she *was* there, and that's something at least." He glanced over to Alex, who was nibbling her lower lip...He'd like to be—*Don't even think about it.* "Sorry, Marty, what was that?"

"Boy, clean your ears," Uncle Marty huffed. "I said the computer that sent the email was using a wireless connection, which makes pinpointing a location harder. I can tell you that based on the configuration, they're using a laptop and not a mobile phone or tablet."

Jake rubbed his neck. "Was there any activity on the other account? Dan's or whoever the hell he is?"

"Knew you were a smart boy!" Marty laughed. "As a matter a fact there was. The dummy account sent an email to a fella named Benjamin Drake."

"Who's Benjamin Drake?" Jake asked and smiled when Alex get out a pen and paper.

"Seems he's one of them crackpot head doctors."

Jake snatched the pen and paper from Alexandra. "Where?"

She glared at him, then went to blow-dry her hair. It was silly, perhaps, but she needed a moment away from Jacob. She enjoyed the warm air until her locks were dry; then she leaned into the mirror and brushed her fingers across the dark circles forming beneath her eyes.

She almost didn't care. She'd lied to Jake when she said that all her dramatics had been an act. She was walking a fine line between calm and calamity. A wisp of a line. She felt ancient, like some haggard crone.

How did her sister look right now? Was she sleeping? Eating? Alexandra swallowed. Was Fletcher still breathing? She shook her head. She knew better than to let her mind wander down dangerous roads.

She walked back into the main room; Jake was going through her suitcase. She marched right over to him and swatted him away. He put the phone between his ear and shoulder and held up his hands in mock surrender. The nerve!

"Thanks again, Uncle Marty," he said, then ended the call. He put his phone in his back pocket. "Sorry."

She zipped up her bag and glared at him.

Jacob shrugged. "PI's are nosy by nature."

Deciding to let the issue drop she asked, "What did he say?" She'd heard his end of the conversation up until he'd taken her pad and pen away from her. More rudeness. She took a seat on the bed and pointed to him. "Spill." She rolled her eyes as he flipped through his notes. At least he was sitting at the small table and she didn't have to sit in the horrid chair.

"Seems the kid's with this Dan guy."

"We suspected as much. Who's Benjamin Drake? And how is he involved in all this?"

"Uncle Marty intercepted an email from Dan to Drake or Dr. Benjamin Drake, as it were. He's, as Uncle Marty likes to say, a crackpot head shrinker," Jake said mimicking his uncle's Scottish brogue.

"He's a psychiatrist?"

Jake squinted at the paper. "Seems so."

She ran her hand over the thin nubby comforter. "That makes sense."

"How so?"

"It's obvious Dan is certifiable."

"Yeah." Jake smiled. "I can agree with that. You want a beer?"

"No, thank you. So where is the good doctor?"

Jake stood up. "I feel like a beer."

"Good for you and good luck!"

He fished his keys from his pocket. "What do you mean good luck?"

"It's a dry county, which means they don't sell alcohol—"

"What the hell kind of place did you bring me to?"

She smiled.

"Uh-oh."

"What?"

He pointed at her. "Hell must have frozen over."

She rose a brow.

He grinned. "You gave me a real smile, and not one of your phony innkeeper smiles."

She frowned. "I don't have a 'phony' smile. I have a perfectly natural smile around my guests because I'm genuinely happy to see *them;* you on the other hand—" She didn't finish the sentence because her mouth was occupied by his. She closed her eyes for a second, then brought her knee up. "Ow," she hissed. "You bit my lip."

"You deserve it!" he said and adjusted himself. "God help you if you give me permanent damage."

"Oh, give me a break." She sucked on her lip. "You shouldn't have kissed me."

"You kissed me first!"

"That was in case someone was watching."

He smirked and tapped his finger on the tip of her nose. "Keep telling yourself that, sweetheart."

"You must have to buy special hats to fit your extra-large head. Just don't do it again," she said when he would have said something else.

"One day you're going to beg me to kiss you."

"Please hold your breath on that one," Alex said on a fake laugh, then sat down on the bed. "Now, where is this Dr. Benjamin Drake?"

"A couple hours west of here, outside of Nashville, Tennessee."

"All right, so we'll leave in the morning,"

"Fine." He went to the door and turned. "Get some rest and lock the door behind me."

She stood. "Good night."

Once the locks were in place, she picked up her cell phone and dialed a number she hadn't wanted to use. "It's me. Yes, I'm calling in that favor. His name's Dr. Benjamin Drake, and I need to know everything about him. Thanks. No, go ahead and put me on hold. I'll wait."

****

There was a soft knocking on his door. Jake groaned and rolled over in the bed. "I'm coming," he growled. He pushed away the covers and slipped on the pair of jeans he'd left on the floor.

He opened the door, squinting at the sun. "Yeah?"

"The lady wanted you to have this," squeaked the maid who handed Jake an envelope and ran off.

Jake scratched his stomach, yawned, and used his foot to shut the door. He pushed the curtain to the side and opened the note.

Jake,

I got a lead on Dr. Drake, and I couldn't wait for you to wake up. I'll be back in Blue Creek in a day or so. Please meet me there, and if you could tell the others the latest, that would be great.

Sincerely,

Alexandra

"Fuck that," Jake said balling up her note. If she thought for one minute she could cut him out of this thing after he'd come so far, then she was crazy. Not to mention he'd given her the information on Drake. But wait…He opened the note again and reread it. How the hell could she have gotten a lead on Drake? "Doesn't matter," he muttered and slipped on his hoodie. He grabbed his duffel bag and headed for the door.

He wasn't going back to Blue Creek as her highness had so haughtily decreed. No, Jake was going to find Dr. Drake and Alexandra. Then *they'd* find the kid. And that was how it was going to be.

Chapter Nine

Alexandra sat in the waiting room of Dr. Benjamin Drake's office and flipped through one of his outdated magazines. Dr. Drake was in his mid-thirties, single, and a well-respected psychiatrist. His father came from old money but had died when Drake was a child. Drake's mother was a socialite who was said to be traveling abroad, but who had been institutionalized five years ago by her one and only son.

"Ms. Madison?"

"Here," Alexandra said standing. Granny Vaughn would have enjoyed Alex using her name in this charade.

The secretary gave Alex a funny look and said, "Dr. Drake will see you now."

"Thank you."

The girl smiled a genuine smile that reached her honest eyes, which made her pretty in Alex's book. Though, referring to her as girl was crass, considering they were probably the same age.

Then again, with her blonde wig, push-up bra, and slutty suit, she herself was surely a spectacle. The fact that she *did* resemble Marylou was a sure-fire way to say "easy" without saying it. A special touch indeed!

Alex had a story planned out; hopefully it would do the trick. If the doctor had come into contact with her sister, then he would be familiar with her background, in which case Alex wanted her bases covered.

"Thank you," the doctor said to his secretary. He ushered Alex inside.

Alexandra controlled her surprise. Dr. Benjamin Drake wasn't drop dead gorgeous. No, he was a bit taller than her, with sandy brown hair styled to look like he'd just rolled out of bed, not to mention his chocolate brown eyes, which were enhanced by his wire-rimmed glasses. He had an aristocratic nose and beautifully manicured hands. He was her ideal of a proper life partner: intellectual, financially solvent, and lowkey sexy. Lastly, easily maneuvered; that was critical. No one, especially a man, would dictate to Alexandra McKay.

"Won't you have a seat, Ms. Madison." He pointed to one of the two chairs in front of his large oak desk.

"Yes, thank you," she said, taking a seat. "And call me Lexis." She smiled at him, and he smiled back. Charming.

"Nice to meet you, Lexis. Please call me Ben," Dr. Drake said. He leaned back in his leather chair. "Now, I'm told you need my help."

"Is this where you see patients?" she wondered aloud. It was a nice office, though somewhat clinical, and there was a faint odor of perspiration. Gross.

"No, this is my personal office. The room in which I see my patients is less formal." He gave her a patronizing smile, so she batted her eyelashes.

"Oh, I see." She crossed her legs. "To answer your question, yes, I need your help."

He tented his hands on top of his desk. "I'm all ears."

"I'm looking for my coworker—"

"Is he a patient of mine? Because I can't talk about patients."

"I don't believe *she* is, no." Alex was caught off guard. Fletcher wasn't seeing a psychiatrist. Was she? "Her name is Jamie McKay." His face contorted for a split second, but then he pasted on a smile. It was empty and fake. Fine.

"No, I'm sorry the name doesn't sound familiar."

She pulled out a handkerchief and fiddled with it. She'd play his game. "We received an anonymous tip saying you've been in contact with a man named Dan—no last name—who's with my coworker." She bit the inside of her cheek, and her eyes watered. "You see, Jamie's not stable, and he could be in terrible danger. We need your help to make sure she doesn't do anything to harm herself or anyone else. Jamie is a good person, Dr. Drake—"

He waved a finger. "Ah, ah, ah. It's Ben, remember."

The arrogance! She gave a shy smile. "Ben…you see Jamie hasn't been the same since her boyfriend committed suicide. Work had been helping, but then she left town out of the blue. So, you see, we need to find her."

He came around the desk, sat next to her, and took her hand with his clammy one. "Who's we? You said 'we' before about the anonymous tip."

"Oh, our local sheriff's department. She's a deputy or—or she was until her boyfriend's death." The doctor caressed her hand, and bile filled her throat. She would have thought saying she worked in law enforcement would discourage…Had the man never heard of sexual harassment? She hoped he wasn't like this with his patients. Not only was he unethical, but he was horrible at reading people.

"I see."

"Can you help us?" He'd ruined her entire fantasy; liars were not attractive to her, nor were sleazebags, and Dr. Drake was both. Pity.

He let go of her hand and sat back. "I'm afraid not. I don't think I personally know anyone by the name of Dan. It would seem you were all misinformed."

"But how can that be!" With southern flare, she brought her handkerchief up to cover her nose and mouth. If he needed a weak hysterical woman to get his rocks off, then she'd give it to him. "What am I going to do now? How am I going to go home and tell the sheriff? Not only are we no closer to finding Jamie, but we have someone doling out false information to the department."

Dr. Drake shook his head. "I'm truly sorry."

"Oh, I'm sure if you could help me you would. So please don't be sorry." But he would be. "I should go. I apologize for taking up your time."

He rose when she did. "Do you have a place to stay?" he asked.

"Yes, thank you."

"I would like to make it up to you if I could, Lexis," Drake said giving her his charming smile again.

"Please, don't feel obligated."

"No, not at all. I would enjoy the pleasure of your company." His expression actually turned sheepish. "Would you join me for dinner?"

She ducked her head and gave him a demure smile. "Oh, I don't know, Ben."

"Tell me where you're staying, and I'll pick you up around seven."

Alex rattled off the name of a hotel. "I'll see you tonight, then?"

"Oh, absolutely." Dr. Drake took her hand in his

and kissed her folded fingers. "I look forward to it."

"Me too." She might vomit.

He walked her to the lobby. "Until this evening."

"Bye," Alex said and hit the button to the elevator. She glanced over her shoulder not surprised to find Drake hovering in his doorway with a lecherous grin. The nerve.

She stepped into the elevator as soon as the doors opened and stabbed the button for the lobby with her index finger. That lying, dirty snake! No one played Alexandra McKay. No one. Least of all Dr. Benjamin Drake.

The elevator doors opened, and she swore under her breath that he would get his. With every click of her heels on the marble floor, she came up with a different way to exact revenge on the good doctor. By the time she reached her vehicle, she was smiling again.

Alex arrived at her hotel two hours later. She had done some shopping to prepare for tonight's excursion. She used her key card to open the door, then locked it behind her.

She put her bags down on the bed and was about to take off her wig when someone grabbed her.

"Who the hell are you?" said the gruff voice behind her.

Alex bit her captor's hand and swung around to slap him. "Damn it, Jacob! I told you to go back to Blue Creek."

"Princess?" Jake snickered. "Why in the hell are you dressed like that?"

"You're a private investigator! Surely you've gone undercover before," she said taking off her wig and shaking out her red hair.

"Yeah, but I'm a professional. Don't laugh. Damn

it, I'm a great PI!"

"I never said you weren't, Jacob." She'd hurt his tiny male feelings. Go figure.

"You implied it." Jake took his hair out of its ponytail and tied it back up. "Look, I thought we were in this together."

"Of course we are," she assured him and went into the bathroom.

"Couldn't prove it by me," Jake said standing next to the closed door. "That's why you left me at the motel—"

"I left you a note."

"Did you honestly think I would go back to Blue Creek without you?"

"I wasn't sure."

"What do mean you weren't sure? It sounded like a royal fucking decree," Jake said following her. He looked back at the bathroom when he realized she'd changed while she was in there. Now she had on a cream sweater and green skirt. The tight dress she had been wearing was lying on the bathroom floor and the spiked heels were behind the toilet.

She rolled her blue eyes. "It wasn't a decree…just simple instructions I hoped you would follow."

"But you weren't sure I would?"

"Lo and behold, here you are. In my space and in my way."

"Like I said, we're in this together." He sat on one of the double beds.

"How did you find me anyway?"

He smirked and motioned toward her suitcase.

Her eyes widened. "You weren't being nosy last night; you were planting a tracker."

"Good thing too."

"You have some nerve," she murmured.

He scoffed. "Yeah, yeah, I'm the dickhead, when you're the one who tried to ditch me! But that's beside the point. What I want to know is how you found out about Dr. Benjamin Drake."

"You told me." She glanced at the desk where she'd left her notebook.

"That's right, princess. I read your notes, which were interesting. How the hell did you come up with more information than Uncle Marty did?"

"I have my ways."

He stood and took hold of her arm. "Answer me!"

"Will you quit grabbing me?" She yanked her arm from his grasp.

Jake glared at her, then sat down back down with a grunt. "You're not being straight with me, and it's pissing me off!"

"As you wish," she murmured and sat on the bed next to him. "Granddaddy—"

"Don't give me that bullshit; your granddaddy's dead."

"Could I finish my sentence? Thank you. As you know Granddaddy Vaughn was a well-respected judge. He had a lot of influential friends, and he often invited these men and women to lavish parties at his home. I was usually the hostess at these soirees, and I was introduced to some powerful people."

He snorted. "And these people still talk to you now?"

"Granddaddy said to never burn bridges. In this world, who you know, and your connections, are keys to success. People need people, but more importantly they need people to—"

"You blackmail them?" Jake stood and began to

pace the small confines of the room.

"I've never blackmailed anyone."

"You know it's a crime, right?"

She scoffed. "My grandfather would never suggest blackmail."

"Explain it to me then."

"I've kept in touch with most of the people Granddaddy was acquainted with. By doing so, they've introduced me to the people they know and so on. I don't blackmail anyone. If they need something, I help them find it. Nothing illegal…I do have a conscience. I do people favors, and they do me favors in return."

He stopped his pacing to look her up and down. "What kind of favors?"

"Nothing you're thinking, I'm sure. I find them priceless antiques or point them in the right direction. I help them find the best of the best for whatever they need, and I do it with the utmost discretion."

"And what is it you get in return?"

"Guests."

"Huh?"

"They send me guests. You know, patrons for my B and B, or they come to stay themselves." She shrugged. "Networking."

"All right. Then what kind of favor did you do to get"—he pointed to her notepad—"that kind of information on someone?"

She slid off the bed and maneuvered past him. "I know a judge."

"That's not what I asked you." Jake huffed out a breath. "Look, we need to be honest with each other if we're going to work together."

Alex shrugged. "I was honest."

He rubbed his hands over his face. "What did you

do for this *judge*?"

"If you must know, I found her daughter." She got a bottle of water from the mini fridge and took a sip.

"Got any beer in there?"

She smirked and retrieved a beer for him. "Just in case you showed up," she explained.

He hesitated but took the beer and asked her how she'd found the judge's daughter.

"The girl was seventeen and into some deplorable activities. She ran away from home."

"And you found her how?"

"One reverts back to what they're used to."

He eyed her over the rim of his beer. "Explain."

"The girl was used to finer things, so when she arrived in Blue Creek, there was only one establishment she could go to."

He pointed his beer bottle at her. "Yours."

She smiled. "Precisely. Now, as I said, I've kept in touch with the people Granddaddy introduced me to, so I was familiar with the girl and her situation. The guy she had with her on the other hand was a cretin, but he only stayed for a few days."

"What did you do with him?" Jake sipped his drink, letting the cool liquid sit on his tongue for a moment, and tried not to notice how Alexandra lit up when she shared a story. Her blue eyes were bright—engaging even.

"I had my father scare the boy, enough so that he up and left without so much as a note. Heartbreaking for the girl."

His lips quirked upward. "Then you turned her over to her parents, right? Ryan and I have had a couple cases like that." He didn't particularly care for scaring kids straight, but he did enjoy it when families reunited.

She took a seat in the desk chair. "Not exactly."

He paused midsip. "What? Which part?"

"I called the girl's mother and let her know her daughter was safe and in my care. As a respected member of the community, I have quite a good reputation, and the judge was aware of it. We worked out a deal that I would have her daughter back on track and back home within a month."

He stared at her. "How the hell did you do that?"

"I had her mother cancel the girl's credit and debit cards; then after she had racked up quite the bill at the B and B, I informed her that her cards were declined."

Jake killed his beer. "You made it so she had no choice but to go running home to Mommy."

"No." Alex smiled. "She went to work."

"Work?"

"Yes, I told her if she couldn't pay me, she would have to work it off or I'd have to call the police."

"She worked at the B and B?"

"Yes, and she did a couple of shifts at the diner. Fletcher took her to the juvenile detention center; it's amazing how that cleared her head."

Jake grunted. "I bet it did."

"By the time she worked off her bill, she had a new outlook on things, and a lot more self-respect. She went back home on her own accord."

"Or so she thought?"

Alex shrugged a shoulder. "She did the work and made her own choices. I gave her the tools."

"So the girl's mother, a judge, owed you one."

"I didn't make a demand, just asked for a simple favor."

He crossed his arms over his chest and leaned against the TV console. "But she did it."

"Yes," Alex said sipping her water.

Jake rocked back on his feet. "How's the girl?"

"She's doing quite well. She graduated from high school last year, and she's in college getting a degree in hotel management."

"I'll be damned," he said shaking his head. "It's moments like these when I think you might actually have a heart."

She tsked him. "See, here you thought I'd done something underhanded and illegal."

"Like you haven't prejudged me, princess." He scoffed. "Sorry, not sorry."

Alex rolled her eyes.

"I'm assuming you met the good Dr. Drake; what did you think of him?" This he couldn't wait to hear. He took a seat on the edge of the bed.

"Yes, I met him, and he's dirty." She made a face.

"Not your type? That's surprising. He's smart, rich, good breeding; hell, I bet he even speaks French."

"Yes, those things are qualities I look for, but I can't stand liars or sleazy creeps. It's unfortunate too because he's quite nice to look at."

He shook his head. "Really?"

"I do have standards." She glanced at her watch and stood. "I need to get ready soon."

"For what?"

Alex went through her bags. "I have a date with Dr. Drake."

She'd gone shopping? What the hell? "I thought you said you didn't like the doc? Now you're going on a date with this ass hat?"

"If you would let me finish—"

He raised his hands in mock surrender. "Who's stopping you?"

"What *is* your problem?"

"I'm just saying if the guy was such a creep, why go on a date with him? Does he even have information to give? Does he know the kid or this Dan lunatic?"

"Oh, he knows. He pretended like he didn't, but he knows and he's hiding something."

"So you know he's a bad guy—" He jumped when she threw her water bottle at him. "What?"

"If you would let me finish my sentence! I swear your head is as thick as Casey's—"

"Hey, now." He sat back down and pointed a finger at her. "That's not nice."

She gurgled her words, which made him smile. Was it wrong he liked that he could get under her skin? She sure as hell got under his.

"Fine," she began again between clenched teeth, "Dr. Drake will come to pick me up for a date, but I won't be there!"

"Where will you be?"

She pulled a long piece of black fabric from one of the shopping bags. "I'll be breaking into his house."

He was on his feet. "*What!*"

She tsked him again. "Honestly, Jacob, how did you think I was going to find out the truth? Ply Dr. Drake with sex? Seduce him, then pick his brain? Give me a break."

"What about when he finds out you stood him up? You don't think he'll go crawling back to his house?"

"First of all, I didn't stand him up; Lexis Madison did. Besides, there will be someone waiting for him at the hotel."

"This hotel?" He crossed his arms over his chest. "And who's Lexis Madison?"

"No, the hotel where Lexis Madison, aka yours

truly, told him she'd be staying."

Jake scratched his jaw. "If you're not going to be at the hotel, who will?"

"An undercover officer," Alex said smiling.

"Undercover as what?"

She bit her lip. "A call girl."

He threw his hands in the air. "That's entrapment."

"Not if they don't coerce him into it. If it's his idea…" She shrugged. "Besides, all he has to do is say no."

Jake stared at her. "You don't think he will?"

"No, I don't."

"So we're just going to break into his house while he's being"—Jake waved a hand in the air—"whatever."

"I like to think of it as being brought to justice. I have a nasty suspicion the good doctor has seduced plenty of his patients, and I'm hoping this will have them coming out of the woodwork. Nothing like a public scandal to create chaos, am I right? Wait, I never said you were breaking in with me—"

"Now hold on a damn minute." He blocked her between the wall and the bed. "I thought we were in this together."

"We are."

"Good." He moved out of her way. "I *am* going with you."

She began pulling things out of her shopping bags and piling them on the bed. "Fine, you can wait in the car."

"Fuck that! I'm going *in* with you. I am a PI for Christ's sake; I've done this before, you know?"

"I'm aware of that, Jacob."

Oh, he hated that tone. "What do you know about

breaking into a house, anyway?"

"You forget Craig ran a securities firm. He's taught us all a thing or two about security systems." She set the empty bags aside. "And, if you must know, Casey and Fletcher were never satisfied with a simple game of hide and seek. There had to be obstacles like locked doors and booby traps."

He shook his head. "After some of the stories I've heard from Ryan, I guess I'm not surprised." He picked up a utility belt from the bed. It was a nice one, but— "Where the hell did you find all this stuff?"

She gave him a droll look. "I typed 'where to buy spy gear' into my phone's search engine. And like magic"—she snapped her fingers—"a list of shops appeared."

"Funny." He tossed the belt back. "Do you even know what you're going to look for at the doc's place?"

"The truth."

He snorted. "And you think it will be there plain as day?"

"No, I'll have to search for answers, but I *will* find them."

"Is that your phone?" Jake asked pointing to where the incessant ringing was coming from.

"Yes… Hello. Hi, Craig. Yes, I'm perfectly fine. I know. I knew it. In the fan pull right? That's what I thought. Cameras too, I know. Okay, I'll call you when I have something. I love you too. Thanks, Craig," she said and hung up the phone. "He found the bugs and the camera."

"You don't have to look so damn happy about it," he said at the same time she said, "Right where I told you they were."

Figures. He puffed out a breath. "What's done is

done…Now, about the doc's house, I'm going in with you and that's final."

"Whatever you say, Jacob."

Chapter Ten

After meeting the man, Dr. Drake's house was everything Alexandra thought it would be. A beautiful Edwardian home with a well-kept lawn, but the minute she picked the lock to the back door, disabled the security system, and turned on her night-vision goggles, the truth was undeniable: the man's taste was as loathsome as his character. The back room was reminiscent of an old-fashioned bordello and a cheap one at that.

"Can someone say 'sleaze'?" Alex whispered into her mic.

"That bad, huh?" Jake laughed from his end, which was in his vehicle.

"Like someone regurgitated a lovely Italian meal on the walls."

"Yikes!" His words were gruff, but his voice played over her skin like warm velvet.

She shook herself. "You're not fooling anyone, Jacob. It's right up your alley."

"Come on, princess. You saw my place."

"Sorry, no bullet holes here...I found the office." She entered the room, careful not to bump into anything. She took a seat behind a desk identical to the one in Dr. Drake's office and began going through his files.

"Find anything?"

"No, but I confirmed Dr. Drake is a moron."

"How so?"

"The man is so arrogant he doesn't even keep his documents secure." Presumptuous prick. There were piles and piles of folders on his desk.

"That's not arrogance. That's plain ignorance."

"True." Alex shuffled through more papers. She wouldn't pry into his patients' medical histories, but she did stop at a familiar name. "Oh, my—"

"What is it? Did you find something?" Jake's tone was anxious.

"Sort of. Not about Fletcher. Remember Drake's mother is in an institution?"

"Yeah, but they're telling everyone she's traveling the world. Right?"

"That's the one." Her eyes widened, and she reread the page.

"So?"

"She's not mentally unstable."

"Depressed?"

"No. He's treating her for schizophrenia."

"Poor woman, and to have a criminal for a son too."

Alex bit her lip, then read through Evangeline Drake's medical file. She went over it twice. "There's zero history of schizophrenia in any of this documentation."

"Wait, what? She's not off her rocker?"

"Where did you attend finishing school? Jerk University?" She rolled her eyes and flipped pages.

"Hah. Hah."

She pulled out her phone and did a quick search for the medications listed on the post-it note stuck to the inside of the folder. She scrolled through the long list of side effects that were listed and gasped. "He's giving her a combination of drugs to induce psychosis." Was it a coincidence someone had done something similar to her sister almost two years ago?

"Hold up…you're saying by giving his mother this shit he's making—That's fucked up."

"I couldn't agree more." Alex used her phone to take pictures of Dr. Drake's notes. She would help Mrs. Drake.

"Anything else?" Jake asked a few minutes later.

"Nothing to help us find Fletcher, but—" Alex's gaze shot to the ceiling where a floorboard creaked above her head.

"But what? Alex? Are you there?"

"I heard something upstairs," she whispered. She crept out of the office and stared up the ornate staircase.

"Get the hell out of there, Alexandra. Get the hell out or I'm coming in," he warned.

"Just stick to the plan," she hissed.

"I will if you will. Shit!"

She got to the first landing. "What now?"

"Neighborhood security. Damn it all to hell."

"Show your PI license." She cocked her head to the side. Was someone up here?

"I know that, princess, but I'm going to have to cut off communication so we don't get arrested. Get out of the house! Good evening, officers…"

Static filled her ears, and she slipped the earpiece out. There was no way she wasn't going up to the second landing. Jacob would have to get over it. The wood under her feet groaned; she cringed. She glanced up the last few steps. Nothing. She tiptoed into the hall; it looked like some creepy maze. Wonderful.

She walked with her back to the wall until she came upon the only room with light shining under the door. Putting her ear against the cool wood, she tried to make out any movement; again nothing. Dr. Drake didn't have any pets or girlfriends, so what in the hell was going on? She took off her goggles and hooked them onto her belt; she didn't want the light to make her hesitate.

She took a deep breath, put one hand on the knob, the other on the door, and pushed it open. Her breath came rushing out of her. The blue-green gaze staring back at her belonged to her sister.

"Fletcher?" Her knees went weak.

"It's about damn time!" Fletcher headed toward her, then stopped midstride.

The door shut behind her as Alex closed the gap and took hold of her sister. "I am *so* not speaking to you for a month after the hell you've put me through."

"What are you babbling about? *I'm* still not talking to *you*," Fletcher said, tightening her embrace.

"Let's get you out of here. How the hell did you get involved with Dr. Drake anyway?" Alex checked the earpiece to see if Jacob was back online. He wasn't.

Fletcher crossed her arms over her chest. "Who?"

"Dr. Drake?" Alex took a good look at her sister. Fletcher had always been disgustingly tiny, but her big mouth made up for it as far as Alex was concerned. Right now, her sister was being swallowed up by a…"Fletcher? Why the hell are you dressed like you're going to a ball?" Her sister never wore dresses. Ever. She was a total tomboy. Her signature look hadn't changed much since she was a child—overalls, T-shirt, and pigtails—but this was—

"Not by choice. Course I've never seen you in a recon outfit. Suits you."

Alex ran a hand down the sleek black leotard she'd

purchased for this endeavor. “Of course it does!”

“Pulled out all the stops too. Recorder, radio, night vision, and a camera. I’m impressed.” Fletcher looked Alex up and down. “But where’s your gun? I’ve never known you not to come packing.”

“Jacob didn’t think I needed one and wouldn’t let me bring it.” Alex rolled her eyes; this was what happened when you listened to the male of the species.

“Jake’s here? Where?”

“He’s being questioned by the neighborhood rent-a-cop, so we broke off radio contact.”

“Makes sense. Well, Alex this is fun.” Fletcher made a big production of twiddling her thumbs.

“Are you coming or not?” Alex asked annoyed. Here she’d come to rescue her sister and the little beast wasn’t helping any.

“Did you bring a blowtorch?”

“Why in the hell would I bring a blowtorch?”

“How else are you going to get me out of these?” Fletcher lifted up the skirt of the dress to show the shackles around her ankles. They were attached to a longer chain which was hooked into a wall.

“What in the world?”

Fletcher shrugged. “Insurance.”

“What?” Alex bent down on the floor to get a closer look. This did not bode well.

“So I couldn’t escape. Come on, Alexandra, get with the program. Hell’s bells, some rescue this is. Berating the victim should be against policy.”

How could her sister joke at a time like this? “Well, excuse me.”

Fletcher smirked. “Don’t be a bitch, Alexandra.”

“I’m not being a bitch. Damn it, Fletcher,” she practically screamed as she stood up.

"Shut up. Jeez, are you trying to blow my escape?"

"Don't tell me to shut up—oh, never mind. Did you try to pick it?"

Fletcher sent her a droll look. "Do you think I would still be stuck in this stupid ass dress if I could pick the damn thing. Get real! If I can't do it, then it can't be done."

"I'll have to find a blowtorch then." Where in the hell was she going to find one? Fletcher fell onto the bed, her chains clinking as she did so. "At least it's a nice room, much better than downstairs," Alex said, knowing she'd get a snort out of her sister.

"How's Jasper? Don't go into uptight bitch mode, Alex. I'm not trying to bring up shit. I heard he had another heart attack and was wondering."

"How did you hear that? The bugs in my house!"

"No, he's been keeping an ear out and thought he'd be nice and let me know. The bastard." Fletcher hissed, then looked at her sister. "So…is Jasper okay?"

"Jasper's going to be fine. He had to have surgery, but he'll be better than new in no time."

"That's good then."

"Wait, when was the B and B bugged?"

"After the lodge—"

"But why *my* house?" Alex was relieved that she hadn't been spied on for long.

Fletcher huffed. "Maybe I mentioned that Granny Vaughn's is kinda our center."

Alex tried not to let the pleasure of her sister's words show on her face. This was not the time to preen. "I see."

"Heard how you don't give a shit about finding me."

Her cheeks heated. "I said, quite clearly to whoever

had bugged my home, that I didn't care about *Jamie*."

"Yep." Fletcher smirked. "I caught that too."

"You knew I..." The understanding on her sister's face said that Fletcher knew exactly what Alex had been doing. "Well." She cleared her throat. "How did Drake get you here, anyway?"

Fletcher sat up. "Who the hell is this Drake guy you keep yammering about?"

"The guy who owns the house. The one who's been keeping you chained to a wall?"

"Oh, Benji." Fletcher nodded, then stared at her sister. "Benji isn't the one who captured me. Jake got the email—I got his. I paid for it too! Lost my privileges and everything."

"Wait...what are you saying—"

A door slammed downstairs.

All the blood drained from Fletcher's face. "He's back!"

"Who? Dan?"

"Hide. I can't believe...Oh, fuck." Fletcher pulled on Alex's belt.

Alex swatted Fletcher's hands away from the recorder. "What in the world is going on?"

"Hide, please." Fletcher pushed her down toward the floor. "Quick, get under the bed and breathe like Granddaddy taught us on our hunting trips. If he finds you—Alex, *please*."

Alex swallowed, then contorted herself under the bed, brought her side to the wall, and barely breathed. A pair of black leather loafers entered the room, and she closed her eyes.

"What have you done?"

There was something familiar about the man's voice, but Alex couldn't place it.

"Pardon?" Fletcher said.

Her brow pinched. Fletcher's tone was odd; it was breathy and—

"You don't know?"

"Know what, my darling?"

Alex's eyes flew open, and she stared at the chains keeping Fletcher prisoner. *My darling?*

"You truly don't know, do you, Jamie, my love. Ah, I am sorry for making the accusation. I should have known better."

The man walked closer to Fletcher, and Alex clenched her fists. He was no doubt touching her sister.

"No, darling. I understand your distrust. After last time."

Alex blinked at the guilt in Fletcher's tone.

"But you learned your lesson, my sweet. I told you punishment often brings clarity. Did I not?"

"Yes. As always you were correct. The scars are healing nicely—"

Scars? What the hell had this bastard done?

"Ah, ah, ah, not scars; for I would never scar someone so sacred to me. They are merely a testament of my love for you."

"Of course."

"I do these things because I love you and love is forever."

Alex winced when Fletcher sat on the bed.

"You said there was a problem? That I've done something?"

"No, not you, my love. However, our host has compromised our position."

Alex almost smiled. One sleazebag down…

"Benji? How?"

"Why he insisted you call him that I don't know."

The man's sigh was heavy. "He was caught in a compromising position with a woman of questionable moral standing."

"You don't mean—"

"Deplorable, I know. He's only human. Now, we must take our leave, for our welcome has ended."

Leave? No! Alex bit her lip. What could she do? If she had brought her gun, this would already be over. Surely, between the two of them, she and her sister could take this guy.

"Yes, of course. I do believe some things should remain hidden under the beds of man."

Okay, she needed to stay put. *Real subtle, Fletcher.*

"Your words so often astound me, Jamie. You truly are the most remarkable creature."

And you're a psycho.

"Thank you. Where will we go?"

Good, Fletcher, get us something to go on.

"We will go where I had originally planned. I thought you had given it away in your confusion, but you did not."

"The email said nothing of our secret place."

"Don't upset yourself. I couldn't bear to see you cry. You gave nothing away. Our secret is safe. We are safe." He sighed. "Now, can I trust you enough to unlock you?"

"Yes, do I have time to change? I would rather wear something more appropriate for travel."

"You do please me. Yes, of course. Shall I choose?" She must have agreed because the psycho went to the closet, then handed Fletcher something to wear. He wasn't going to watch her, was he? The creepy voice made agreeable noises, and Alex swallowed hard to keep down the bile that rose up in her throat.

"Beautiful. Absolutely exquisite. Now we must leave out the back. Lord knows what kind of trouble Benjamin has gotten into."

The same kind you're in, you sick son of a bitch.

The man moved closer to the bed to unlock Fletcher's chains, and Alex held her breath. His pasty white hands were steady as he unlocked the padlock.

"Did you pack the rest of my things?"

"I'll get you new things. Now don't argue; money means nothing next to your happiness, my sweet."

Alexandra kept still while they exited. She was about to move when Fletcher came back into the room. Her sister knelt by the bed.

"Alex?" Fletcher whispered.

Alex tapped her nails in a small tattoo against the hardwood floor.

"I have to talk fast. He's going to burn down the house—fire's his thing. I'm going to knock down a vase downstairs. You have exactly four minutes to get out of the house from then. There's a bathroom three doors down with a balcony and a tree right outside—that's your way out. You can do it. I'm still pretty pissed at you, but I love you 'cause you're my sister and all that crap. I love you and the family and Jasper and Jake, Okay. Tell them that just in case. Shit. And…"

The floor creaked. The man's loafers came back into the room.

Fletcher cleared her throat. "I thank you God for sending the love of my life to show me the right path. Amen."

"I'm sorry to interrupt, but we must go."

"Yes, of course."

Alex lay helplessly under the bed. The room went dark, and two sets of footsteps descended the stairs. A few breaths later, a crash resounded from downstairs. Four minutes. She slipped her night-vision goggles back on and put her earpiece back in. "Jacob?" she whispered, but there was no answer. With as much stealth as she could manage, Alex got out from under the bed and made her way to the hall. She opened the third door, as her sister had told her.

The bathroom was luxurious, the bouquet of rose and jasmine inviting, but there wasn't time to stop and enjoy. Taking every precaution, she opened the french doors and snuck out onto the balcony. She ducked down when a car pulled out of the back drive without lights. "Fletcher," she whispered. She squeezed her stinging eyes shut for a moment; she'd been so close. So damn close.

Alexandra hesitated. The car parked up the street and wasn't leaving. What had Fletcher said? Fire was his thing or something like that. He's going to watch? Alex didn't have a choice there wasn't any time for a choice. She had to get away from this house.

"Are you out of the damn house yet?" Jacob's voice hissed across the radio.

"Thank God, Jacob! Do you see that sportscar up the street?"

"The silver one?"

"Yes, follow it. Fletcher's in that car," Alex choked out. He didn't answer her, but the revving of an engine and squealing tires was enough. "Don't make it obvious, Jacob. The guy's not stable."

Alex took a deep breath and grabbed the nearest tree branch. She swung herself into the tree and prayed it would hold her. She went down as fast as humanly possible; but it wasn't fast enough. As soon as her feet hit the ground, the earth beneath her feet shook, then everything went black.

Chapter Eleven

Jake sat in one of the chairs in the hospital waiting room and tried to put the events of the last few hours in order. He'd gotten up this morning pissed off at Alexandra, and now he was praying she would be all right. He'd been chasing down the sportscar when the reflection in his review mirror lit up like the Fourth of July.

Jake rubbed his hands over his face. He had been torn by the two choices he'd had in front of him. One, follow the kid, or two, make sure Alexandra was still in one piece. His first instinct had been to keep following the kid, but when he wasn't able to reach Alexandra over the radio, he'd made an illegal U-turn and gone back to the Drake house. Then he'd set about finding her.

He clenched and unclenched his fists to quell the tremor. He'd found her all right, lying semiconscious underneath a pile of branches. Jake couldn't remember the last time he had been so pissed or sca—

"Mr. Keller?"

Jake jumped to his feet. "Here!" The doctor's smile did nothing to comfort him either.

She held out her hand. "I'm Dr. Thatcher. Your wife is perfectly lucid now. She has a couple mild lacerations and a few bruises, but no concussion."

Jake breathed a sigh of relief.

The doctor patted his arm. "She'll be fine."

"Can I see her?" Jake looked toward the corridor of rooms.

"Of course, this way."

Jake stared at the curtain and shifted from foot to foot. Antiseptic perfumed the place, and it made him want to hurl.

"Go on in. I've already gone over everything with your wife. In fact, she's already filled out the paperwork; all you need to do is check out with the discharge nurse."

Jake stood back as Dr. Thatcher and Alexandra said their good-byes. He knew Alex wasn't paying much attention because she was staring at him. Jake didn't mind because he was staring right back.

"Did you get her?" Alex asked once the doctor left. She got off the bed and straightened the scrubs they'd given her to wear.

He shook his head.

"No?" Her fists clenched at her sides. "What do you mean no?"

He opened his mouth, but she pushed past him and went to the desk.

He grabbed the plastic bag containing her things and followed her out. "I didn't have much of a choice, did I?" He waited until she finished signing and headed for the elevators. "I could keep going after Fletcher or make sure you weren't dead."

The elevator doors slid closed and she glared at him. "*I* was fine!"

"You looked near death to me," he said through gritted teeth. They weren't alone in the elevator.

She stood back to let someone off. "See…I was fine."

"Can we talk about this later?"

"Oh, absolutely." She tapped her bootie-clad foot until it was their turn to exit. "Okay, how about now?"

"What?" he hollered, the sound echoing in the parking garage.

"Don't you dare take that tone of voice with me, Jacob Keller!"

He opened the passenger side door and guided her in. He tried to buckle her seatbelt, but she swatted at him. "Fine," Jake grumbled and walked to his side of the vehicle.

He climbed in behind the wheel. "And I'm not the one here who has a *tone*." He started the engine and glared at her. "You could have been dead. One might say, 'Thanks, Jake, for coming to my rescue,' or 'I'm grateful you made sure I was alive.' Try one of those."

"Fine! Thank you for coming to *my* rescue. I'm *so* very grateful to you for making sure I was alive. But *I* was perfectly fine. *Fletcher's* the one who needed to be rescued. *Fletcher* is the whole reason we're in this mess!"

"Well, excuse the fuck outta me, your highness!" Jake said, speeding up. She was lashing out at him because she was scared for the kid, he got that, but for fuck's sake, a guy could only take so much. "You're a real piece of work, you know that? Do you really think I wanted to go back and look for you when the kid was so close? Think again, sweetheart."

"Slow down," she hissed and turned toward him. "If that's the case, why did you come back for me? Why didn't you keep going after Fletcher? I mean, if that's what you wanted to do?"

He pulled into the hotel parking lot. "I have no fucking idea why I chose to help *you*, but I regret the decision."

She shook her head and got out of the SUV. “As do I.”

He followed her through the rows of vehicles. “You need a key card, you know?” he said holding up the card. She turned abruptly and tried to snatch it from his hand.

“Give it to me.”

Jake raised his arm above his head.

She narrowed her eyes. “I don’t have time for your childish games, Jacob.”

He walked ahead of her, then looked over his shoulder and said, “I’m staying with you.”

“You most certainly are not!”

“Yes, I am.” He stopped again. “Despite what you think, you could have died. And it wouldn’t hurt to watch over you just in case.”

“That’s ridiculous.”

“I don’t think so, sweetheart. I’m staying with you and that’s that. You want the keycard?” He made a production of slipping it into his boxer briefs. “Then you can come here and get it.”

“You really need to grow up,” she said and strode past him.

He had to do a double take; surely his eyes were deceiving him…was she trying not to laugh? Had that been a slight smile on her lips?

Alex glanced over her shoulder, her mask of cool indifference back in place. “Well, come on. You have the card, and I need some sleep.”

Jake couldn’t help but grin. He’d won—he’d finally won. Hot damn!

****

The water slid over her body. She was exhausted; sleep had been far from coming last night. Not only were thoughts of Fletcher, and how close Alex had come to saving her, consuming her, but Jacob snored. She sighed and shut off the water. If they didn't find Fletcher again, she didn't know what she'd do. How would she look her family in the eyes? How would she look at herself, for that matter?

She swallowed. She had been fooling herself for some time now. Wanting to believe Fletcher wasn't in real danger. Maybe because it was her fault they were in this mess in the first place.

Thoughts of Fletcher being "punished" by that psycho played over and over again in Alex's mind. Her sister had enough scars—inside and out. But she was alive, and that was enough to keep Alex going. And maybe she had been somewhat tough on Jacob; he had come to save her. If she was honest, that's more than she had expected him to do.

She stared at her reflection and bit her lip to quell her smile. She shouldn't find his antics amusing, but—no, no buts. Alex straightened her shoulders; she wouldn't lighten her resolve when it came to Jacob. Couldn't.

Slipping on a sweater and a skirt, she opened the bathroom door and shook her head. There he was passed out in the chair, drooling. He could sleep. Taking out a pen, she wrote him a short note saying she'd be back. There was something she had to do.

It only took half an hour to find the sanitarium. She got out of her vehicle, straightened her skirt, and headed for the intricate doors. It was a beautiful location; money made this place more like a resort than an institution.

"May I help you?" the woman at the front desk asked.

"Yes, I'm here to see Evangeline Drake, please."

"Do you have an appointment?"

"I'm with the law office representing Dr. Benjamin Drake." Alex ignored the woman's widening eyes and glanced down to see this morning's newspaper lying on the desk. Dr. Drake was on the cover trying desperately to hide his handsome face. The caption read *Doctor of Depravity?* Alex pursed her lips, fitting.

The woman looked between Alex and the paper, then leaned in and whispered, "Is it true?"

"I'm not at liberty to say," Alex said, but she made sure her face spoke volumes.

"I knew there was something wrong with that man," the woman said.

Alex looked at the woman's badge. "Can I speak frankly with you, Patricia? You strike me as an honest woman."

She nodded. "People tell me that all the time."

Alex pursed her lips, took a good look at the woman's desk, and made a decision. "I'm not really with the law office…" She waited until Patricia gasped. "But I am a private investigator. I've come across information indicating Evangeline Drake is here under false pretenses."

Patricia's slouch turned ramrod straight. "That's simply not possible."

"Not by anyone here, I assure you." Alex waited a beat. "But by her own son; if you can believe it."

The woman's face drained of all color. She was horrified—good.

"We also obtained information about the, shall we say, extracurricular activities Dr. Drake was involved in; we informed the police." She pointed to the paper. "They were watching him."

Patricia looked from one side of the room to the other. "What is it you want me to do?"

"First, I need to see Evangeline Drake; then I'm going to need your help."

Fifteen minutes later, Patricia whispered, "I'll be right outside."

Alex waited until the door closed to look at Mrs. Drake. The former socialite's hair was white and unkempt, her clothes hung off her frail frame, and there was a slight staleness wafting around her. Alex had seen a picture of the woman in the society pages; she had been beautiful once. Her mind shot to her own grandmother and her eyes squeezed shut. If anyone had done this to—that man would pay.

Patricia said the doctors kept Mrs. Drake heavily sedated, so Alex whispered her greeting.

Evangeline struggled to lift her head. "Do I know you?"

Alex pulled a chair next to the other woman. "No, you don't know me. My name is Alexandra McKay, and I've come to help you."

She rocked back and forth in her chair. "That's what they all say. We're here to help you, Evangeline. This pill will help you." She took hold Alex's hand. "I'm not crazy!"

"I know, Evangeline. I know all about what your son has done."

"Benji." Evangeline nodded. "Troubled boy. Never could get through to him." She dropped Alex's hand.

"I understand."

"I tried to get him away from the demon creature."

"Demon creature?" Alex squeezed her eyes shut and prayed it was the meds making Evangeline hallucinate.

She shook her head. "Never any good. Never liked him."

"The demon creature was a man? Do you mean Dan?"

"Things get fuzzy." Evangeline tapped her temple. "Dan…sounds right. Came here to see me with Benji, he did—no good, that one."

"You don't remember anything else?"

"Doctors and pills. Needles, lots of needles."

"I'm going to get you out of here."

Evangeline cackled. "They'll never let me go."

"Trust me," Alex said, and then called for Patricia to come in. "Evangeline, you know Patricia?"

"Yes."

"We're going to help you!" Patricia promised.

Mrs. Drake picked at the sash on her robe and mumbled something under her breath.

Alex pointed to Patricia. "Can you get me to a computer?"

"Sure thing."

An hour or so later, Alexandra sat in the waiting room while detectives served a warrant to the head of the sanitarium. Alex had taken the notes from Drake's home, scanned them, then emailed them to an old college friend of her grandfather's, a retired judge who still carried a lot of weight in this part of Tennesee. He had then sent them along through the proper channels, and within an hour, the good men in cheap suits showed up.

"Patricia, could you come here please?" asked the chief of staff.

"Yes?" The woman walked over to him with her head held high.

"Do you have something you want to tell me?"

Alexandra took the opportunity to say good-bye to Evangeline. The former socialite didn't have a home to go to, but she had rich, powerful friends. Alex had no doubt once the truth was out, those friends would be coming out of their fancy homes to help.

****

"So how did Patricia explain herself?" Jake asked Alex when she returned to the hotel and told him what had happened. He was impressed. Fuck that! He was downright astonished. There may be hope for her yet.

"Just as I told her to." Alex toasted him with the mimosa she'd ordered from room service. She sipped, then stared at him in a sexy kinda way. Which he normally would revel in, but right now he wanted answers.

She handed him a champagne flute, but he set it aside. "Alexandra?"

She rolled her eyes and sat on the bed. He sat a safe distance away in the chair.

"Well, you see, Patricia is a trusting person who usually keeps to herself, but something about Dr. Drake bothered her. She never told anyone; after all, Patricia is not a gossip."

"Got it." Jake kept his grin to himself. Her storytelling was a treat. Hell, her wall of ice was melting, and what he was seeing…Jake shifted in his seat; nope, he wasn't going there.

"Good. Now, Patricia, being of kind heart, decided to hire a private investigator to look into Dr. Drake. Lo and behold, the investigator was able to find the documentation proving Drake's criminal activities. The investigator informed Patricia, and she, being the upstanding citizen that she is, informed an old family friend."

“Who happened to be one of the city’s most prestigious judges?”

“Why, yes!” She grinned and sipped from her glass. “This friend was indeed a judge, and he took the information to the local authorities with a warrant and”—she snapped her fingers—“faster than you can say ‘felony,’ Evangeline Drake was released into police custody.”

“And that’s it?”

“Patricia is a hero or heroine as it were. Evangeline is free and will be found sane. Dr. Drake will be brought up on more charges and will rot in his cell for years to come.” She lifted her glass. “I love happy endings.”

“I hate to break it to you—”

Her face fell. “Then don’t.”

“Alex, what you did for that woman was fucking awesome, no question, but we’re no closer to solving our own problem. You know your sister. Kidnapped. Any of this ringing a bell?” He ducked in time to miss the champagne flute she threw at him.

She stood. “How dare you suggest I’ve forgotten about my sister.”

“That didn’t come out right.”

“Oh, you spoke so eloquently I couldn’t have misunderstood one word!” She shook her head. “I just wanted…never mind.”

“What?” Jake came up to stand behind her. “What did you want?”

“I wanted to be able to help someone in all this.”

“You *did* help someone. Mrs. Drake is a free woman because of you. Dr. Drake is in jail where he belongs. Even Patricia will probably lead a happier life because of you. I wasn’t making light of what you did,

Alexandra. I'm impressed."

"Oh, goody, I have your approval; now I can sleep."

And there was the ice! "I'm trying to be nice here." He sat his ass back down. "What the hell do you want from me?"

"I don't want anything from you, Jacob. As I've told you several times." She sighed. "This is getting us nowhere. We may as well drive home this afternoon."

"It's hours away."

"Your point is?"

"You haven't had much sleep," he pointed out.

She pulled out her suitcase. "I can sleep when I get home."

Chapter Twelve

"You mean she was right there in front of you?" Casey snapped.

Alexandra sat back in her chair. "What could I have done?"

"I don't give a flying—"

"Casey," Ryan began, "I understand you're upset, but Alexandra did everything she could. She almost died, for heaven's sake."

"Fletcher could be dead now!" Casey turned to her father. "Pops?"

"He's right. Alex put her life on the line." He put an arm around his wife's shoulders. "This has gone on too long. I think I may need to contact the FBI."

"What could they do that we haven't already done?" Jake shook his head. It was like the seventh circle of hell around this table, and he wasn't even being blamed for anything. That fell on Alexandra. They all seemed to be accusing her without *actually* accusing her, which pissed him off.

"Not a damn thing," Craig said.

"They don't have the connections Uncle Marty or, apparently, Alexandra have," Ryan said, and Jake appreciated his brother's attempt to help their cause.

"Yeah, I'd like to know what the hell you did to get those connections, too, Alexandra—"

"That's enough!" Savannah shouted. "I'm scared too, Casey, but your sister doesn't deserve your anger."

"Everyone needs to calm down," Charlie said and got up to refill people's drinks.

"I agree," Savannah said.

"Look, Mrs. Drake said Benjamin knew Dan. That's at least a place to start."

"The woman wasn't even lucid yet. You said so yourself."

"I remember what I said, Casey. Thank you very much."

"You know, Alexandra, if you didn't want to find Fletcher, why the hell are you wasting our time?" Casey said, rising from the table.

Alex opened her mouth, but Jake held up a hand, then pointed to his sister-in-law. "I think it's time you shut the hell up, Casey."

"Jake!"

"No, Ryan, I'm going to have my say. Now, Casey, you're right, Alex didn't want to go on the hunt for Fletcher, but she did it anyway. Did you ask yourself why? I bet you didn't. You know, I'm not a big Alex fan myself," he said and smirked at Alex. "Sorry."

She shrugged. "Sure."

He ignored the glares from around the table. "None of you ever wondered why?" Casey opened her mouth, but Jake cut her off. "She's doing it because despite what you think, she loves Fletcher. She almost died for her. She helped save a perfect stranger. She's trying; why don't you give her some fucking credit? And if you want to point the finger at someone, point it here! I stopped following a car I knew Fletcher was in to get Alex. So I'm to blame."

"No one blames you," Charlie huffed out. "Don't be silly."

"Why the hell not? I was as close as Alex was—"

"Jacob, you're wasting your breath," Alexandra said.

"I don't think so—" Jake began.

Jebb came running into the kitchen. "I've got it," he hollered.

"What?" Emmit asked over everyone else.

Jebb took a deep breath, then blew it out. "Alex said she had a recorder with her, but it got messed up. Well, I was able to retrieve the file. And I can tell you Fletcher *told* Alex to hide."

"Wait a minute, Jebb. If you're here, who's watching Mack?"

"Good question, Craig!" Charlie sat up. "Jebb?"

"No worries, Mack's watching a movie in one of the guestrooms upstairs. Plus, I put up a camera." He pulled out his phone. "I'd know if she moved."

Charlie pursed her lips. "Thanks a lot."

"Enough," Casey began. "Okay, Bullfrog, let's hear it."

Jebb played the recording, though Alex didn't actually want to relive the entire thing. She kept her gaze focused on the chains of her fan. Craig had gotten rid of all the surveillance equipment, but she was still upset her handmade fan pulls were nowhere to be found. Now she would have to get new ones…of course that could mean redecorating—

"That sick son of a bitch!" Her father jumped out of his seat and headed for the bathroom. It was no secret intense emotions upset Emmit McKay's stomach.

Savannah shook her head. "I have to agree with your father."

"She mentioned the email, so it must contain more information than we've been able to figure out," Jebb said.

Craig crossed his arms over his chest. “We’ve all read and reread the email, and none of us has come up with a damn thing.”

“But wait a minute.” Alex sat up. “They had to have been at the lodge, so obviously that wasn’t his final destination.”

Charlie nodded. “I’m with you there. Do you think Fletch may have left a clue at the lodge?”

“It would make sense. The first part of the email led us to the bunker, the second part to the lodge. Logic dictates the final entry of the email would lead us to another location,” Ryan said.

Jake grabbed a beer from the fridge. “But we searched the damn lodge, and all we found was a dead body.”

“Noah sure as hell won’t let us up there either,” Casey said.

Craig sighed. “I could get him up there.”

“I doubt that,” Emmit said coming back in the room and taking his seat next to his wife. “Noah’s under a lot of scrutiny with the murder of an officer.”

“Larry was retired.”

“Doesn’t matter, Jebb. An officer is an officer, plain and simple,” Emmit told his son.

Jake leaned against the counter. “We need to go up there.”

“We can’t,” Alex began. “Noah’s watching. It’s a crime scene, after all.”

“Putting it off isn’t a great idea, either,” Casey said.

“What if Fletch was doing what Ryan suggested?” Charlie asked. “What if the lodge was one of the locations she knew about, and the last part of the email was where they had been planning to go?”

Casey pointed to the recorder. "But we just heard her tell that creep that 'the email said nothing of our secret place.' So I'm guessing she was also telling us or Alex."

"She's right," Savanah said and everyone agreed.

Alex pursed her lips. "What if instead of telling us a direct location, Fletcher was trying to guide us to a clue that would lead to the next location. Does that make sense?"

Jake nodded. "It does to me."

"Anyone have a copy of the email?" Emmit asked.

"I do, Pops," Jebb said and pulled a folded piece of paper from his pocket. "I've kept working on it, just in case.

"All right, the last part says, 'Maybe you should take her on a treasure hunt. Oftentimes the key to finding truth is to figure out where your heart lies. Nothing new here. I'm well, if not a little antsy.' "

"That's putting it mildly," Alex murmured.

"Okay, where does the heart lie?"

Jebb tapped his chest. "Right here, Pops."

"I'm not sure she was being literal, Jebbediah," Emmit said. "Any other suggestions?"

"What about the words 'treasure hunt'? Could that mean anything?" Craig asked.

"I was thinking about that…the word 'hunt,' as in hunting, as in lodge. Been there, done that," Jebb said. His phone vibrated on the table. "Gotta go check on Mack."

Charlie motioned for him to stay seated. "I'll go see what she's up too."

Casey turned the paper toward her. "That makes sense, Bullfrog."

Jebb nodded. "I also think we should take 'where

the heart lies' to mean chest."

"Okay, if Jebb's right—"

"Wait!" Jake shouted interrupting Alex. "That locket thingy." Jake waved his hand in the air. "The one you say she never took off. The one you said meant something significant. That lies on your chest, right?"

Casey sucked in a breath. "Holy shit!"

"Good job." Ryan slapped Jake on the back.

"I might not be right."

Alex shook her head. "No, Jacob, it makes perfect sense. Why else would she leave it behind?"

"Where's the locket, Alexandra?"

"Upstairs. I'll get it."

They sat around the table passing the locket around for what seemed like forever. Each of them turning it round and round until one by one they gave up.

Ryan shook his head. "I don't understand what it could possibly open."

"This may seem like a stupid question," Jebb began, his cheeks pinking. "But did any of you open the locket?" He slunk down in his seat when everyone stared at him.

"I didn't," Casey said, then everyone admitted they hadn't either.

"I will," Craig said. Using his thumb nail, he popped the round locket open. "It's a picture, but I don't understand its relevance."

"Let me see." Ryan took the locket and turned to Jacob. "We've seen this before, on Fletcher's computer. Remember, Jake?"

Jacob squinted at the photo. "I'm with you, bro, but that's the lodge."

Casey took the locket from her husband. "It is…another dead end."

"It has to be here. We can't give up," Jebb said, taking the locket and looking it over. "We can't give up; we've got to find her!"

"Jebb, honey, take it easy." Savannah went over to rub her son's back. "No one's giving up. We'd never give up." She used her thumb and forefinger to tilt his chin down so they were eye to eye. "Never. Is that understood?"

Jebb nodded.

Alex bit her lip when her mother gave her father *the glare*.

Emmit cleared his throat. "I say we take a break. We can meet back here tomorrow bright and early. No sense sitting here going 'round and 'round and getting more frustrated. Time to call it a night." His word being law, everyone made their way home for the night.

When all who remained were Alexandra and Jacob, she shrugged and said, "I wanted to go check on Jasper tonight anyway."

"Yeah, that's a good idea. Do you want company?" Jacob asked.

Alex rubbed her hands over her arms. He had been on her side, standing up to her family—to Casey—on her behalf. But she couldn't let it matter, could she? Keep it simple, no attachment. "Sure, why not?"

****

"She seemed all right though? When you saw her, I mean?" Jasper asked from his hospital bed. The doctors had decided to keep him an extra day for observation.

"Other than the chains, she looked good actually," Alex told him smiling. "I think the dress bothered her more than the rest of it." She was glad when Jasper laughed. He was a mess, but she expected anyone would be after going through surgery. He looked even older than he had after Fletcher left. It was her own fault, of course, but that was a recurring theme of late.

"I can believe that," Jasper sighed. "Noah stopped by—"

Jacob grunted.

"Told me about Larry."

"Did he?" Alex asked, though she wasn't surprised.

"Larry and I were friends, went fishing with the man the first Sunday of every month for more than twenty years. I'll miss him."

"Alex told me he and the kid didn't get along?"

Jasper reached up to fiddle with the badge that was no longer there, then dropped his hand and fiddled with the blanket instead. "Wasn't a secret. More my fault than Fletcher's."

"How so?" Alex asked.

"I reckon it doesn't matter if I say anything now. It was quite a few years ago. See, Larry worked for me before moving to the city precinct, and one night we had a break-in at the station. It was the second time, I believe."

Alex bit her lip. She knew where this was going.

Jasper grinned. "On the previous break-in, nothing was stolen and there wasn't damage, but this time the person responsible knocked Larry's football trophy over. He was a big star in college, but he didn't make the draft, so that trophy was his pride and joy. To make a long story short, even though we were able to fix the trophy, Larry never got past it."

Jacob scratched his head, making his man bun bob. "What does that have to do with the kid?"

"Fletcher was the one breaking into the station," Alex said.

Jasper cackled. "Oh, the night I caught her was

something else altogether. I almost pissed myself, ah, begging your pardon, Alexandra."

"Quite all right, Jasper. I remember."

"She broke in?" Jacob looked at Alex. " 'Locked doors and booby traps.' "

Alex's lips quirked. "I told you."

He shook his head. "How old was the kid?"

" 'Bout eight, I reckon. It took a bit to get her to confess; with Fletcher, yah have to ask the right question. We were there for a while."

Alex rolled her eyes. When they were kids, Fletcher would leave the house late at night to do whatever it was Fletcher did; Casey went with her sometimes, but that was no one's business.

"She didn't do it again after I caught her. Course, it might be a coincidence Savannah came to Blue Creek around that same time." Jasper shook his head. "What days those were. Anyway, she admitted the truth, said she'd come to fix it herself. Larry happened to come in that night and put two and two together."

"Let me get this straight; he hated her 'cause she broke his trophy when she was a little girl?"

"Larry was an only child and didn't have no kids of his own. He felt Fletcher was a thief, and he never changed his mind. Never trusted her."

"That must have been hard on your friendship," Alex said. Fletcher would have felt guilty about that if that were the case.

Jasper nodded. "For a time, but Larry didn't have anyone else to fish with."

"All this over a trophy," Jake scoffed.

Alex sat up. "It makes Larry being at the lodge that much stranger. If he hated Fletcher as much as you say, then why would he be there?"

Jasper hung his head. “It’s my fault.”

“How could it possibly be?”

“Well, Alexandra, Fletcher gave me free rein to go to the lodge whenever I wanted. She said I needed some male bonding time and would let me and Larry stay there. He might not have liked Fletcher, but he loved that old lodge.” He reached for the box of tissues on the bedside table.

“He went up there a lot?” Jake asked.

Jasper blew his nose. “At least once a month.”

“Wrong place, wrong time,” Jake said. “Isn’t that always the damn way.”

“I told Noah all this too. And I told him Fletcher wouldn’t have killed Larry.”

“How do you know that?” Alex wished she hadn’t asked when Jake kicked her chair. What? Jasper hadn’t been there; he couldn’t know for sure. It was a valid question.

“Noah asked me the same thing. Larry was my friend. Course he wasn’t much of a friend, to tell yah the truth, but he was important to me nonetheless. Fletcher wouldn’t have killed him based on that and that alone. And I know that all the way down to the bones of my toes.”

“Is that what you told Noah?”

Jasper squirmed. “No, but I told him the truth.”

“Which is?”

“Fletcher wouldn’t have slit his throat; it’s too messy. And as you well know, Alexandra, she wouldn’t have had to get that close.”

“I know no such thing! She had no qualms about holding a knife to Craig’s throat a few months ago.”

Jasper snorted. “She caught him breaking into my place; she was fired up, but she wouldn’t have killed him. He's too important to you and Charlie. It was a threat. An empty one."

"I—"

Jasper pointed his finger at her. "Your problem is that you don't understand your sister."

"And everyone else does? Give me a break, Jasper. Really!"

"Fletcher wouldn't kill nobody in cold blood, and yah know it. Dagnabbit, Alexandra McKay, when are yah gonna get it through that head of yours that Fletcher's not a murderer?"

Bile rose in her throat, but her gaze didn't waver from Jasper's. "Like me, you mean?"

His cheeks got ruddy. "I didn't say that. You did what you had to do to protect your life and the lives of your family. Fletcher's done the same."

A nurse came rushing in. "Excuse me? Is there a problem in here? Your heart rate is elevated." She turned to Alex and Jake. "You two will have to leave."

"Fine." Jake stood. "Come on, princess."

She was at the door when Jasper called her name. She squeezed her eyes tight for a moment. "Yes, Jasper?"

His gaze was piercing. "You never really murdered nobody."

"Sir, please calm down," said the nurse.

"I'll calm down when I'm damn good and ready, and not a moment before, missy!" Jasper said, then pointed at Alex. "You've never murdered anyone. Self-defense isn't murder."

She looked him up and down. "Whatever you say, Jasper. Get some rest."

"I'm not finished, dagnabbit!" He swatted at the nurse's hands. "Your sister's never murdered nobody, and neither have you!"

Alex stopped in her tracks. "What?"

"I'm sorry, you'll have to leave now."

"Just like I said. Neither of you've ever murdered anyone. She's going, she's going, no need to get rough," Jasper said to the nurse, who was poking at him. "Go on now and think on it. I said that hurts, damn it. Do you know who I am? I'm Sheriff Jasper Hart…"

Alex didn't hear the rest; she joined Jake, waiting by the elevator doors.

"You ready?"

"Yes," she said. "Maybe we should take another look in Fletcher's bunker."

Chapter Thirteen

Jake glanced between Alexandra and the darkened forest path leading to Fletcher's cabin. He didn't mind driving in the woods; that's why he'd made sure his SUV had four-wheel drive. What he didn't like was navigating the woods at night, during a storm, while his passenger remained silent. The latter annoyed the crap out of him.

Jake had gone straight to the elevator and hadn't heard whatever Jasper had said. It must have been something to confound the princess because he'd leaned on the gas the whole way and she hadn't complained once, even when he almost fishtailed; she just looked at him and went back to thinking about whatever it was. He wished she'd talk to him or confide in him. Hell, he would be fine with her yelling at him, anything other than staring out the window.

Alex's hand went to the door handle. "Stop."

Jake made no move to slow down. "We aren't there yet."

"I said stop the car."

"Firstly, this isn't a car. It's a souped-up SUV, and it's raining. We're almost there."

"Jacob, stop the freaking SUV then."

"Do you have to pee or something? Can't you hold it—"

"Stop the vehicle!" she shouted.

"Fine," he grumbled.

Alexandra hopped out of the SUV and slammed the door.

What in the hell was she doing? He grunted and followed her out. His head was instantly drenched. Shit. Cold water sluiced down his back, and he shimmied. Damn it! He called her name a few times, but she didn't answer. Where the hell was she?

He turned in a circle, then said, "Fuck this!" He got back in his ride and put the gear in drive. Moving at a snail's pace, Jake found her walking toward the cabin. "Crazy broad," he muttered.

He put his window down a couple inches. "I'll meet you there." If she wanted to walk in the pouring rain, that was her business.

Jake parked, then ran to the porch and unlocked the door so he could hit the lights. He went to the bathroom and grabbed a couple of towels. He patted himself down a few times, then went back to the porch just as Alex came around the bend. What the hell was wrong with her?

"Are you crazy?" he asked the moment she stood next to him. She was soaked through. "You're gonna get hypothermia or some shit. Then what good will you do me?" He was rattled when she did nothing but stare at him with those big blue eyes. Fuck!

He took her hand and pulled her into the cabin. Her wet hair looked brown, and it started to curl. He used one of the towels to wring out most of the water from her hair. Still, she just stood there. "Shit, shit, shit," he muttered. He glanced at the fireplace and wondered if he could actually start a fire in it. Pinching the bridge of his nose, he decided it was better to be safe than burned alive.

"Damn it, say something. You're creeping me the

fuck out!" Was it twisted that seeing her dripping wet turned him on? He hoped not. He also hoped she didn't notice he was rock hard.

"Princess? Come on, talk to me." Nothing. "You have to get out of those soaked clothes, or you'll get hypothermia. Then how will it look? Huh?"

She pulled her sweater over her head.

He turned around and gulped. Forget a match—there went the whole damn matchbook! Whoosh. Sweat prickled his brow.

"Jacob?" Alex whispered.

Jake glanced over his shoulder, then swung his head back and stared at the floor. Oh, man, she was completely naked. He closed his eyes, but all he saw were Alex's full breasts with pink nipples and the triangle of red trim at the juncture of her thighs. Shit! What would Ryan do?

Alex pressed her body against his back; her heat radiated through the damp fabric. She pressed her face between his shoulder blades and ran her hands up his sides, then under his shirt. He shuddered. Her icy fingers traced a path over his abs and up to his chest. Fuck.

What would Ryan do? Jake took her hands out from under his shirt. "Alexandra, I don't think this is a good idea." That sounded more like his brother. Yep, the hitch in his voice was definitely more Ryan's than his own.

Alex trembled against him. "Jacob, please."

He clenched and unclenched his fists, then turned around. She wouldn't meet his eyes, so he cupped her cheeks and brought her gaze to his. "Be sure, princess, because I'm no gentleman." He hadn't realized he'd been holding his breath until she spoke.

She stared at him for a moment. "Yes, I'm sure," she said and moved back while he stripped off his shirt. They stood there watching each other until Jake leaned in to kiss her.

Alexandra closed her eyes when his lips touched hers. She was again surprised by the softness of his beard. Amazing how someone whose mouth was so crass could have lips so smooth. She brought her arms up around his neck, which pressed her naked breasts against his bare torso.

She needed this. Between everything going on with Fletcher, her family, and Jasper, the messy emotions were threating to overtake her—to erupt within her like some volcanic nightmare. She would take the physical outlet instead. *This* she could handle; *this* she could do without burning it all down.

He groaned, and Alex savored the sound.

Jacob ran his hands up and down her back, then moved lower to caress her backside. He tilted his head and deepened the kiss. The woodsy scent that was all him flooded her senses, and she indulged in the feel of another human being—the intimacy.

Alex moved her tongue with his. A dance as old as time—potent and primal. She shivered when he sucked on her lower lip, then gasped when he wrapped her arms more tightly around his neck, put one of his arms under her knees, and picked her up without breaking the kiss.

He set her down in front of the bed, letting her body slide down his. "One sec."

She stepped back toward the bed, the cool material of the comforter grazing her thighs, while Jacob lit the candles on the dresser. The small flames danced on their wicks as a different heat coursed through her veins. Alex licked her bottom lip when he came to stand in front of her again.

Jacob's body was reminiscent of a painting she'd seen once. His shoulders were strong and broad. His abdomen tight, his arms sinewy, and his chest had a rakish thatch of brown hair that stopped at his jeans—and no doubt led to other impressive and erect parts of his anatomy.

He brushed her hair to the side, then kissed her collarbone. His hands paid homage to her entire body. Starting at her shoulder, then down her arms, and back up to caress her breasts.

Alex closed her eyes and rested her forehead on his chin. She shivered when his fingers brushed her hardened nipples. She relished his touch for another moment, then slid her hands down his chest until her fingertips grazed his erection.

He paused, and she undid the top button of his jeans, then slowly lowered the zipper, surprised to feel flesh instead of more material. She looked up, and he grinned.

"No boxers or briefs today."

Alex pursed her lips and slid her hands into his jeans. She took the waistband between her fingers as she pushed his pants down, releasing his impressive erection. He kicked off his boots and pants.

"Better," she said when he was completely naked in front of her.

He straightened fully. "Thanks."

There wasn't an awkward moment of silence, just reverence. Then Jacob bent down and picked her up again, this time laying her on the bed. He slid down beside her, reintroduced his mouth to hers, and his fingers wandered.

Alex didn't stay still. She glided her hands down to his more impressive attribute and began caressing him. He froze.

"Do unto others…" he said and swept one hand down to her sex.

Alex sucked in a breath when his fingers found her most sensitive spot. She was ready for him; her body gave away just how much she wanted him. She opened her eyes when he stopped.

Alex was riveted by his movements as he brought his fingers to his mouth and sucked. She swallowed. Sitting up she kissed him with abandon, then lay back down and pulled him on top of her.

He shifted off her and then off the bed.

Alex leaned up on her elbow. "Wh—"

"Condom," he said and held up a silver packet. He got back on the bed and knelt between her legs while he sheathed himself.

"What?" Alex whispered when Jake made no move to continue.

"You're beautiful. I mean, I know you've heard it a thousand times, but—"

She sat up and kissed him. She waited until he closed his eyes, then took hold of his shoulders and straddled his thighs. She moaned low in her throat as she welcomed him into her body. He grabbed her waist with one hand, positioned himself with the other, then began to move.

He leaned in to latch onto one of her nipples, and Alex's head fell back. He moved to the other breast to give it equal attention, and she panted. Wanting his mouth, she grasped his hair and pulled his lips to hers.

They clung to each other. Their bodies glistened with sweat, and they moved achingly slow against one another. Her orgasm was coiled within her, just out of reach, and Alex squeezed her inner muscles around him. Jake groaned, ripped his mouth from hers, grabbed her hips, and set a punishing pace. Alex crested first, then Jake held her in a vise-like grip until he too had climaxed.

They sat joined, each trying to get their bearings. Jacob placed light kisses across her face until he found her lips. Alexandra sank into him again. He shifted their position so they were lying side by side. He smoothed her hair from her face, then moved away from her and off the bed.

Alex stretched like a cat while he went to throw away the condom. And she didn't resist when he came back to the bed and pulled her body on top of his. She rested her head on his chest, and he ran his fingers up and down her spine.

"Do you think I should blow out the candles?" Jake asked sometime later.

She smiled against his skin, then slid her hand from his chest to his sex. "If you want," she murmured. He sucked in a breath as she took hold of him.

"I'm good," he said, and they began again.

Chapter Fourteen

Alex opened her eyes and lifted her hand to block the sun. Yawning, she sat up and grabbed the sheet to cover her nakedness. She ran her hand along the empty side of the bed and closed her eyes for a moment. Shaking her head, she went to raid her sister's sorry excuse of a wardrobe.

Coming out of the bathroom, where she had used her finger to brush her teeth, Alex tried to smooth out the jeans she was wearing. It was a good thing Fletcher never wore anything that fit. Alex was taller than Fletcher and a size bigger, so the clothes fit her perfectly. Thank God. She hated wearing jeans, but it was better than wearing wet clothes. She'd also borrowed one of her sister's rubber bands for her hair. She was a mess, but for some reason she didn't care.

She followed the whistling into the next room and found Jake in the kitchenette. His chest was bare, and his jeans were zipped but unbuttoned. His hair was wet and up in its man bun. He looked…tempting, if she was honest with herself.

Jake turned and grinned. "Good morning." He motioned to her with his mug. "You look hot in jeans."

Before she could reply, Jake was kissing her. Alex didn't try to stop him, just enjoyed his lips.

"Good morning," she said when he moved back around the counter.

He handed her a cup of coffee. "It's not as good as

yours, but it'll do."

She took a sip; it was good. "Thank you, for the coffee and the compliment." She took a seat at one of the barstools and winced.

"Sore?"

"A little. You don't have to look smug about it."

"If you say so," he said and grinned. "Did you sleep well otherwise?"

"Yes, and you?" She so loathed idle morning-after chitchat.

He scratched his chest with his free hand. "Better than I have in a couple of weeks."

"That's good then." This was why she always went to the man's house and left before he woke up. These conversations were generally a waste of time and uncomfortable. Not that it was uncomfortable with Jacob; she squashed the thought. No good ever came from ideas like that.

He looked at her over the rim of his mug. "You're not having second thoughts, are you?"

Here we go. "No. I knew perfectly well what I was doing. What we were doing. Look, Jacob, the sex was good."

He raised a brow.

"Okay, it was very good." Amazing. It had been amazing, but she couldn't and wouldn't tell him that.

"But?"

"But it was just sex."

He smirked. "Fucking great sex—all four times."

Alex laughed. "I can't argue with that."

Jacob stretched his neck, then looked her up and down. "What happened last night?"

She rolled her eyes. "We already covered this."

"No, I mean before"—he waved a hand in the air—

"getting out of the SUV in the pouring rain."

"Oh, that…" She looked down into her coffee cup.

"Yeah," Jake said. He came over to her and tilted her chin. "That."

"Nothing, I—"

"Don't give me that crap. It was something."

"Jasper said I never murdered anyone and neither did Fletcher."

"You killed in self-defense, Alex. I agree with Jasper; that's not murder. And the courts agreed too."

"I understood what he was saying about me." People had told her often enough. "But Fletcher killed her mother—"

"In self-defense. And even then, she was a baby."

"That's just the thing; the only person who didn't see it as self-defense was Noah. He held it against Fletcher."

"That guy has got some balls on him. I wouldn't mind taking him down a peg or two myself."

"He *is* my cousin, so in his defense I'll say he didn't have all the facts. But he was the only person who ever thought it was murder. It's not even that really…"

He topped off their coffees. "Okay, what?"

"It was…" She struggled with the words. She looked up to meet Jacob's steely green gaze. "Jasper was so…unwavering about it. Not just about Fletcher but—"

"But about you too?"

"Exactly!" Thank God he was on the same page as her. "I don't understand why."

"You think he knows something we don't?" Jake asked and slipped a T-shirt over his head.

"I think Jasper knows a lot of things we don't, but

if I've learned anything, it's that the secrets he keeps are kept to protect us." Fletcher had taught her that. It had been a hard lesson, but Alex *had* learned it. "As far as Fletcher's concerned, if Jasper knew anything that would help us, he'd tell us." She rubbed her temples.

"The kid told me all kinds of funny stories about the old sheriff. They have a connection."

"Trust me, I know. All too well."

Jake took her shoulders. "Don't do that."

"Do what?"

"Put up the wall," he said, then kissed her.

Alex welcomed Jacob's lips, his touch. Wrapping her arms around his neck, she tilted her head for better access. The door opened, and they jumped apart.

"Well, isn't this special. Ryan, don't you think this is just something," Casey said from the doorway.

"Shut up, Casey," Alex said.

Jacob's nostrils flared.

"I'm not the one sucking face—"

"Casey," Ryan said coming fully into the cabin. "We were worried when you weren't at the B and B. Jebb tracked your phones."

"See, we were *worried*," Casey hissed and swung her long black hair over her shoulder. "Everyone is on their way out here; figured we'd bring the party to you. Course we had no idea you were engaging in your own form of entertainment."

"You know what, Casey?" Alex moved to stand in front of her sister. She was two inches taller than Casey in bare feet. "I'm getting sick and tired of you pointing your finger at me. You're not so damn innocent, and you know it. I suggested Jasper may have been hiding things from us—"

"Well—"

"Let me finish, Casey! I *suggested* it after careful consideration; while you on the other hand took two seconds to agree with me. But we didn't tell Fletcher all that, did we? Hell, no. God forbid she knows the truth about her beloved big sister."

"That's enough, Alexandra," her father said. Her mother was behind him, but Alex didn't care.

"No! Not this time," she said, her tone going cold. "Years ago, I kept a secret to protect the sanctity of this family. And I accepted the brunt of the blame when Casey left; and I still seem to be shouldering that now, which is fine. I can live with that. But *this* time is different; I didn't do it alone!"

"Alexandra, please," her mother said, reaching out a hand.

She flinched away. "No, Mama, I'm not through! Fletcher may blame me for what happened with Jasper and that's fine; I deserve *her* anger. But how dare *you*"—she pointed to Casey—"act like you had no part in it."

"Alex, we could hear you from outside—"

"I don't care, Charlie! We're in the middle of the damn woods."

"Enough!" their father shouted.

"What's wrong, Dad? Am I upsetting your favorite daughter? Don't give me that look either," Alex said, unable to stop herself. "Everyone knows she's your favorite."

Her mother stepped forward. "That's just not true!"

"Oh, please, you have no room to talk; we all know Fletcher's yours," Alex said, looking her parents in the eyes. Craig joined the group. *Wonderful!* "Thank the Lord I had Charlie or I would have gone insane."

"Alexandra, why didn't you say anything to me?"

"You could never understand. Who doesn't love you, Charlie?"

Casey's gaze was piercing. "So you feel unloved?"

"No, I know I'm loved." Could a person embarrass themselves out of existence?

"I've loved you since the day you were born, and I'll never stop."

"I know, Craig." God she was making a scene. She'd be mortified later.

"Wait a minute, so that's why you hate Fletcher so much?" Casey asked. "Because she's Ma's favorite?"

"I do not have favorites!" Savannah shouted and left the cabin.

"I'll go," Charlie mumbled, taking Craig's hand and going out the door.

Alex slipped on her shoes. "No."

Casey grabbed Alexandra's arm. "You're not going anywhere until you answer me."

"Take it easy," Ryan warned.

"I'll take it easy when I get an answer."

"You're pregnant, Casey. Take it easy *now*," Ryan said, and Casey let go of Alex.

"Fletcher's my sister. Of course I love her," Alex said.

Casey pointed a finger at Alex. "But you hate her too; admit it."

"Fine, you want the truth?"

"Yeah, Alex, I do…for a change."

"Yes, I carry some resentment toward her."

Their father held up his hand. "This has gone on long enough."

"In a minute, Pops. I want answers. Fletcher never did anything to you, Alex."

Her cheeks heated. "Didn't she?"

Casey crossed her arms over her chest. "What then, if you have the answer. What'd she do?"

So many emotions roiled inside her that she opened her mouth to evade them, but the truth slipped out instead. "From the moment Ms. Tina put Jamie with us, you didn't give a shit about me."

Casey's arms dropped to her sides and her face drained of color. "What? How can you say that?"

"Easily. Since that moment, it's always been Casey and Fletcher." Alex turned from the door and looked at her sister. "You know, the first time I met Granny Vaughn I was running away from home."

Casey shook her head. "You're making that up."

"Am I? Dad, you remember, don't you?"

"Yeah," her father said and rubbed his stomach. "Gracie said you were adjusting to your new life. And it was love at first sight for Sadie."

"Yes, she loved me, and I stayed. Then we got Charlie, and she loved me. I could never mean as much to Dad as you did. Or as much to Mama as Fletcher did. I had Charlie and Granny Vaughn. But I knew you'd never love me the way you did before Fletcher came along. So yes, I resent the hell out of her for that. Happy now?" She slammed out of the cabin, ignoring the others as she passed them. For once, she didn't care; let them talk. She'd let the truth off its leash, and it took a big ol' bite of the situation. Unfortunately, in this instance, she'd only hurt herself.

Chapter Fifteen

"Alexandra, wait up," Jake hollered, trying to catch up with her long legs. He hadn't known what to say in the cabin. If he were honest, he'd wanted to know why Alex felt the way she did toward the kid. But he hadn't expected all that. He'd been so wrong about her. She had a heart, and it had been broken a long time. "Alex!"

She spun around to face him and ran into his chest. "What could you possibly have to say to me right now?"

"I wasn't planning on saying anything." He hoped she wasn't expecting him to say something profound. Ryan was the emotional one, always knew what to say, always a shoulder to cry on, all around nice guy, and, well, Jake wasn't.

"Wonderful." She moved to turn around, but Jake took hold of her arm and kissed her. She kissed him back for a moment, then stepped away and started walking again.

"What?" He'd given Emmit the keys to his ride, so he could follow Alex. Now he was rethinking the idea.

"I'm not in the mood."

"Because you were crying?"

She turned around to swat him.

He dodged her. "What? You *were* crying, weren't you?"

"I swear, you have no tact!"

"I'm not supposed to notice you're upset?" Where

was Ryan when he needed him?

"You can notice, but must you feel the need to comment on it?" She picked up her pace.

"Wait? I'm required to notice but expected to keep my mouth shut?" Women were fucking confusing. He sidestepped a tree root and followed behind her.

"Exactly," she hollered.

"Well, that's stupid."

"I don't make the rules."

"That's fine," he began, catching up with her in time to catch her smile. " 'Cause I'm not known for following them."

She made a face. "You really are dumber than you look."

He took no offense. She needed someone to take it out on. He didn't mind being that person. "That's funny. You're as bitchy as you look."

She laughed, then sobered. "Is everyone going to be at my place when we get there?"

"Nah, just your dad." He put his arm around her shoulders. "He's got my ride, so he best be there."

She sighed. "That's all right then."

"Alexandra…" He waited until she looked at him. "You have nothing to be ashamed of. I know, I know, I have no tact, but seriously. You were being honest about how you feel, so if anyone has a problem with that, fuck 'em."

She leaned into him a bit. "Thanks, Jacob."

"Sure…So now that we've had sex, am I your boyfriend?" He moved in front of her, wiggled his eyebrows, then, in his best dumb jock impression, asked, "Whatcha say, princess? Are we going steady?"

Alex put her hand to her forehead and tilted her head back. "I do declare, Jacob Keller wants to court me. Whatever shall I do?”

Jake laughed, then tripped over his own feet and fell. “Damn.”

Alex stepped over him. “You should watch where you’re going.”

“Not so fast,” he said and pulled her down on top of him. He didn’t know who was more surprised when she kissed him. Him or her. Instead of dwelling on it, Jake rolled them over in the wet leaves and kissed her the way she should be kissed. Long and soft. After enjoying her for a few minutes, Jake got up and helped her stand.

She glanced at him, then back to the path. “That was nice.”

Jake swallowed. Things were getting heavy. She’d let out a lot of crap at the cabin, emotional shit. It was only fair he did too, right? Something to level the field. He cleared his throat. “I don’t like hospitals.”

She turned to him with a raised brow. “Um, okay.”

He rolled his neck. “No, I mean…I hate them.”

She stopped and crossed her arms over her chest. “Why?”

“I don’t know if Casey or Ryan told you about how our parents died.”

Her face softened. “It was a car accident, right? Drunk driver?”

He shuffled the leaves with a booted foot. “Yeah. They’d gone out to celebrate their tenth wedding anniversary and got sideswiped.”

She touched his arm. “I’m sorry, Jacob.”

“Dad died on impact, but Mom…Mom lasted two days.”

“The hospital?”

He sniffed. He didn’t talk about this, not with

Ryan, the kid, no one, but he wanted her to know. "Yeah, we were eight, Ryan and I, when it happened—just a couple of clueless little dudes. Our grandparents let us stay in the hospital with our mother. Ryan had gone with our grandfather to get us some snacks. Grandmother was home getting a change of clothes. So it was just me in Mom's room; I held her hand."

Her blue gaze never wavered from his. "You don't have to tell me this, Jacob."

Jake stared back at her. "Mom opened her eyes for a second—looked right at me—I was holding her hand. I squeezed her fingers; I couldn't breathe, couldn't speak…and then the alarms started blaring and she was gone. I blinked, and she was gone." He shivered.

"And that's why you hate hospitals?" She rubbed her arms.

He nodded. "They make me itch."

She looked him up and down. "I get it." She started walking again.

Jake followed her. He hadn't meant to make things worse. Maybe he shouldn't have—

"I keep one of Granddaddy's ties, and one of Granny's silk scarves in my dresser."

He eyed her. How was he supposed to respond? "That's—"

She laughed. "Strange? Maybe. My grandparents meant the world to me. I like having a piece of them near. Aside from Charlie, Granny was my best friend. The first grownup I ever loved."

Now that was a surprise. Knowing what he did about the McKays. "Before your dad?"

She stopped again. "I had a hard time trusting these strangers who adopted us; in my brief experience, grownups couldn't be trusted. I put on a good show—I seemed to know how to do that innately. But with Granny…" Alex shrugged. "She was called the Widow Madison then, a southern lady with all the bells and whistles. I'd never met anyone like her, and the second she hugged me, I loved her—trusted her. It was instant. It took only a little longer to love my father."

"My grandmother taught me to cook," he said. "Ryan and I would split time with our grandparents, and anytime Grandmother was in the kitchen, I was right there with her. Cooking, baking, you name it. I loved it."

She glanced at him over her shoulder and smiled. "She taught you well."

"That she did." Enough of the heavy crap! Jake wanted to lighten the mood, so he asked her what some of her favorite shows were. She rattled off a few, but he wasn't familiar with them and he said so.

"What do you expect? You are several years older than me."

"Several?" Jake swallowed. He hadn't realized…

She smirked. "Yes, old man."

"You don't seem that young."

"No"—she pointed to him—"but you do."

He made a face.

"It doesn't matter, Jacob."

"What?'

"Age. In the long run, it doesn't matter. Besides, women mature faster than men."

"I've heard that."

"Is my age a problem for you?"

"Hell no," he said and to prove it he kissed her. "See, doesn't bother me at all."

"That's good then." She shook her head. "Any other questions?"

"Nope, you ask one."

"If I asked you how many girlfriends you've had would you tell me?"

"No. Would you tell me?"

"Sure…I've never had a girlfriend."

"Funny, what about boyfriends. How many have you had?"

She shook her head. "It's none of your business."

"You asked me."

"And you, like myself, declined to answer."

"Fine, let's not talk," Jake said smirking.

She grinned. "I thought you'd never ask."

He shook his head, took hold of her, and they walked hand in hand the rest of the way.

The path cleared to the B and B. Jacob's SUV was parked by the door. "Here we are," she said. Her father was sitting on the back steps. Alex sighed. Wonderful.

Jake kissed her hand, then let her go. "I'm going to go busy myself inside."

"I'd like to speak with you," Emmit said once they were alone.

Oh, goody. "I figured as much." She took a seat beside him, jumping when he hugged her. She tightened her arms a moment; this man was her father, no matter what her birth certificate said.

He let her go and looked her in the eye. "You know I love you, right?"

"Dad, I—"

"Because I do. So does your mother. I know you think we have favorites, but we don't. I love all my children the same. As far as my relationship with your sister goes, I understand Casey. She's not like you." He rubbed a hand over his stomach. "You know, girly. Now…I mean that in a good way, Alexandra."

She gave a small smile. "I'm aware. Not that I look girly right now, you have to admit."

"Don't change the subject."

She shrugged. "Just making an observation."

He held up his hand. "An observation you were going to turn against me to change the subject. You may not think so, Alexandra, but I do pay attention."

"I never said you didn't." She was torn between annoyance and pleasure that he did in fact pay attention.

"I didn't say you did. I don't know how to react to what happened at the cabin. I have no idea where to go from here or what you need me to do."

"Forget it and move on," she suggested, knowing he wouldn't.

"Not this time. You know, you're a lot more like Casey than you realize. Don't get defensive," he said when she squirmed. "I was going to say you're a lot like your sister in the way you bottle up your emotions. It would seem you just have a bigger bottle. One that holds twenty years of hurt. I never would have guessed."

"What? That I have feelings too? Sorry—"

"You're better at hiding your emotions than I ever would have believed. Hell, you sucker-punched all of us. I want to know why."

"Why what?" She needed to take a shower and get out of these clothes. In fact, she was seriously considering blaming the clothes for her emotional outburst.

"Why you, in all these years, never said anything? Why didn't you come to me or your mother? What about Charlie? Did you tell her?"

"I didn't want to hurt her."

Her father rubbed his neck.

She sighed. "Charlie's my best friend, but she's Casey's sister. Her real flesh and blood sister." She was making things worse. "Really, Dad, I'm stressed, and Casey set me off. Things came out of my mouth that I didn't even know were there."

"Why don't I believe that?"

Because you're a smart man. "It's trivial, truly."

"No, Alexandra, it's not. I think it means a great deal to you."

"You're right, it does, but I'd rather not discuss it. Can you respect that?"

His nod was slow. "I can."

"Good," she said and stood.

"But there's something you need to know." He waited until she looked at him. "I admit I may give Casey more attention and your mother does the same with Fletcher. But they need it. We've never had to worry about you, Alexandra. We've—*I've* believed you were perfectly happy. You never gave the slightest hint you needed more. And, yes, I guess that had an awful lot to do with Sadie and J. T. I didn't realize you felt like I didn't love you or love you enough. And for that, I am sorrier than I can say."

Alex stared. This was what happened when you showed your true feelings. "I know you love me, and I know Casey and Mama love me too. I love you all as well."

"That's something then…" He rubbed his hands over his thighs. "As far as blame—"

"Dad, you've done your job here, okay? I feel reassured of your love. Now, I don't want to talk about this anymore. I'm going to go take a shower."

"Fair enough." Emmit stood.

"Dad?"

"Yeah?"

"If you're going to be sick, go by the bushes." She smiled when her father smirked but headed toward the hedges. At least that never changed.

Chapter Sixteen

Jake moved away from the window and got back to cooking. He glanced at Alex when she came in. "You good?"

"Yes, you?"

Jake nodded. "I'm in the zone. The cooking zone, that is."

"Wonderful," she said with a sigh. "I'm going to go freshen up."

"Sounds good." He almost asked if she wanted company, but he had enough sense to give her some time to herself. He turned when the back door opened and his brother came in.

"What in the hell do you think you're doing?" Ryan asked.

"What's it look like, bro?" Jake lifted himself up on the counter. "Cooking. What are *you* doing?"

"You know damn well that's not what I mean."

"I'm your twin, Ryan, not a fucking mind reader." He knew exactly what his brother was getting at, but Jake wasn't going to make it easy.

Ryan pulled on the lapels of his jacket. "I'm talking about Alexandra!"

Jake shook his head. "You're way too predictable."

"And you're deflecting!"

"Sorry, what's your question?" Jake asked and jumped down to stir his sauce. Was it too early for a beer? He glanced at the clock. Yep. "Huh?"

"Are you even listening to me, Jake? I said why, for once in your life, can't you keep you dick in your pants?"

"See, I've heard that speech from you before—"

"I swear you're going to give me a stroke one day, you know that? You're purposely being dense. This is different."

"How?"

"She's Casey's sister, for goodness sake!"

"Lighten up. I know what I'm doing."

"You don't know her, Jake; she eats men for breakfast and is done with them by brunch. She doesn't give a shit about you and never will."

"Wait just a fucking minute…" Jake stared at his brother, incredulous. "You're worried that she'll hurt me, *me*? Your big brother Jake. You think she's gonna leave me alone and brokenhearted?"

Ryan sat down hard. "Yeah."

Jake burst out laughing. "That's rich!" He got his mirth under control by the time Casey walked in.

"What's so funny?" she asked, then pointed to her husband. "You know it's rude that you walked away when Pops wasn't finished talking."

"Honey, he wasn't talking to me." Ryan pulled his wife on his lap and kissed her neck.

"True, but you're going to make him think you don't like him."

"You know I like your father."

"I don't want Pops to feel ignored."

Jake looked between the couple. His brother was so whipped.

"I'll make a point to remember."

"Good; he's coming over for lunch. So what was so funny?"

Ryan shook his head.

Casey pointed to Jake. "You speak."

"He's a man, not—never mind."

"I resent that almost remark, little brother. I was laughing 'cause my bro was warning me away from Alexandra; he's afraid *I'll* get hurt."

Casey looked at Ryan. "Good call."

"*What?* Not you, Casey!" Jake shook his head. "You can't be serious. I'm a man—a womanizer—a no-good rotten rogue!"

Casey snorted. "Did someone actually call you that?"

Ryan nodded. "In San Francisco, he—"

"That's beside the point," Jake snapped.

Casey stood up and headed toward the stove. "What *is* the point?"

Jake poked himself in the chest. "You should be warning her against sleeping with me."

"You have done the deed." Casey shook her head, then tasted the sauce. "That's good."

"Thanks." Jake slung a towel over his shoulder and pointed to Ryan. "Help me out here."

"Normally, I'd agree with you. You are a no-good rotten rogue, but in this instance, you're the lesser of two evils."

Casey took another taste, then said, "Look, I know how my sister is with men…or more to the point how she isn't."

He crossed his arms over his chest. "Did you not hear the same conversation I did this morning? You don't know your sister at all."

"Jake," Ryan warned.

"It's okay." Casey sighed. "Think what you want, Jake. Just don't come crawling to me with your dick in your hand when she emasculates you."

Jake's mouth hung open. Emasculate?

Ryan winced. "Cas—"

"Don't worry, Ryan. Seriously," Casey said and left the room.

"Where's she going?" Jake asked.

"To talk to Alexandra."

Jake gasped dramatically. "And you're letting your wife be alone with her?"

Ryan smirked. "Shut it."

****

Alex came out of her bathroom to find Casey sitting on her bed. Wonderful. First, she'd had to listen to her dad now her sister. She ignored Casey and went about getting dressed.

Casey put her arms behind her head and lay back against Alex's throw pillows. "I know you can see me, Alexandra."

"Oh, I thought you had invisibility powers; you're so good at disappearing."

Casey snorted. "I'm not taking *that* bait."

"Fine." Alex fastened her bra, then pulled out her matching garter belt.

"How the hell do you wear that crap? Those things make me itchy. Not to mention they're always snagging on shit."

"I wear them well." She hooked the stockings to the garter. Now, what to wear? A skirt and cashmere sweater set sounded good.

"I don't get you, Alex. You're a fucking puzzle."

"I'm not complicated at all."

"Yeah, and Blue Creek sits on the damn ocean."

"If you say so."

Casey growled. "Damn it, Alex. What the fuck do

you want from me? I mean, all that shit you spewed this morning. Mind explaining it to me?"

"There's nothing to explain." She was afraid to have this conversation. What if something else slipped out? Needing a distraction, she went into the bathroom to blow-dry her hair.

Casey followed and unplugged the dryer.

Alex tried to get the cord back, but Casey wouldn't let go. "Let me finish, Casey."

"Not until we've talked."

She refused to give into her emotions. "I told you, I have nothing to say."

"Don't do that. I came up here to do the right thing and clear the damn air. The least you can do is put down your freaking brush." Casey shook her head. "You can't say the things you said this morning and not expect me to ask questions."

"Put your two cents in more like," she said and put on her moisturizer. Avoid and evade. "Look, I had a bad moment and said things I didn't mean—"

"Oh, you meant them all right, Alexandra. I'm not stupid."

Alex pulled open her makeup drawer. "If you'd ever let me finish a sentence, you'd hear me say that I didn't mean to say those things."

"Ryan thought I was bad." Casey huffed. "Seems you're worse than me at keeping people from knowing who you really are. Imagine my surprise."

"You don't know everything." She applied her eyeliner, then moved on to mascara.

Casey shook her head. "I never claimed to."

"No, your personality does it for you."

"Does what?"

She shuffled through her cosmetics until she found

her eyelash curler. "Arrogance."

"Arrogance?" Casey crossed her arms over her chest.

"You're rarely, if ever, wrong. That's who you are. The protector must be on the straight and narrow."

"Are you trying to say I always think I'm right?"

Alex shut the drawer hard enough to make the cosmetics roll inside. "Basically."

"Why didn't you just say so?" Casey threw her hands in the air. "Where do you get off accusing me of that anyway? You're the one who always makes decisions for people and expect them to bow down."

"I can admit that." Though she'd made some lousy choices in recent memory.

"Good." The bed squeaked when Casey took a seat. "Now, let's get to the sticky part. About this morning—I had no idea you felt that way."

Alex looked up from choosing a pair of shoes to scoff. "Of course not!"

"You could have said something. You're notorious for your opinions."

Alex looked at Casey, who was murmuring under her breath. "What are you babbling about?"

"I was telling the baby that he'd better be more like his dad—laid-back and easy. Don't look at me like that. Ryan's baby books say it's good to talk to the baby."

Alex bit her lip. "You said 'he.' "

"We're thinking boy; the guy's genes determine the baby's sex—"

"What if you have twins?"

Casey paled. "Don't even go there; I told Ryan that isn't even an option."

Alex fastened her bracelet around her wrist. "Just a thought."

"Well, keep it to yourself."

"Fine." She headed for the door.

"Where are you going? We're not finished here." She patted the bed. "Sit your flat ass back down."

"I do not, nor have I ever had a 'flat ass.' I have a very nice backside." Jacob was quite fond—*stop it!*

"Whatever. The fact is we're gonna hash this out, even if it takes all night."

Alex pursed her lips. "Did Ryan give you a specific schedule?"

Casey grimaced.

"I don't have time for this."

"If I have to get all emotional and open up, then so do you." Casey sighed. "I love you, Alexandra. Do you honestly think I'd hang out with you if I hated you? Give me a fucking break here, huh?"

Oh, this was going to be uncomfortable. "I know you do."

"Then what's the problem? You and Charlie are tight. Me and Fletcher are tight. That's just how things worked out; you can't blame Fletcher for that."

She picked a make-believe hair off her sweater. "I don't 'blame' anyone."

"Then why all this freaking drama?"

"I was angry, and it slipped out." Alex seriously considered burning the clothes she borrowed from Fletcher. It had to be the clothes.

"Some slip." Casey rolled her shoulders. "Ryan said I should let my feelings do the talking, so here goes...You never gave the impression that you needed me or anyone. You've always seemed to be in perfect control of everything. You're your own person, and I thought that's the way you wanted it."

"Absolutely." Secrets were her specialty.

"God, you're confusing. If that's the way—oh, fuck it! I don't know."

"It wasn't until after you left that Fletcher and I even got a chance to really get to know one another. We have a lot of history between us—the three of us—but don't you get it?"

"Honestly, it's like we're talking in circles."

Alex sighed. "Before Fletcher entered our lives, it was just me and you. Then it was Dad and the wicked witch, then Charlie."

"I know all this."

"Charlie's your sister by blood. By sheer genetics she's closer to you."

Casey sat up and pointed a finger at Alex. "You're jealous! You, Alexandra McKay, are jealous. Hot damn, now we're getting somewhere. Jealousy, I get. Not that I have first-hand experience on the subject or anything, but I understand it."

Alex fiddled with her charm bracelet. Was she genuinely resentful of Casey's relationships with the other members of their family? It sounded that way.

"Alexandra," Casey whispered and took her hand. "No one could replace you in my life. You were there before anyone; the first person to need me, the first person I ever cared about—loved—for goodness sake!" Casey shook her head. "That's it, isn't it? I was the first person to mean anything to you, and then Fletcher came along and you felt like I didn't want you around or whatever. Then Pops and I got along like two peas in a pod, and there was another person to take me away from you."

God, it sounded so trite when Casey said it. "I—"

"And it's all bullshit. Don't give me that look. Don't you get it? I didn't think you needed me anymore. Once Fletcher came, you took care of her too. Then you were always with Granny Vaughn. I assumed you were fine. That was my mistake. Alex, you mean a lot to me. And I mean more to you than I ever—"

"I wouldn't go that far." Alex hugged herself.

Casey looked down at her hands. "I know I'm hard on you about what's happening with Fletch—"

Alex took her sister's hand. "Casey, I know." Her sister put all the blame on her because it was easier than to admit *she'd* done something to hurt Fletcher. Knowing it didn't make it any more comfortable, but she wouldn't bring it up again.

She nodded. "So we're good, right?"

"Yes, you can tell Ryan you were successful in your mission." Alex returned her sister's hug.

Casey headed for the door, stopping with her hand on the knob. "You know, I was jealous of Charlie too."

Alex raised a brow.

"It's true, she understood you better than I ever did and I'd known you longer. So, you see, Alex, I missed us too."

"Well, nobody's perfect," she said after the door had closed. She rubbed her hands over arms. She was in control again, or more than she had been in the last twenty-four hours. She glanced out the window and bit her lip; now what was she going to do about Jacob?

Chapter Seventeen

Jake was finishing the muffins when Alexandra came downstairs. Casey had come down about fifteen minutes earlier, then left with Ryan. Jake hoped the sisters had settled their differences.

"I talked to Jasper; he got home from the hospital okay."

"That's good."

"You hungry?"

"A little," she said and took a seat at the table. "What's all this, Jacob?"

He had set the table with a tablecloth and candles. Jake set a plate in front of her. "Brunch!" He took a seat across from her, happy with his presentation.

She stared at him, then took a bite. "It's good; you're a wonderful cook, Jacob. But I meant what's going on with the candles?"

He scratched his beard. "I thought you like the fancy shit." Chicks like her usually dug the romantic crap.

"Yes, but why?"

"Why what?"

"Why go to all the trouble?" She shifted in her seat. "We had one night of steamy sex, one night that meant nothing." Alex set down her napkin and rose from the table.

"Okay, I can agree—on the steamy sex part, but you want to have sex again, right?"

"Were you raised in a barn? God, Jacob, you have the courtesy of a pig."

"Pigs are smart; I like pigs," he said.

"Last night was a fluke. I was distraught and needed a warm body; you were there."

"Wait, you're telling me you would have slept with anyone who was there?" 'Cause that was—he didn't fucking like that. He stood from the table too. Another meal ruined.

"Within reason. You're single, attractive—when you're not speaking—and yes, you were there. Sex is sex, Jacob. And one night do not candles make."

He took hold of her arm before she could make her grand exit. "I get having sex because you've had a shitty day. And I get having sex for sex's sake alone. But what I don't get is what happened to the woman I slept with last night and the one I walked in the woods with this morning? The one I told—I don't get this one-eighty you've done. I was good enough for you last night and this morning, but all of a sudden this afternoon you can't dirty your hands on me?"

"Yes, that's exactly it. Now, remove yourself from my person."

"Oh, hell yeah!" He dropped her arm. "And don't worry, princess, my hands won't be coming near your high and mighty 'person' again."

She gave him a dismissive look, then walked away.

"Damn it!" He kicked the leg of the table, sending everything, including the burning candles to the floor. He cursed and stomped out the flames with his booted feet. He didn't care if he was breaking her fancy china.

Alexandra came back into the room and sent him a death look. "You *will* pay for all of those things to be replaced." She turned on her heel.

"This is what they meant, huh?" he shouted after her. "This is what they meant when they said I should stay the hell away from you? Don't worry, I'm leaving; I need to get my dick disinfected. God knows what you've done to me!"

She went rigid and spun around. "Me? I should order a complete workup. Considering this is the first time I've ever slept with someone like you."

"Someone *like* me? What, trash, Alex? Don't deny the label you've attached to my ass."

"Fine." Her voice turned to ice. "I have never been with someone as undignified, slovenly, and sleazy as you. Last night was the first time I've ever lowered my standards to the bottom of the barrel."

He crossed his arms over his chest and smirked. "You enjoyed it."

"If it makes you feel more like a man, then yes, I enjoyed it. You're honestly my favorite mistake."

Jake seethed as her footsteps echoed up the stairs. Was this emasculation? It sucked.

He looked at the mess and snorted. "This is what you get for playing with matches, pal." He bent down to start cleaning up the wreckage, but her words replayed in his head, and he dropped the plates back to the floor. Fuck it! He didn't need this shit. He wiped his hands on his jeans, grabbed his keys, and slammed out of the door.

He pulled up to Ryan's and hit the brakes. His brother's house was fucking great. A smaller version of the McKay family home. The place looked like a log cabin but bigger.

"What's with all the noise?" Emmit asked.

"What are you doing here?" He'd come to see his brother; not the father of the woman who'd cut off his balls.

Emmit scuffed the ground with the toe of his boot and squinted at Jake. “My daughter lives here.”

“Yeah.” He sighed and weighed his options. Jake didn’t want to complain about Alexandra in front of her father. “I just remembered I need to do something. Can you tell Ryan I’ll talk to him later?”

“No problem.”

Jake jumped back in his ride, pulled out of the driveway, and drummed his fingers on the steering wheel. He needed to get this shit off his chest. Who could he talk to? Ryan was out. The kid was still missing. Jake smiled. Fletch would get him a beer and set his ass straight. Craig wasn’t a candidate since he was Alex’s brother. Jake only knew two other men around here, and he sure as hell wasn’t going to get chummy with Noah Reed.

Jasper Hart’s house was a small ranch-style home. There was a nice wide front porch with four white rocking chairs scattered about. The siding was white, the shutters were a dark blue, and Jasper’s beat-up truck was in the driveway. Bingo!

He rang the doorbell and waited. It took several minutes for Jasper to open the door, and Jake had a moment of regret. The man probably needed to be left alone.

Jasper sighed. “Why am I not surprised, boy? Well, don’t just stand there, come on in,” he said and stood back so Jake could pass him. “Don’t mind the mess. My wife was the one who kept the place in order, Lord rest her soul. Come on into the kitchen.”

“Looks good to me,” Jake said, getting a smile out of the older man. Jasper looked like hell. “How you feeling?”

"I'm fine, thanks. Though I have a strong suspicion you didn't come here to see about my health. Not that I mind." He poured a cup of coffee and offered one to Jake.

"Thanks. You wouldn't happen to have any food? I made brunch, but it didn't turn out well."

Jasper pursed his lips. "Hate it when that happens. I've got tons of food. The women of Blue Creek fixed up a bundle and dropped it by after I got home this morning. Help yourself to the fridge."

Jake whipped up a meal from the different offerings the local ladies had brought. He and Jasper made small talk as they ate; when they finished, Jake cleared the plates. "That hit the spot."

"It did. Now, what do you really want to talk about?"

"You ever slept with someone you don't even know if you really like? Then after you have the best sex of your life, you're reminded of what a bitch she is. That ever happen to you?"

Jasper shook his head. "You and Alexandra, huh?"

"How the hell did you know that?"

"All that bickering and carrying on between the two of you."

"Wouldn't that say more like we don't like each other than—"

"Reminds me of me and the missus."

He could only stare at the older man. "How so?"

Jasper took a swig from his mug. "The bickering and back and forth; sometimes it lights a different kinda fire."

Jake blinked. "I'll be damned. It's foreplay."

Jasper sputtered.

He rubbed a hand over his beard. "Makes sense

now that I think about it."

The older man pursed his lips. "You should know Alexandra has a reputation for being somewhat of a…"

"A bitch," Jake offered.

Jasper shifted in his seat. "A slayer of men. She doesn't date anyone from Blue Creek. I asked her once about that, seeing as we have some fine men 'round here. She told me and not in these words, but basically you don't shit where you live. Not in those words, like I said. It was more complicated but came down to the same thing."

"Tell me about it!" Jake sat back down and rested his head on his fist. "I'm not like my brother."

"You don't say?"

"Funny." Jake grinned. "All kidding aside, Ryan's the sensitive one. Me, I go with the flow. Or whatever woman is flowing my way."

"And Alexandra put a dam in your flow, so to speak?"

"That's one way of putting it. I mean, I'm the one—"

Jasper pointed to him. "Who usually walks away without a backward glance. The one who's gone before she wakes up. Am I on the right track?"

"Yeah. I just don't get it. I mean, we were great together." Jake ignored the shiver and reminded his dick that they weren't getting any. "I'm not talking preseason here; I'm talking championship." Jake shook his head. How the hell was another woman going to live up to what he had shared with Alexandra? He was so screwed.

"I get the picture, son."

"Damn, is this making you uncomfortable? The kid listens to my crap, and you listen to hers…" Jake shrugged. “She said she turned your hair white.”

Jasper laughed. “True. But it’s more her antics and tendency to get into trouble that have made my hair white. If she talked to me about men trouble, I’d probably go bald!”

It was Jake’s turn to laugh. “So you don’t mind shooting the breeze?”

“No, it don’t bother me none.”

Jake refilled their coffees. “That makes me feel a bit better.”

“I’m glad. Now, I have a question for you?”

“We’re no closer to finding Fletcher,” Jake said wishing he had a different answer. “Oh, for fuck’s sake. Alex and I have been working together to find the kid.”

Jasper ran his hand over the cotton tablecloth. “Son, your mouth’s gonna get you in trouble one of these days.”

Jake smirked. “Already has, Jasper.”

He sighed. “But—”

“I don’t like the sound of that.” Sounded ominous to Jake.

“But…the question is why are you so bent out of shape? You got what you wanted with no strings attached, as the kids say these days. Is it because Alex did the ending, or is there something more to this? Ask yourself this: why do you care?”

“I knew I was gonna hate this question.” Jake ran his hands through his hair. “Got any beer?”

Jasper shook his head. “Nope.”

“Well, this sucks.”

****

Alex put the mop up, then placed a clean tablecloth on the table. It had taken her over an hour to clean up the mess. Jacob’s mess. Then another hour to return things to the way she liked them. The backdoor opened, and her heart hitched for a moment until Mack and Charlie came in.

"Auntie Alex, Auntie Alex, look at this," Mack cried, holding out a piece of paper. "I drew it in school."

"It's beautiful, Mackenzie!" She knelt down to Mack's level. The picture had eleven stick figures standing around a big house.

"That's you and that's me. Mama and Daddy are here. Grandma and Grandpops are here. That's Jebby." She pointed to the boy with a box around his head. "That's his…"

"Computer?"

"Yep, Jebby's computer. This is Uncle Jake, and this is Auntie Fletch." Mack looked up from the page, her dark eyes shining. "I miss Auntie Fletch bunches and bunches."

"Me too, sweetie." Alex kissed the top of Mack's blonde head and stood up. "Do you want to put your picture on the fridge?"

"Yep!" Mack said and went about finding just the right magnet.

"What happened here? Or did you just get the urge to clean?" Charlie asked pointing to the trashcan.

"Jacob had a male tantrum."

Charlie rubbed her hands over her face. "Oh, Alex, you didn't, did you?"

"Didn't what?" Alex narrowed her eyes.

"Mack, why don't you take your doll baby and go play?"

The little girl thought about it for a moment, then nodded and ran into the other room.

When they were alone, Charlie said, "I wasn't

going to bring it up—"

"Too late." Alex crossed her arms over her chest. "What is it you think I did?"

Her sister shifted from foot to foot. "Did you sleep with him and then treat him like the rest?"

"Are you accusing me of something?" Oh, she wanted to hear this.

"No, I'm stating a fact."

Alex raised a brow. "Please, enlighten me."

"You have a tendency to trample the guys you sleep with…and…well, that's putting it mildly."

"Give me a break," Alex said. She wasn't that bad.

Charlie shook her head. "Not this time, Alex. You messed up. Jake's Ryan's brother. He's not going anywhere. He's here in this family forever. You won't be able to avoid him or pretend nothing happened. Jake's not your usual type. He's not weak."

"No, he's a brute; hence, destroying my things."

"What do you expect, Alex? For someone who prides herself on reading people, you really stink." Charlie's blonde curls bobbed when she shook her head. "You never should have gotten involved with Jake!"

"Thank you for that wonderful observation."

"Any time." Charlie smirked. "And for the record, I knew you liked him—I said so, remember? I didn't think you'd *act* on it, but…"

How could she forget? "Is this your way of saying 'I told you so'?"

Charlie's grin fell from her face, and she pointed to where Jacob was coming up the back steps. "Looks like you got trouble."

"Wonderful," Alex mumbled. "Did you come to wreck more of my things?"

"We need to talk, princess. Excuse us, Charlie," Jake said taking hold of Alexandra's arm and pulling her upstairs. He didn't let go of her until he shut her bedroom door.

She glared at him. "I have nothing more to say to you."

"Good, I have plenty to say."

"I don't care to hear it." She tried to move past him but he was blocking the door. "Move!"

"No," he said and pulled her against him. "You're going to listen to me." He backed her toward the bed.

The back of her knees touched the mattress. "What do you think you're doing?"

"Proving a point," he murmured and kissed her.

Alex was still swearing at him when his lips played upon hers. Then she closed her eyes and opened her mouth. She pulled at her hands, grateful when he released them. Instead of smacking him, she took down his ponytail and ran her fingers through his hair.

He kissed her deeply, and she relished the feel of him. She was not the type to deny her sexuality, nor could she stop her body from reacting to his. His hands slid over her covered breast, down her thigh, and up her skirt. His fingers stopped at her garter belt.

He let go of her lips to look at what he'd found. "That's fucking sexy."

She rolled her eyes.

"Now…" He pushed her onto the bed.

Alex sucked in a breath when he took hold of her legs, pulled her to the end of the mattress, tore off her silk panties, and began to use his tongue on her. She covered her mouth with her hands. It was only a matter of minutes before he had her arching, gasping, and reaching sweet release.

He took his time putting her clothes to rights, stroking her thighs with his hot hands, then working his way up. She scooted on the mattress. "Did you prove your point?"

Jake smirked and got on the bed with her. He caged her head in his hands, and kissed her.

She moaned. His erection pressed into her, but he didn't veer away from the kiss. She sighed and wrapped her arms around his back, bringing him closer. Wanting his weight on top of her.

Alex wasn't sure how long they lay there, but eventually Jacob released her lips. The mattress dipped as he stood.

She took a breath, straightened her hair, and sat upon her elbows. "What was this, Jacob?"

He shrugged. "A guess?"

"So you *did* have something to prove."

"You want me, Alexandra. You want me so much you can't stand it. I know that for certain now."

"Conceited much?" She stood and straightened her skirt, tensing when he pulled her against him. "You proved your point. I want you. So what! I also want to buy designer clothes, but I'm practical enough not to."

His arms tightened around her. "But you *do* want me?"

So, so much. "Fine. Yes! Happy now?" 'Cause she wasn't. She had the urge to cry, and that pissed her off. Tears were a weakness.

"Why?"

She tried not to relax into him. "Why what?"

"Why all the bullshit this afternoon? Why cut my dick off?"

She bit her lip and pressed her nose into his chest. There was that scent she couldn't resist; she could get addicted to it—to him. But she wouldn't. "This can't go anywhere, Jacob. Don't you see that?"

"Why not?"

She practically jumped out of his arms. "You can't be serious?"

"I don't say things *I* don't mean, Alexandra. That's not my style."

"You don't seriously think this…thing between us could be more than sex, do you?" He didn't say anything for a moment, and a giggle slipped past Alex's lips. She straightened her shoulders. "You're crazy!"

"Tell me why then. Give me a reason. And"—he crossed his arms over his chest and planted his feet—"give me an honest one. Not the bullshit you were touting earlier."

"We're two completely different people. Not to mention your brother is married to my sister. And—and how does that look?"

He scoffed. "Like I give a shit *how* it looks. If that's the best you can do, princess, then the only person you're fooling here is yourself." He tapped her nose with his index finger and left the room.

Alex found him downstairs playing cards with Mackenzie and Charlie. Not knowing what else to do, she sat down and joined them. They played several rounds when Mack got up and let out a hoot.

"I won!"

"How'd she do that?" Jake wanted to know.

Charlie smiled. "Fletcher taught her how to play."

Mack blew a raspberry. "I sure miss my auntie Fletcher."

"We do too, kiddo," Jake said winking.

"She promised we'd have lots of fun next time we were together."

"I'm sure you will," Charlie said, looking at Alex for help.

"Absolutely. You'll do all the things you usually do with your auntie Fletch."

"Yeah," Jake added.

Mack pouted. "But I want to go on a treasure hunt now."

"You will, shug. She'll be back before you know it." Charlie rubbed her daughter's cheek.

Jake was on his feet so fast the others flinched. "Wait a minute, kiddo, what did you say?

Chapter Eighteen

"I can't believe it was under our noses all along," Casey said for the second time since arriving at the B and B.

Jacob shrugged. "How could we have known the kid was being literal when she said 'treasure hunt'?"

"We won't know anything for sure until Charlie comes back with the box," Alex said. "I'll go ahead and start the coffee." She figured with both Casey and Charlie pregnant, she better make decaf too. That was the lucky thing about being a bed and breakfast, she had multiple coffee makers. She hit the on buttons and turned when the back door opened.

"Where's Charlie?" she asked, surprised by her father's appearance.

Emmit held the door for Jebb, who was holding a medium-sized wooden box. "She brought Mack by the house for your mother to watch, then decided she'd stay—"

"She sent us instead!" Jebb said and hauled the box onto the table.

Alexandra sucked in a breath and pointed at the box. "That's what Fletcher went back into the fire for."

"The fire at Charlie's house a few months back?" Jake asked.

Alex ran her hand over the smooth stained wood; their father had made it for Mack's fourth birthday. "Fletcher and I were inside when the fire started. We got out through a window, but Fletcher went back in. No one knew it was for the box until later."

"Yeah, this is Mack's treasure chest," Emmit said.

"Wait!" Jake dug his cell out of his pocket. He pulled the email up on the screen and held it out. "The truth is where the heart lies"—he pointed to Jebb—"in the chest. Not a literal treasure hunt, but a treasure *chest*!"

"Hot damn!" Jebb shouted, his voice echoing in the kitchen. His cheeks got ruddy, and he apologized.

"What are you waiting for?" Jacob asked. "Let's open the thing."

Jebb shuffled his feet. "Mack said Fletcher has the only key."

"So we pick the lock," Ryan suggested.

"Yeah, right." Jebb laughed. "Fletch put the lock on it. That means only she can open it."

"A sledgehammer would work," Jake murmured, then held both his hands up in mock surrender when everyone glared at him.

"We're not going to ruin Mack's prized possession if we don't have to," Alex said.

"Let's not give up," Ryan said.

Casey took a better look at the chest. "What about the locket?"

"The heart lies *in* the chest," Jebb repeated aloud. "And the locket lies *on* the chest."

"It's upstairs," Alex said. She retrieved the locket from her room, then paused on the steps, at the angry voices coming from the kitchen. *What now?* She followed the commotion, and there, taking up more space than necessary, stood Noah. And Casey was about to assault an officer. Wonderful.

"Noah, what brings you here?" she asked. All eyes

turned to her, and she lifted a brow.

He inclined his head. "Alexandra."

Casey mumbled something and sat down.

"As I was telling your family, I came by to see if you'd found your sister."

"No…" She cocked her head to the side. "Why?"

"She's his lead suspect in Larry Hines's murder, that's why," Casey spat.

Alex rose a brow. "You spoke with Jasper, didn't you?"

"I did, yes." The floor creaked under the weight of his shifting feet. "But I still need to speak with your sister."

"I'd be happy to assist you, Noah, if I knew where she was. You see, you should want to find my sister because she is *with* Larry's murderer, not because you think she *is* his murderer."

"I have no one who can corroborate your theory, Alexandra. I have the facts; Larry was found murdered on Fletcher's property, and she's mysteriously absent. You claim she was abducted, but you have no proof."

"You want proof?" Jake asked leaning back on the legs of his chair. "We can take a drive to my condo, and I'll show you proof."

Noah crossed his arms over his chest. "You didn't report the break-in to the police."

"How do you know that?" Casey sneered.

"I know how to check a lead, Mrs. Keller. And if in fact someone *did* break in to your place, then why didn't you call the police? And if you *knew* Fletcher was missing, why not report it?"

The legs of Jake's chair slammed down against the linoleum. "She left a note."

"Ah, the infamous note. The one you told me

about, Alexandra?"

She didn't care for his tone, but she nodded.

Noah grunted. "I thought so. As far as that goes, it seemed she was trying to get away. Perhaps go to the lodge she owns for a little R and R."

Casey's cheeks tinged pink. "Can you honestly say, knowing this family as you do, we would be sitting here with our thumbs up our asses if we knew where in the hell Fletch was?" Casey was once again on her feet and in Noah's face. "If my sister is still alive, God willing, she's with some nutjob who thinks chaining her to a wall is the best way to show his eternal love!"

"Calm down, sweetheart," Emmit said.

"If this sorry sack wants to point his finger at someone, he should point it at himself. Mr. Always Blaming Fletcher for Everything. You, *Sheriff Reed*, need to stop accusing my sister of murder and start trying to find the man who's probably going to murder her!" Casey stormed out the back door.

Ryan jumped to his feet, but Alex held up her hand. "I'll go, Ryan; you fill Noah in."

Her brother-in-law opened his mouth, then he must have thought better of whatever he was about to say and nodded.

Casey was pacing the confines of the screened porch.

Alex rubbed her arms. "Do you want me to grab your jacket?"

Her sister hugged herself. "I'll go in in a minute."

"Okay." Alex pulled the sleeves of her sweater down over her cold fingers and studied the state of the porch. She needed to purchase fresh cushions for this spring, perhaps a floral pattern. She shivered; they really shouldn't be out here in the cold. She glanced at

Casey, who was muttering to herself. "How does a hot cup of decaf sound to warm us up?"

"Yeah, that's probably not a bad idea," Casey said with a heavy sigh.

The coffee pots were sputtering out the last of their brews when they came back inside. Ryan was just finishing up telling Noah what they'd learned, so no one spoke when they entered the kitchen. Alex went to the counter, prepared Casey's beverage the way she liked, and handed it to her.

"Be careful, it's hot," Alex said more from habit than anything else.

Casey snorted.

"What's everyone waiting for?" Noah growled. "Get the locket, and let's open the damn thing."

She looked him up and down. "Why do you care?"

"Because, Alexandra, if what you say is true—"

Her father pinched the bridge of his nose. "It's the truth, Noah." He took the mug Alex handed him and set it on the table.

Noah declined coffee, then said, "If that's the case, I need to find Fletcher as much as you do."

Jacob gripped the edge of the table. "So you can arrest her?"

"No, to arrest Larry's murderer. If what you say is true, then the man who has Fletcher is the same one who killed Larry. So let's open the damn box!"

"Alexandra, the locket?" Ryan asked.

She put down the coffee carafe, took the locket from her pocket, and handed it to her brother-in-law. Ryan gave it a try but was unsuccessful.

Noah held out his hand. "Give it to me."

Emmit nodded. "Go ahead, Ryan."

Ryan passed it to Noah, and Alex moved next to

him. Noah took a breath and opened the locket. His hands stilled before he stuck one half of the locket inside the keyhole and turned. The lock released with an audible click, and everyone moved in closer.

Jebb stared at Noah wide-eyed. "How did you know?"

Alex pursed her lips. The last thing she needed was for her little brother to start hero-worshiping Noah; Fletcher would never—

Noah shrugged. "I guessed."

"I guessed," Casey mocked, then shrugged when their father glared at her.

Alex pursed her lips and pretended not to have noticed the exchange. She did wonder why Noah was lying; which she was sure he was. But why? Given his history with Fletcher, how could Noah know about the locket? Unless…Was there more to their relationship than—

"Well?" Emmit stood. "What's in there?"

Casey nudged Noah out of the way and reached into the box. She pulled out a framed photo of Fletcher with Mackenzie, some costume jewelry, little trinkets, and a small stuffed black bird. Casey motioned to the contents. "Any ideas?"

Alex would have taken a closer look, but Noah lifted the box and took it to the other end of the table. Keeping an eye on the sheriff would probably be a better use of her time, so she moved beside him. The small hinges creaked as he turned the box over and ran his hand along the inside.

"What are you looking for?" Alex asked.

"Just…looking." His brow creased, then he paused and dug a penknife out of his pocket. He opened the blade, then used it to cut into the supple velvet lining.

Alex narrowed her eyes. "Another *guess*?"

Noah shrugged.

Alex moved over when Casey crowded next to her.

"What's he looking for?" her sister whispered in her ear.

Alex shrugged. She hadn't a clue.

"There's something here," Noah said.

Beneath the lining, an envelope was taped to the inside of the box. Alex snatched it out before Noah could touch it. Adrenaline flowed through her veins as she ripped open the seal. She took a deep breath and emptied the contents onto the table.

Feet shuffled, and everyone picked up a piece of photo stock.

"Who is it?" Jebb asked, turning the picture in his hand this way and that.

Alex looked over his shoulder. "Daemon Randle."

"Another one?" Jake made a disgusted noise.

Casey shook her head. "How many pictures of the guy does she need?"

"The man was a criminal," Noah reminded them. "But that's neither here or there; he killed himself."

"Fletcher didn't think so," Alex and Casey said at the same time. Her father winked at them, then asked what else was there.

Jake held out his hand to Alex. "Look familiar?"

She took the picture he offered. There were four young men posing together. "That's Daemon and his brother Rick," she murmured, then sucked in a breath and looked up at Jacob. "And Dr. Benjamin Drake."

Casey moved closer. "What the hell?"

"Wait?" Noah turned to Ryan. "That's the guy who had Fletcher stashed in his house, right?"

Ryan nodded.

"He was a sleazebag," Jacob said.

"Yes, the worst kind," Alex said, thinking of Evangeline. She handed the picture to Casey, who then handed it to Ryan. "Any guesses on our mystery man number four?" she asked.

He shook his head.

Jebb tossed another photo on the table. "Who's this guy?"

Alex took a closer look. "I have no idea?"

Noah stiffened. "I do."

"Don't keep us in suspense," Jake began. "Who is it?"

Noah placed the picture back on the table. "I don't know what he has to do with any of this. Probably a new way for Fletcher to fuck with me."

"If you have any information that can help us find my daughter, you best be telling me."

"And me," Jasper said coming in through back door. "I hadn't heard from anyone in a while, and I wanted to be brought up to speed."

"How'd you get here, Jasper?" her father asked.

"Same way as you, I reckon."

Jacob crossed his arms over his chest. "Should you be driving?"

Jasper grumbled that he'd do what he damn well pleased, then nodded toward Noah. "You want to be telling us who that is, boy?"

Alex pulled out a chair. "Jasper, are you sure you shouldn't be resting?"

"Rested all dagnab day," he said and took a seat. He pointed to Noah. "Well?"

Noah sighed. "It's my father."

"Weird," Jebb said and returned to the picture of the four boys from the pile.

"That's John?" Emmit picked up the photo. "We worked together at the Bureau, but this doesn't look like the man I remember."

"That's my father after my mother's death," Noah explained. "He hit the bottle pretty hard—let himself go. This is probably the only picture of him before he died. I don't know how, or why, she has it."

Alexandra patted his shoulder. "I'm sorry, Noah."

Her father shook his head. "I don't understand why she'd have a picture of John in here. It makes no sense whatsoever."

"Name me one thing about Fletcher that has ever made sense," Casey said.

Alex pursed her lips. "It has to mean something, doesn't it?"

Jacob rubbed his beard. "Like be connected?"

"Yes." Alex moved aside when Jasper reached past her to get a cup of coffee. Should he be having coffee? "There's decaf, Jasper."

The older man mumbled something under his breath, but he poured from the decaf carafe.

Casey toasted him with her mug. "They got me on the stuff too, Jasper."

Alex pointed to Noah. "Any other ideas?"

"As to why my father's picture was in there? No, I don't."

"We can get back to that," Ryan suggested. "Noah, who was your picture of?"

Noah dropped the photo faceup on the table. "Some woman."

Alex turned in time for Jasper to spew coffee on the floor. "Jasper, are you all right?" She helped him back to his seat.

The old man gulped. "I think I…well, I think I

may, ah, pass out."

Jacob got to his feet and hurried over to Jasper. "Put your head between your knees."

"Careful, the man just had surgery, for goodness' sake."

"Excuse the fuck outta me, princess." Jake held up his hands and sat back down.

She glared at him. "Don't you dare start—"

"Will you both shut your yaps? My Lord, McKay, you sure do have your hands full. I'm fine, missy." Jasper swatted Alex's hands away.

Fine. She would clean up the mess instead.

Her father shook his head. "You don't even know the half of it, old friend. Casey," he warned, and her sister stopped laughing.

Ryan cleared his throat. "Jasper, you recognized her?"

"The picture…" He took a couple sips of coffee, then cleared his throat. "It's her…it's Fletcher's birth mother."

Alex's hand stilled from where she was cleaning up the spill.

"Come again?" her father said.

Alex quickly rinsed the rag in the sink and tried to settle her nerves. She turned to meet her sister's gaze. They both recognized that tone in their father's voice. Alex swallowed. He wasn't just angry, he was calm too, which was worse.

Noah sat down, put his feet up, and his hands behind his head. And without even realizing it, he defused the situation by saying, "Now *this* I'm dying to hear."

Alex exhaled and returned Casey's relieved smile.

"I think we'd all appreciate an explanation," Ryan

said.

Jasper sighed. "Fletch would say it's *Jamie's* birth mother to be more accurate."

"How the hell do you know that?" Casey asked.

Jasper gave them a funny look. " 'Cause. I looked into it, that's how."

Her father blanched.

"All right, this is…a bit shocking, but what we need to figure out is why the pictures are in the box," Alex said. Her father hadn't looked into their origins—not that she could blame him—but Jasper had; she didn't know how to feel about that.

Casey took a seat. "One thing can't have something to do with the other. Can it?"

"Why else would she put the pictures together? There has to be a connection," Emmit said.

Jasper nodded. "Agreed."

Jebb waved a photo in Alex's face. "Is your laptop in your office?"

She stilled his hand. "Yes, why?"

"I want to check something out."

Alex eyed the people in her kitchen. She needed a reprieve from the crowd anyway. "Come on."

Chapter Nineteen

Jake went through the dining room and parlor and past the massive check-in desk in the front of the B and B to get to the princess's office. He didn't know how she was able to make everything look both fancy and comfortable at the same time, but she did it. And the place always smelled somewhere between lemons and laundry, all fresh and shit. He didn't know how she did that either.

The light from the office cast a shadow on the floor, and the clicking and clacking of computer keys echoed from the room. Jebb was sitting in the chair behind the Queen Anne desk, and Alex was hovering at his side. She moved a loose tendril of hair behind her ear, and Jake held back his groan. God, she was hot. He licked his lips imagining he could still taste her there.

"Jacob?" she said as if sensing his thoughts.

He would have given her a lecherous grin if Jebb hadn't looked up, instead he asked, "What are you two up to?"

"Come see." Alex motioned him forward. "Jebb's onto something."

Jake hurried around the desk. The photo of the Randle brothers, Drake, and the mystery man sat next to the keyboard. "What is it?"

"Take another look at the picture," Jebb said, his gaze not veering from the screen.

Jake picked it up. "Okay?"

Alex's body brushed his, and she pointed at the boys. "Their shirts all have the same emblem."

"Some fancy boarding school," Jebb said.

"They went to school together!"

Alex nodded. "Exactly. Jebb is looking into the alumni now."

"He's hacking—"

"He's not hacking," Alex began. "It's not his fault the school's firewall is mediocre."

Jebb looked over his shoulder and grinned.

Jake shook his head. "Whatever you say, princess."

"Got it!" Jebb shouted. Jake and Alex both leaned in. The same photograph of the boys appeared on the screen. "It's from their yearbook, which means—"

Alex sucked in a breath. "Which means the names are listed."

"Exactly!"

Jake slapped him on the back. "Damn fine work, Jebb."

"Daniel Henderson," Jebb read aloud.

"Dan!" Jake and Alex said in unison.

"That's my guess. Give me a minute…" Jebb's fingers flew across the keys.

Alex straightened. "We have to assume that Daniel Henderson is the same Dan from the emails, don't we?"

Jake nodded. "It's a lead." The first real lead in a while. Hot damn!

"Here we go," Jebb said. "Daniel Henderson is a doctor."

He rubbed his beard. "Another one?"

"What kind of doctor?" Alex asked.

Jake leaned in to read the article Jebb had found. "Plastic surgeon, is what it says." He didn't get it. "Does that matter?"

"I don't know," she said.

Jebb shrugged. "It's more than we knew before."

Jake straightened. Maybe his brother would see something they weren't. "Let's go fill in the others."

****

Alex tidied the counter while Jebb and Jacob rehashed their findings. She came back to the table when Jacob asked his brother if he had any ideas.

Ryan shook his head. "Figuring it all out is the hard part."

Noah lined up the pictures side by side. "We have to make out the connection."

Everyone murmured their agreement.

Jebb pointed at the first photo. "Daemon and Rick Randle—"

"Are both dead." Alex sighed.

"My father and Fletcher's birth mother are also deceased," Noah said.

"Who's not dead?" Jake asked.

"Drake and Dan are the only two alive," Casey pointed out.

"Benjamin Drake is rotting in a jail cell," Ryan said.

Jake nodded. "Yeah, thanks to Alexandra."

Alex inclined her head. "That leaves Dan." Which took them no further than where they were.

"We keep going in circles," Casey said around a yawn.

"What do these people have in common?" Ryan asked.

Jacob scratched his beard. "The dead people, you mean?"

Alex rolled her eyes.

"Rick was murdered," Jasper said.

"So was Fletcher's mother. Deserving or not," Noah added when the entire table glared at him.

"That's a place to start. Your dad, Noah, how'd he die?" Jake asked.

"He jumped in front of a bullet, in the line of duty."

"Jumped?" Jake's gaze shot to Alex's.

"Noah, I don't mean to upset you by asking you this, but do you think your father's death could be construed as suicide?" Alexandra waited for him to look at her, then touched his arm. "Honestly."

He shrugged his massive shoulders. "After what my mother—yeah."

"Does it say killed in the line of duty on his death certificate?" Ryan asked, pinching the bridge of his nose.

Noah rolled his neck. "Yeah, so?"

"Wait—" Casey pointed to Noah. "—what did you say earlier about Fletcher's mother?"

"Case, drop it," Ryan pleaded.

"I'm not trying to start shit, Ryan; I'm asking a perfectly reasonable question. Noah?"

"What? About her mother deserving it?"

"That's it!" Casey stood to move the pictures around. "I think I've got it. Rick—"

"Died in a robbery," Jasper said, sipping his coffee.

Emmit motioned to the other man with his mug. "Which we know was staged."

"Exactly! What about Jamie's mother's death certificate?" Casey asked. "Jasper, do you know what it said?"

"Accident," Jasper spat out.

"Where are you going with this, Casey?" their father wanted to know.

"I think I understand," Alex said. "Noah's father

killed himself, sorry. But his death was labeled homicide. While Daemon Randle's death was labeled a suicide, and we're pretty sure he was murdered. We have four dead people who died under different circumstances than what was recorded on their death certificates."

"See?" Casey nudged Alex's shoulder. "We *are* a lot alike."

"But what does that tell us?" Ryan asked.

Noah rubbed a hand over his face. "That there's a lot of paperwork to be updated.

Jasper shook his head. "Best let the dead lie, boy. Less of course you're planning on going to the feds with your suspicions about your daddy."

"No."

"That's settled then," her father said. "What else do we know?"

"The day of Daemon's death, Dan emailed Fletcher and said Daemon had been murdered."

"We covered this, Jebb. The only person who could know Daemon was murdered was the person who did it." Emmit got up to refill his coffee.

"What if it was a test?" Jebb said, holding out his hands like he was offering a present.

Ryan sat back in his chair. "What kind of test?"

"I'm with you, Jebb." Jake nodded. "Dan was colluding with Daemon, is what you're saying; he wanted to see if Fletcher was as true to Daemon as she appeared."

Noah's legs dropped from the table. "He set her up."

"That's my guess." Jebb hopped on the counter.

"But why?" Casey began. "Why would it matter if Fletch was true to Daemon or not? I mean, the guy's dead, what's done is done? Why set her up?"

Ryan sighed. "Valid question."

Alex nibbled her lip. Casey was right. Why would it matter?

"If my buddy was murdered, I'd want to know his girlfriend really loved him," Jebb said. "But I don't see why—"

Casey snorted. "You're in high school, Bullfrog, so of course that makes sense to you."

"Yeah, like having your friend ask the girl you like if she likes you." Jacob grinned and pointed to Ryan. "Or your twin."

Ryan toasted his brother with his mug.

"Hard to ask a favor like that from six feet under," Jasper said.

Alex smirked. "Indeed."

"Maybe Daemon asked Dan before he killed himself or was murdered," Jebb suggested.

"Weird ask," Casey mumbled and fiddled with the flowers in the centerpiece.

"If Daemon asked Dan to do this before he died, and he didn't kill himself, then are we saying Daemon knew he was going to be murdered?" Jacob asked.

"Like he was preparing just in case, you mean?" Jebb asked.

Casey dropped her hand and sat back in her seat. "If he knew he was going to die, then why did he ask Fletch to marry him?"

"That was one of the reasons Fletch thought Daemon had been murdered in the first place," Emmit added. "Because why ask someone to marry you, then kill yourself before they give you an answer?"

"Right," Casey agreed. "Who does that?"

Jasper set his mug down on the table. "Could it

have been another test?"

Emmit nodded. "What shows more loyalty to a relationship than marriage?"

"Yeah," Casey began, "but Fletcher didn't pass or fail because she didn't give an answer."

Noah pointed to the photo of the four boys. "Enter old school pal Dr. Daniel Henderson with a new test."

Jacob grunted. "We're going in circles again."

Alex nodded and looked again to the array of photos on the table. Murder, suicide, accident; round and round and round they went. The labels were almost interchangeable because no one died how they were said to have—"That's it," she shouted.

"What?" the group asked almost in unison.

"No one's death is as it appeared to be."

"We know that," Jebb said.

Alex shook her head. "No, I mean, *that's* what connects them."

They were all quiet for a moment, then Jebb said, "So Daemon *was* murdered?"

"You're thinking the plastic surgeon did it?" Jasper asked.

"I…" Alex's brows puckered. Was Dan the killer?

Jebb's phone chimed breaking the silence. He held it up. "It's Ma. She says they're watching a movie but wanted to check in."

"Text her what we've got so far," Emmit suggested.

"Will do." Jebb's thumbs played across the screen.

Alex hid her smile. Of course they were watching a movie; Charlie was a lover of the silver screen. It had been a while since she and her sisters had watched a movie alone together; the last time had been months ago. Fletcher had won the toss that night and had chosen a horror movie—of all things. Like they hadn't enough horror in their real lives. It had been a remake…something sinister. What was the name of it? She pursed her lips and stared at the photo of the boys. She gasped. "Demon creature—ohmygod!"

Jacob stretched his arms over his head and rested his hands behind his neck. "Care to enlighten the rest of us, princess?"

They were all looking at her like she'd lost her mind. Alex took a breath and pointed to Casey. "Last time the four of us watched a movie alone together—"

"Fletcher picked that creepy-ass horror movie *Omen*," Casey said. "What does this have to do with anything?"

Adrenaline flooded Alexandra's veins. "Evangeline Drake said her son was corrupted by a demon creature. That they visited her *together*. I asked if she meant Dan, and though she said yes, she seemed confused. Now, I think she meant *demon* as in—"

Casey shot to her feet. "Daemon! Like the creepy kid in the movie."

Alex nodded and opened her mouth to talk, but Jacob held up his hand.

"Wait," Jake began. "So Dan didn't kill him—"

Jebb jumped down from the counter and shouted, "A plastic surgeon! What if *Dr.* Daniel Henderson gave Daemon a new face!"

Alex pointed to her brother. "Exactly!"

"Daemon Randle's alive!" Casey shouted, then her eyes rolled back in her head and she crumpled to the floor.

Chapter Twenty

Alexandra sat on the bed next to Casey after she changed out of the coffee-stained sweater. "Feeling better now?"

"Fainting," Casey began with a shake of her head, "who does that? I'm so fucking embarrassed, I might pull a Fletcher and hide. Sorry, not the time to joke about Fletch." She gagged, then jumped off the bed and ran into the bathroom.

Alex waited until her sister finished emptying her stomach before handing her a cool wet washcloth. "Here…now you're just like Daddy. He had to go throw up once he realized you were all right. And your husband got so worked up, Jake had to slap him to calm him down. Noah took the liberty of carrying you up here; he picked you up like you were a peanut," Alex said with a snap of her fingers.

"Gross," Casey said, dabbing her face with the cloth. "Where was Ryan?"

"After Jake slapped him, Ryan retaliated and then the fight was on. Jasper was trying to play referee, and our dear brother made for a decent cheerleader."

"Who won?" Casey asked before she used Alex's mouthwash.

"I think Jasper put an end to the boxing match before any real damage was done. So I'd say it was a draw. I should add, it'll be harder to tell them apart now." Alex tried not to laugh. She enjoyed a good fight.

Casey spat in the sink, then said, "Sorry I missed it. I got worked up, I guess. The idea of Daemon being alive—Fletch must have pissed herself when he showed up."

"If she recognized him," Alex said.

They were only in the kitchen for a second before Casey shouted, "Look at your face!"

Alex winced. Ryan had a black eye and a split lip.

Ryan put the ice pack over his eye. "You should be resting."

"I'll rest when you stop acting like an idiot." Casey shook her head, looked at Jake, then pointed to Alex. "A draw, my ass!"

"Oh, come on, Casey. We were just releasing some steam," Jake said grinning. "Alexandra isn't mad at me; don't be mad at Ryan."

"If you want to act like a barnyard animal, that's your business, Jacob," Alex said taking a seat at the table. "I don't care either way."

"I'm not mad at Ryan. You're the one at fault here, Jake, and don't think I don't know it. And I do believe my little sister bested you, so I wouldn't be bragging."

Jasper hooted. "She's got you there, boy!"

Jacob smirked. "By the balls, I know."

"Can we please get back to the part where we find Fletcher?" Jebb said. "She needs us now."

"Daemon Randle blew his brains out," Noah reminded the room. "His sister gave a positive ID."

"Not much of his face was left though," Jasper put in. "If I remember correctly, she identified him by the ring he wore."

"I read the file, Jasper. Yes, part of it was his ring, but he also had a tattoo."

"What kind of tattoo?" Jebb asked.

Noah shrugged. "I don't remember, right off. His sister said it was new. Not that I particularly trust that backstabber…Jasper, do you remember what it was?"

Jasper sipped his coffee and stretched his neck. "It was snakes forming a circle."

"Sick bastard," Emmit hissed.

The image prickled something in Alex's memory, but she couldn't quite—

"It's a positive ID," Noah said.

"Did you run his fingerprints?" Jake asked.

"I wasn't sheriff. Jasper?"

"It's like Noah said, Daemon's sister gave us a positive ID." He shrugged. "There wasn't a need to look into it any more than that."

"Then what are you waiting for, Noah?" Casey asked.

"What do you want me to do?"

Casey threw up her hands. "Go dig up the body."

"I can't go exhuming bodies. I need a court order and permission from the next of kin." Noah shook his head.

Jasper drummed his fingers on the table. "Ain't no family left."

"I still need a court order."

Alex shook her head at Noah. If Jasper were still sheriff, he'd already be on the phone. She sighed. "I know a judge." Before anyone could respond, she went to place a call; a few minutes later, she came back in the room. "The order will be emailed to you within the hour."

"How the hell did you do that?" Noah shook his head. "You made one phone call, and it's done?"

"I'm a well-respected member of this community, Noah. I'm also on the town council, not to mention our grandfather was a judge."

"That's nice, but where am I going to find the manpower?"

Jasper stood. "Now, that I can help you with. Come on, Noah, we got a lot to do. Time you started getting to know my secrets. We'll see y'all later," Jasper told the group as he led Noah out. The back door banged shut behind them.

Alex smirked. "Think Noah's upset?"

Casey patted her on the back. "You're something else, Alexandra!"

They sat around the kitchen, some at the table, some propped against the counter, discussing the possibility of the body in Daemon's plot belonging to someone else. What-ifs went 'round until Jake got hold of the little black bird from Mack's box and started messing with it.

"What kinda bird is this anyway?" Jake asked his brother by shoving the little stuffed animal under his nose.

Ryan swatted Jake's hand away.

Alex shook her head; would he ever grow up? "It's a raven, I believe."

Ryan sighed. "More Poe."

"Poe," Jacob mumbled, then sat straighter in his chair and started pulling at the little stuffed toy. "That damn kid!"

"What?" the room said almost in unison.

Jacob grinned and held up a small golden key.

Alexandra shook her head. "You can't say Fletcher doesn't have a knack for hiding things."

Casey snorted. "No shit."

Ryan leaned closer to his brother. "Looks like it goes to a safety deposit box."

Jebb took the key out of Jake's hand. "Yeah, but remember what Fletcher said: it's also the key to finding truth."

"I'll be damned," Casey whispered.

"We have two problems," Jake pointed out. "First, we don't know which bank—"

"Blue Creek Bank," Alex said after she got a look at the key.

"How do you know?"

"They're the only bank around here with a shamrock engraved on their keys." She shrugged. "Something about leprechauns guarding their money."

Her father nodded. "Hal O'Conner owns the bank; his family's from Ireland. He's big on their legends."

"Okay, we still have two problems," Jake said. "One, a small-town bank will know none of us is Fletcher, and unless she authorized one of us, the bank can't let us into her safety deposit box. And two, they'll be closing any minute now."

"Not a problem," Emmit said and pulled out his cell phone. "Hal, McKay here. No, not yet, as good as can be expected, I reckon. I'm glad you said that, Hal. Yes, I could use your help. I found a key…Yes, that's the one. I know. I'm not asking you to break the law. No, Hal. I just wanted to know if you remembered who…Could you say that again please. Did she? Yeah, I guess that makes sense. You're right, of course. Thanks, Hal. Alexandra will be with him. Yeah, I know she is. Thanks again. Say hello to Dot for me. All right then, bye." Emmit stuffed his cell in his pocket and stared into space.

"What'd Hal say, Pops?" Casey asked.

He scratched his head. "He remembers who Fletch authorized to get into her box."

"Dad? Who was it?" Alex didn't like the look on his face. Please let it not be someone deceased because apparently she was going with them.

"Noah."

"What? Why would she—?" Casey blew out a breath. "Never mind."

"Hal said he thought it was strange too and asked her about it." Emmit shifted in his seat. "She said the information concerned a case she was working on, and who better than the sheriff to have access. Sounded reasonable to Hal."

"Not that I particularly care for the idea," Casey began, "but it looks like we'll need Noah again."

"I'll call him," Emmit said. "Maybe Jasper can oversee the exhumation while Noah opens the box. The vault's on a timer, so if you don't go now, we'll have to wait until the morning."

"Trust me, Noah will come," Alex said. "His curiosity alone would guarantee it."

Their father left the table for a couple minutes, then came back saying, "Noah will meet you at the bank."

Alex nodded. "All right, I'll leave now. Is everyone going to wait here?"

Casey snorted. "Duh!"

"Fine then." Alex grabbed her keys and, with her father following her, went to her vehicle. "Are you coming with me?"

"No," her father said smiling. "You did good, sweetheart."

"Oh goody, is that why I get to go with Noah into the big bad bank?" She winced. "Sorry, Dad."

"I never realized you were such a smart-ass."

Her cheeks flamed. "I—"

"Noah trusts you; that's why I want you to go."

She rose a brow. "He trusts you too."

"Not as much here lately." Emmit shrugged. "He knows he pissed me off. It's not a secret I don't like people making accusations about one of my girls. I would have asked Craig, but he's at work. You're the next best thing. He is your cousin, after all."

"True." She sighed and looked at her watch. "I guess I'll go solve the big mystery."

"Be careful." He started to walk away but then turned back around. "Noah needs to be watched, Alexandra, and you're the only person I know who's savvy enough to do so."

She couldn't help but smile. "When you say it like that…"

He nodded and walked back to the house.

Savvy? Yes, she liked that. Cheered, she pulled out of her parking space, then slammed on the brakes when Jacob jumped in front of her vehicle.

He hopped in the passenger seat and opened his mouth to speak, but she smacked him. "What were you thinking? I could have hurt you, then Ryan would never forgive—"

Jake kissed her thoroughly, then sat back in his seat. "Now we can go."

She blinked. "Who invited you?"

"I'm your boyfriend, remember?" He buckled his seat belt. "We're going steady."

Alex shook her head and put the small SUV in drive. "Not this again."

"You want me, and we both know it!"

She pursed her lips to suppress a smile. "Who could forget with you mentioning the subject every few minutes?"

"Did you get a chance to put your panties back

on?" He reached across the console and up her skirt.

She swerved. "What do you think you're doing?" She took one hand off the wheel to swat at him. "Do you want me to kill you?"

His hot hand stroked her thigh. "Just doing my own research."

"Get your brain out of the gutter, and your hand out of my skirt," she hissed. Though, if she was honest, she was undeniably turned on.

Jake nodded. "Fun later. Work now."

"Stop staring at me."

"Sorry."

It didn't take long before Alex pulled into the bank parking lot. "You stay."

"If you're not out in fifteen minutes, I'm coming in."

"If you insist."

He took hold of her hand.

She stared at their linked fingers. "What?"

"I don't trust Reed."

"I'll be fine, Jacob, I promise," she said, then gave him a quick kiss.

"What was that for?"

"Just because." She flashed him a smile, then locked him in the SUV.

Noah was waiting for her by the bank's entrance. "Let's get this over with," he said and opened the door for her.

Alexandra made idle chitchat with Hal as they walked into a small room with a table and a couple chairs.

"You can wait in here, Alexandra," Hal said, then pointed to Noah. "Do you have the key?"

Noah held out his hand to Alex. She handed it to

him without reluctance, then took a seat.

“We’ll be back in a jiff,” Hal said.

Alex tapped her foot and stared at the door the men had gone through. She hadn’t wanted to let Noah out of her sight. Not that she didn’t trust Noah; she did—to a degree. She glanced at the entrance with a tilt to her lips; Jacob was probably going stir-crazy waiting in the SUV. Her smile turned downward; what was she going to do about him? She’d tried shoving him away with ice, but he’d gone and heated things up again. She could do the whole leech thing: hang on his every word, be sickly gushing toward him—smother him. But that would annoy *her* during the process. So that was out. Maybe…

“Here we are,” Hal said. “Now, I’ll leave you two alone.”

“We won’t be long,” Noah assured the other man.

Hal glanced at his watch. “Bank closes in fifteen.” He gave a wink and a wave.

Alex waited until Hal had left the room before turning to Noah.

“You’re sleeping with Keller?” Noah asked.

“Not that it’s any of your business, but yes,” she said, more annoyed by the fact he wasn’t opening the box than by the question. “I have nothing to hide when it comes to Jacob.”

He shrugged. “I didn’t say you did or should. I’m surprised, is all.”

“This from the man seeing Marylou Thomas?” She laughed. “You have no room to talk.”

“What is everyone’s problem with Marylou? The whole damn town is giving me shit about it.”

“Honey, if you haven’t figured out why that is, then you’re not as smart as I keep giving you credit for.

Now open the box!"

"Fine," he grumbled. He opened the box and pulled out a manila envelope.

Alex bit her lower lip and gave up a silent prayer for Fletcher to be safe, wherever she was.

Noah ripped open the seal and emptied the contents onto the table. There were two letters inside, one with his name and one with Alex's.

She snatched up the one with her name on it.

"Aren't you going to read it?" Noah asked.

"Read yours first."

Noah muttered something under his breath and pulled out his letter.

"What does it say?" Alex asked when he didn't read it out loud.

"Nothing but 'fuck you.' " Noah hit his fists down on the table. "All this crap. All these fucking clues just to tell me to go to hell." He ran a hand through his short hair. "I'm going back to the cemetery with Jasper. We've got the city's medical examiner coming in later tonight, so hopefully will have some straight answers soon."

She stared at him a moment, then said, "I'm sorry, Noah."

"It's not your fault, Alexandra. I'll tell Hal we're finished here." He headed for the door. "I'll see you when I know something."

"No problem," she said to his retreating back. She gathered her things and went out to where Jake was waiting.

Jake squirmed in his seat the minute she opened her door. "You were gone long enough."

"Not even ten minutes." It was starting to get dark, so she turned on the overhead light.

"What's that?"

"There were two letters in the box."

He rubbed his beard. "And Noah let you walk out without opening yours?"

"Yes, he was too busy lying to me."

"What do you mean, 'lying to you'?" Jake swore. "I told you I didn't trust him."

"Fletcher left a letter for me and one for Noah. He read his to himself. When I asked him what it said, he acted like a caveman, banging his fists on the table," she explained and Jake furrowed his brow. "He said it was a 'fuck you' letter."

He deflated. "That doesn't prove he was lying to you."

"But it does!" She sighed. "I've been the recipient of Fletcher's more vulgar letters; she writes 'F you' and signs her name. She may add a few adjectives, but that's it. Not a full page. Secondly, Noah's a gentleman; he doesn't throw little man tantrums. He has a sheer talent for discretion."

Jake crossed his arms over his chest. "That's your fancy way of saying he has tact, isn't it?"

"You're catching on, Jacob." She kissed his cheek. "Besides those things, I know when I'm being lied to. A fact you might want to jot down in that little black book of yours."

He grinned. "You mean, seeing as how I won't be needing it anymore?"

"Perhaps. Now…" She unfolded her letter and read aloud.

"Alexandra,

"Since you found this note, I'm guessing the family left it up to you to find me. Via some psychological bonding ritual they think we need. Obviously, I'm right if you're reading this. But if you've come this far I'm probably in deep shit."

"We know all this; read what we don't know."

"Okay." She looked back down to the page in her hand. "Daemon, Dan, Benjamin Drake, so on and so on. Lodge, check. Benji's house—been there too…here we go. 'Daemon talked about wanting to go somewhere serene, so…' " She looked back up at Jacob. "I seriously doubt they went to a spa."

"Me too. Of course, after we find her, you and I could check it out." He laughed when Alex shook her head at him. "Just a suggestion."

"Where was I? 'I told him about the cabin we used to go to with Granddaddy—' "

"We've been to the damn lodge and I thought you read that part already."

"I did. Would you let me finish?" She raised a brow, and he slumped back down in his seat. "Thank you. '…you remember, Alex, it was the only one of our outings you enjoyed.' " Alex nibbled on her lip. They'd gone so many places with their grandfather. She hadn't really liked any of them, except when they went to the city. "I don't know what she's talking about! Why talk in riddles? Why not just tell me?"

Jake shrugged. "Who knows? Just keep reading."

" 'Anyway'—her words not mine," she clarified for Jacob. " 'I'm still mad at you…' " Alex said. "Well, she goes on to list the reasons she's still upset with me, but that was all concerning the locations."

"Nothing's ringing a bell?" Jake asked as Alex got back out of the vehicle. "Now where are you going?"

"I have to ask Hal something," she said and rushed away.

Jake took the time to read the letter himself,

laughing when Fletch told Alex off a few times. That kid, Jake shook his head, was something else. "Well?" Jake asked when Alexandra came back and started the engine.

She buckled her seatbelt and started the engine. "I asked Hal if he remembered when Fletcher took out the safety deposit box."

"What'd he say?" Jake tilted his head to read the speedometer. She was speeding.

"He said it wasn't that long ago. He remembered because he asked her how many people were coming to stay at the B and B. I had a large tourist group stay at Granny Vaughn's a few weeks ago. Hal knew my guests would be eating some meals at the diner."

"Why?"

"I don't know if you noticed this, Jacob, but I don't cook and when I say don't, I mean can't. I burn everything. I—"

"It's about fucking time!"

"What?"

"That I find out something you *can't* do. Don't worry, I won't hold it against you, sweetheart."

"Thank you so much for that, Jacob. I don't know what I'd do if you thought less of me." She snorted. "Hal asked Fletcher if Charlie would be able to deliver lunch for him and his employees. And that's why he remembered."

He rubbed his beard. "She must have left the condo, come back here, and opened the safety deposit box. But why would Daemon, or whoever the guy's pretending to be, wait for her to go back to my place? If he was following her, I mean."

She drummed her fingers on the steering wheel. "You mean because he brought her back here?"

"Yeah, it seems. I don't know…" He shrugged. "Redundant?"

Chapter Twenty-One

Alex woke the next morning without an answer. She'd been up most of the night trying to figure out where Fletcher had meant. She didn't feel too bad about not knowing because no one else had any ideas either. She and Jacob had come back to find the entire family sitting around the kitchen table eating the meal Charlie had made.

Her mother and Charlie had gotten sick of waiting for an update, so they'd grabbed Mack and headed over. Her sister had made use of the kitchen and the leftovers; the table had been near overflowing.

Being careful with what they said in front of Mack, she and Jacob had told her family what they'd found out. Which was a big fat nothing. She didn't tell them that Noah had lied, which had upset Jacob, but Alex would deal with Noah in her own way.

After taking a shower and getting dressed, she headed downstairs. Jake was at the stove, which made her smile. He'd understood her not wanting him sleeping with her last night. If most of the family hadn't been here, she might have let him. Okay, there was no question she would have slept with him.

Seeing him here in her kitchen wearing only a pair of—Alex closed her eyes at the horror that was his taste in clothes—torn jeans, she knew she was in trouble. Deep shit would be more vulgar but also more appropriate.

"Morning, princess." Jake put down his spatula and came over to kiss her.

Alex let herself enjoy the kiss, ignoring Casey who bumped into them.

"Oh, get a room." Casey yawned. "Is there decaf?"

"Yeah," Jake said, then flustered Alex by kissing her again.

"Good grief, get a room," Charlie said from behind them.

Alex huffed. "This is my house."

"Well, we're guests," Casey said and sipped her coffee. "Wow, Jake this is good." Casey slapped the palm Alexandra held out. "Never known you to high-five someone, Miss Priss."

"No, this means *where's my money*. Only paying guests get to complain." Alex tapped her foot. "Nothing to say?" She turned to Charlie. "You? Good."

Mack came running into the room, and Jake swept her up in his arms.

Something in Alex's chest turned over, but she ignored it. "I have some errands to run, so I'll see y'all later. Behave," she said and hurried out the door.

****

Alex pulled up to Noah's home. Her grandfather used to own the estate, and she still loved it. She did not, however, love the fact that Marylou's bimbo-mobile was parked in the driveway.

"Wonderful," she muttered and parked. She made her way up the walkway and to the front entrance, jumping when the front door opened.

"This is the biggest mistake of your life, Noah! Mark my words, you're gonna be sorry. Nobody, and I mean *nobody*, dumps Marylou Thomas," Marylou screamed, her bottle-blonde hair flying in every direction. She put a hand to her heaving silicone breast when she turned. "Alexandra?" Her face went white. "What are you doing here?"

"I needed to ask Sheriff Reed a question about the upcoming festival," she lied easily. "Are you all right, honey?"

"No, I'm not," Marylou blubbered. "Noah just"—fake sob—"broke"—blubber—"up"—hiccup—"with me."

"Oh, honey…" *It's about time.* Alexandra patted Marylou's sweaty back and tried not to choke on the other woman's overpowering perfume. She opened the door of the bimbo-mobile for Marylou and said, "There are plenty of men in this town who'd slit their own throat to be with you."

Marylou paused in the middle of buckling her seat belt. "That's true."

"Of course it is!" Alex said. Just the other day Jerry Fellows said he'd slit his throat if he ever had to be with Marylou. "And we both know it. You know what you need?"

"No."

"A day at the spa and some serious retail therapy."

"You're right. I'll show that Noah Reed. Bye now."

Alex waved until Marylou was out of sight. "You pathetic creature."

"I heard that, Alexandra," Noah said from the doorway, then motioned for her to come inside.

"You've obviously come to the same conclusion, haven't you?" Alex asked.

He ignored her question and ushered her into the great room. "I believe the last time you were here you broke in."

"Noah Reed, what an accusation!" she said with southern flare, then thanked him for the coffee he handed her. "We had a key."

"Semantics…take a seat."

Alex admired the marble-topped coffee cart he had set up, though it was a shame he'd prepared it for the likes of Marylou; it was a lovely serving piece. She'd helped him decorate the house before he moved in, and everything still looked elegant, yet homey, but that was beside the point. She sank into the lush cushions of the chair across from him. "I'll get right to it."

"I'd appreciate that."

"Why did you lie to me yesterday?"

He settled back against the sofa. "I didn't."

"All right. Why did you lie to me yesterday and again now?" She pulled out a sandstone coaster from the set on the side table, put her cup on it, and shifted toward him. "I know you lied, Noah. So just tell me the truth."

He set down his own mug. "I didn't."

She stared at his coasterless cup and pursed her lips. Unlike the kitchen table in the B and B, this coffee table needed extra care. "Noah, I'm losing my patience, and that's not something you want."

"Are you threatening an officer of the law, Ms. McKay? Because you're well aware that's a crime."

"I'm not threatening anyone. I don't make threats." She stood and crossed her arms over her chest. "Come clean."

"What do you expect to do? Beat me until I admit to something that's false?"

"I don't need to use brutality, Noah, trust me; I have something much better."

"Really?"

"Secrets." Alex picked up her cup once again and took a sip. Jacob's coffee was much better.

"Secrets? You're planning on blackmailing me?" He laughed. "Also a crime, cousin."

"Did I say blackmail? Did I even say my secrets regarded you?"

He stared at her.

Alex reclaimed her seat and kept from smiling. Victory was close.

"I'll bite. What do you know?"

"Honestly?" Alex relaxed against the cushions and crossed her ankles. "Do you think I'll just tell you? You're smarter than that. I want to read the letter Fletcher left for you."

"I didn't read yours," he said, then shut his mouth when she handed it to him.

"Go ahead. I can't figure it out." She waited until he was finished reading to ask if he had any ideas.

He shook his head. "Other than the fact that she's pissed at you…no."

"My turn." Alex held out her palm.

"I won't let you read it, but I'll tell you what was inside."

Alex withdrew her hand and narrowed her eyes. "Fair enough."

Noah got up and poured himself more coffee. Going to his desk he took out a folder and handed the entire thing to Alexandra.

"What's this?" The file hadn't come from the safety deposit box.

"In Fletcher's note, she told me I needed to take a good long look at the file she'd hidden in my floor." He pointed to a corner of the room where slats of hardwood had been taken out.

Typical. Fletcher loved putting stuff under the floorboards. Alex shook her head and picked up the file. Instead of opening it, she looked at Noah. "What's in it?"

"You trust me to tell you?"

"I have it in my hands, and I'm certain you won't try to lie to me again."

"Fair enough," Noah said, using her own words against her. "There are pictures—"

Alex sighed. "More pictures."

"Compromising photos of a former girlfriend."

"Marylou?" Alex couldn't help herself; she opened the envelope. Fletcher had taken or had hired someone to take photographs of Marylou with three different men. Ouch. Two of them she knew from town; the other, she had to take a closer look. "Is that who I think it is?" Because there was a distinct resemblance to a person of public office. A very public, very married person.

"The same," Noah said. "The last photo should be of particular interest."

Alex flipped through to the end. Normally she would feel sorry for Noah, but he'd been warned, many times. She came to the last photo and held it up. "I don't understand. It's Marylou with her father. Mr. Thomas had a heart attack; he's been dead for years."

"Yeah, then explain to me how Marylou's in a picture with her father wearing the necklace I gave her a month ago?"

Alex sucked in a breath.

"I guess this is one secret you didn't know," he said, his face smug.

"My God," Alex said staring at the picture. "Please tell me that diamond's not real, Noah. You wasted your money." She shook her head and handed him back the file. "And on a floozie too; how sad."

"What?" He snatched back the papers. "You knew? You knew Ian Thomas was alive? What about, 'He's been dead for years'?"

Alex smiled. "I was fooled too, for a second. Then I remembered something about Ian Thomas."

"Which is?"

"He looked like what he was…a snake. It was in the eyes. This man has kind eyes."

"You're serious?"

"Very. That is *not* Ian Thomas, but the likeness is uncanny."

"Then who the hell's this guy?"

Alex sipped her coffee. "If I had to guess, I'd say an imposter."

"An imposter," Noah mimicked shaking his head. "Well, it fooled Jasper too."

She pursed her lips. "Oh, I doubt that."

"What do you mean?"

"The only person who could've possibly hated Ian Thomas more than my family was Jasper. Trust me, he'd know the difference. Did he say it was Ian?"

"He said, and I quote, 'Looks like Ian Thomas if yah ask me, boy.'"

"See, he didn't say the man *was* Ian Thomas; he said it *looked* like him." Alex paused for a second. "Why would they need an Ian Thomas look-alike?" Maybe the old stories of Ian Thomas's having stashed a fortune in Switzerland were true. Something to consider. "Is that all Fletcher wrote?"

"Just about the file, and then she told me in about twenty different ways what I could do with myself and where she believes I'm destined to end up."

“At least one good thing came out of all this mess.”

“Care to share?”

“You broke up with Marylou. That’s about the best thing that’s happened in months!” Alex grinned.

“I showed you mine…”

“Ah, yes, secrets. Have you ever noticed secrets are like spiders’ webs?”

Chapter Twenty-Two

It was late afternoon by the time Alex pulled into her driveway. She squinted at the person on her porch and threw the vehicle in park. She hurried toward him. "Jasper? Are you feeling all right?'

"I'm fine, missy." He huffed. "Did yah hear the news?"

She took a seat next to him on the steps. "What news?" She had never taken the time to get to know Jasper on a personal level, and now she was hesitant to do so.

"The body buried in Daemon Randle's plot?"

"What about it?" So that's where Noah had rushed off to, she realized. The jerk. Here she'd told him…oh, who cared.

"It wasn't Randle." Jasper notched up his cap to scratch his forehead. "We got no idea who it could be. Noah's running dental records. Prints weren't worth a damn."

She rubbed her hands over her arms. "We were right then?"

"I reckon we were—to some extent. Doesn't feel so good, does it?"

"What?"

"Being right 'bout this."

"No, Jasper, gives me chills."

"Me too. Feels unnatural." Jasper blew into his clasped hands. "Reckon we'll get one more snow before spring gets here?"

"I hope not." She shivered, her eyes going to the apartment over the garage; so many things had happened over there. It had once been a barn. "Do you remember Granny Vaughn's prize cow?"

"That damn Mabel." Jasper shook his head. "Never did find the blasted animal."

"You know who let her out, don't you?"

He burst out laughing. "Fletcher let it slip one day. Hadn't even realized I was listening to her; then she went pale, and she started cursing me till her face was blue. Funniest damn thing!" He wiped his eyes. "I'd forgotten all about that. You girls…"

"The McKay heathens," Alexandra mumbled. She flinched when Jasper put his arm around her.

"Y'all weren't never heathens. Folks just didn't know what to think." He tilted her chin so they were eye to eye. "You girls woke this town up."

"Gave people something or someone to talk about is more like it."

He let go of her and shrugged. "Small towns are like that. I'll tell you what I used tell your sister. My job was never as exciting as when you girls showed up."

"That's nice." Was all she could say. Jasper wasn't known for his pretty words, but they didn't have to be poetic to be meaningful.

"I ain't trying to be nice. I'm telling you the truth. Without you girls, things round here would have dried up like the creek during a drought. And we can't be having that."

Alex smiled. "Heaven forbid!"

"You two look like you're enjoying yourselves," Savannah said coming down the steps to join them.

Jasper nodded. "I'll leave you two ladies to it," he

said and went inside.

Alex shaded her eyes from the sun. “Hi, Mama.”

“Hi, honey.” She took a seat next to her. “Your father and I talked.”

Alexandra’s stomach rolled. Not this again. “That’s nice.”

“What’s going on between you and Jake?”

She ran a hand down the skirt of her dress. “Jacob and I are enjoying the pleasure of each other’s company.”

“Once you involve sex, feelings tend to follow,” Savannah began.

“I won’t get hurt,” Alex said, amused.

“I didn’t say you would. But Jake was practically prancing around here this morning, which is a sure sign of a man in over his head.”

“You think I’ll hurt Jacob?” Oh, how wonderful. “What kind of woman do you think I am?”

“Someone who doesn’t let anyone get close to you. Someone who hides who she is.”

Alex shifted on the step. “This isn’t about Jacob, is it? This is about what I said to Casey the other day.”

“Yes. Though, your father and I *are* worried about the Jake situation.”

“How sweet.”

“Maybe you’ve been able to fool me before—fooled me and your father for years—but you’re not fooling me now.”

Alex looked at her nails. “I have no idea what you’re talking about.”

“You do, and we both know it. There’s a lot of hurt inside you, not to mention anger toward your sister.”

Heat crept up her neck. “I don’t think we need to discuss this.”

"There's a lot of hurt…"

Alex narrowed her eyes. "I didn't mean to hurt anyone, if that's what you're accusing me of."

"Only yourself," Savannah mumbled. "You're uncannily apt at making people believe what you want them to. I certainly didn't think you ever used your talents against us."

Alex sucked in a breath. "I didn't use anything against you."

"I didn't mean it that way. I'm trying to understand why you kept silent all these years. Why you felt the need to hide your feelings from us. I don't remember you being this way when you were younger."

Alex took hold of the porch railing. "I've always been this way."

"No." Savannah shook her head. "You haven't always been deceitful. I know that for a fact."

"I like to think of myself as cunning, thank you very much," Alex said between gritted teeth. Tears prickled her eyes, but she would be damned if she would let them fall. She moved to leave, but her mother pulled her back down.

"I'm still your mother, Alexandra."

"You have no idea who you're dealing with."

"No one does when it comes to you. Lord, Alex, do you even know who you are or what you really feel? I think you've been pushing your emotions down so long, you don't know what they are anymore."

"You could never understand the way I feel," Alexandra shouted. Why was her mother saying these horrible things to her?

"Then explain it to me because I'm lost," Savannah whispered. "What happened to my sweet little girl?"

Alex's laugh held no humor. "The only sweet little

girl you ever had was Charlie." Her mother wanted to argue? Fine; she could argue all damn day.

"That's not true."

Alex stood and wrapped her arms around herself. "Are you really that fucking naïve?"

Her mother jumped to her feet. "Don't you speak to me that way!"

"Then don't bring up things you have no right bringing up."

"I'll do whatever I need to do to get the truth."

Alex threw her hands up in the air. "What's so great about the truth? Everyone wants to know the truth. Are you happy? Now we have an audience!" Alex yelled when all of her family stepped outside. Even Jacob. Wonderful. "This is no one's business; don't you get that?"

"It's my business when I don't even know who you are or what the truth is behind that mask you wear," Savannah said, then pointed at everyone else. "This is between me and Alex, so please go back inside."

It only took a moment for everyone to retreat.

Savannah pointed to Alex. "Now answer me!"

"What?" Alex swatted away tears. "You want to know what happened to your little girl, is that it? Well, there you go"—she motioned to the house—"she's in there somewhere. Have fun finding her, I couldn't." She spun around when her mother grabbed her. "Let go of me," she snapped.

"Not until you explain yourself," Savannah said with tears in her eyes.

"The girl you're so desperate to find died…" She pulled her mother with her to the tree by the back porch and placed her hand on the rough bark. "Right here, years ago."

"Alexan—"

She pulled out of her mother's grasp. "I became this—how does everyone put it?" She tapped her finger to her lip. "Oh, that's right…cold bitch. I became this person the night I took a man's life."

Her mother stared at her openmouthed. "You bounced right back," she whispered. "The therapist said you had greatly improved. You—you were saving us."

Alex shook her head. "You don't get it, do you? I killed him. I knew what I was doing. I'm an expert marksman. I could have wounded him enough to stop him. But I didn't! I *chose* to take the kill shot."

"You're talking nonsense, Alex; you were ten years old."

"You still don't get it. Casey, Fletcher, and I were never really children—Charlie either. Our lives weren't some fairytale. I knew exactly what I was doing when I pulled that trigger. And I don't care. Do you understand now? I killed a man, and I have absolutely no remorse. I'd do it again to; even knowing he *was* my father. I'd do it again!"

Savannah sucked in a breath.

Emotions threatened to overwhelm her, but she focused on anger. "I know Fletcher told you who my sperm donor was."

"Why didn't you ever say—"

"Let's be realistic. I sound psychotic." Alex shook her head.

Savannah covered her mouth with her hand. "Oh, Alex…"

She wiped her eyes. "You wanted the truth? Well, here you are. We only ever talk about Uncle Evan, but Kyle was our uncle too; he played a major role in our lives. He loved us in his way. And we loved him—*I* loved him—but I killed him just the same. I've done everything to protect this family: lie, cheat, and kill. What does that make me?"

"You're my daughter; that's who. And I love you. Nothing you say or do will change that—nothing!" Savannah said through her tears. "I love you, and I always will!"

Alex choked back a sob and said, "I love you too. But don't you see? That's the problem. These things I've done, these horrible things…I've done them for love…just like he did." She turned and went inside. She ignored all the stares as she passed everyone on her way to her room until Jake stopped her at the top of the steps.

"You okay, princess?"

Alex cringed; he'd heard everything. They'd all heard. "How noble of you, Jacob," she sneered and sidestepped when he reached out. "Don't touch me."

"Fine," Jake said and without another word went down the stairs.

Alex shut her door and stripped off her clothes. She turned on the shower, waited for the water to heat, then stepped inside the stall and let out the sob that choked her. She'd sent Jacob away because more than anything she wanted to fall into his arms. She found safety in his embrace—happiness even. For the first time in so long…

But she wasn't stupid. She couldn't keep Jacob. She couldn't let herself need him. "Alexandra McKay needs no one!" she said into the spray, then put her fist in her mouth to keep the lie down. She'd known better.

The Widow had taught her many things, but a few always rang true for Alex. Firstly, don't let them see you cry; second, discretion is key in intimate encounters; thirdly, true love chooses you, but it doesn't care if it destroys you in the process. The fourth was the most important. A woman must find her own strength, and never let *anyone* find a weakness.

She couldn't let it or Jacob matter. She'd revealed too much, and that was concerning. Her feelings were her own and not meant for anyone else. Her mother had asked why she hadn't told anyone. She had. She'd told the only person who could understand. The one person who knew the weight of keeping a secret, who understood the burden of taking a life; she had told her little sister. "Oh, Fletcher," she sobbed and slid down the cold tiles to the shower floor.

She cupped her face and let out all the emotion she'd been bottling up for weeks. She was responsible for Fletcher leaving. She let everyone believe she didn't care about her sister. But that was another of Alex's secrets. If anything happened to Fletcher…

Alex sat there for a several more minutes, then stood and straightened her shoulders. Tears had never gotten her anything. She washed away all signs of sorrow, shut off the water, and stepped out of the stall.

"Here."

"What in the hell are you doing in here?" Alex snatched the towel out of Jacob's hands. She wouldn't let him know how humiliated she was. "How long have you been playing peeping Tom?"

He shrugged. "Long enough."

She wrapped the towel around her and pointed to the door. "Get out, Jacob."

"You really want me to leave?"

"I just gave you the answer to that." *Leave before I cave. Please.*

"I'll go…downstairs."

Alex waited for him to go, sighing when he stopped with the door open.

"I never knew you were an expert marksman. That's fucking cool." He grinned and left the room.

Alex couldn't help but smile. He was too much. She slipped on her underwear and scoffed. "F'ing cool, he says." She shook her head, then froze.

"Third bullseye in a row! That's so fucking cool, Alex," seven-year-old Fletcher said.

Alex lowered the rifle. Her little sister's admiration warmed her heart, but she wouldn't give that away. "How hard is it to say Alexandra? Hmm?"

Fletcher snorted. "That's fucking cool, Alexandra, then."

She bit her lip to stop her smile, then straightened her shoulders and said, "You better not let Granddaddy hear you curse like that."

Fletcher threw her small arms into the air. "Hell's bells..."

Alex dropped her towel. Holy God! That was it! She got dressed faster than she had in her entire life.

Chapter Twenty-Three

Alexandra ran down the stairs and right into his chest. "Where's the fire?" Jake asked taking in her wet hair and—"Aren't those the kid's clothes?"

Alex looked down at herself. "They were in the clean pile—never mind. Where is everyone?"

"I sent them home. I figured you needed some alone time." That was the gentlemanly thing to do. Ryan had suggested it, but Alex didn't need to know that. Jake couldn't stop staring at her. He'd stood outside her bathroom while she had cried, and his gut had turned over. He had also come to grips with the fact that he was head over heels in love with the princess. He was screwed, and he knew it, but he was too shocked by the idea of it all to care—for the moment anyway.

She pursed her lips. "I guess we can call everyone back."

"You want to tell me what's going on first?" Jake was surprised yet delighted when she kissed him. Leaning in, he cupped her head with his hands and deepened the kiss. Her tongue ran across his lips, and he grew hard. He groaned and made his move.

Jake lifted her up, turned on even more when she wrapped her long legs around his hips and her arms around his neck. She took his hair down and ran her fingers through it. God, he loved that. He brought her closer, held her tighter, needing more, wanting—

Alex pulled her lips away. "I figured out where Fletcher is. Ow," she said when he dropped her butt on the counter.

"Sorry." He took the elastic band from her and put his hair back up. "But this is great. Where? When? How?"

"You made me think of it."

He puffed out his chest. "How?"

"The only cabin trip I ever truly enjoyed was when Granddaddy taught me how to shoot a rifle. Cool, huh?"

Jake swept her up off her feet again, making her yelp. "My idea? Hot damn!"

She laughed as he set her down.

"So where are we going?"

"You're not going to believe this," she began. "It's not even an hour away."

"Just where the hell is it?"

"On Blue Creek. There's this deluxe cabin we—"

"Wait, who owns the place?" Jake wanted to know. *Don't say the kid; don't say it.*

"Blue Creek does. There's a grouping of cabins that you can rent for the weekends during the summer or fall. The one Granddaddy rented was the largest—he reserved it every year, but the place would be a virtual graveyard right now." Alex cringed. "Sorry, bad choice of words."

"No shit."

"How about we not dwell on it and get ready," she said and rushed to the pantry door behind him.

Jake couldn't see what she did, but a panel on the inside wall of the pantry slid open revealing a weapons stash. This chick had more secrets and secret hiding places than anyone he'd ever met.

Alex pulled out both a pistol and a rifle. She set her things on the counter, then began pinning up her hair. "You have your gun, right?"

Jake glanced between her and the pantry. What the hell did she have in that thing? "What? Oh, yeah, I've got my gun." Looked stupid compared to hers, but what the hell.

"And we'll give this back to Fletcher." She pulled out a wicked-looking blade.

"Who should we call?"

"We'll call on the way. Let's go."

"Now?"

"Yeah," she said and hurried out the door.

"You failed to mention we'd be walking in the woods," Jake said several minutes later. He followed right behind her. Now, what did this remind him of?

"I said it was on the creek. Why drive up and take away the element of surprise?"

"So you know where you're going?"

"My sisters and I took this path almost every day during the summer. The creek's like a big swimming hole."

"That means you *do* know where we're going?"

"Yes, Jacob," she drawled. "If you feel the need to talk, why don't you get on your cell and call your brother or someone. That way if we die, they'll know where to look for our bodies."

"That's twisted, princess." He pulled out his cell phone and prayed for a signal.

****

It took longer to get there than she remembered, but the lights of the largest cabin glowed against the darkening sky and the soft hum of music echoed on the wind. Fletcher was in there. She signaled to Jake to go around. He didn't hesitate. They'd called Ryan and Noah. The latter had asked them not to make a move. Well, he'd *told* them not to, but as Noah had said to her earlier, semantics. Ryan was getting everyone else together with a backup plan if they needed one. Until then, they'd all be at their parents' house. She'd save her sister or die trying.

Holding up her rifle, she looked through the scope, then blinked and looked again. *What in the world?* They were—"Dancing?"

"What was that?" Jake's voice was staticky over the mic.

"They're dancing. It's creepy," she whispered and lowered the rifle. She couldn't get a clear shot. Damn. She told Jake they'd have to take them by surprise.

"Alexandra?"

"What?" Alex crept up to the only window unlit. She slung the strap of the rifle across her back so her hands were free.

"I—" He didn't speak for a moment, mumbled something about matches, then said, "Just be careful, okay?"

"You too." She cut off the connection as they'd planned. She tested the window, wincing when it creaked a bit. "Please, God, a little help here." She got it open without incident and let out a breath.

She lifted herself up to the windowsill and put one leg in. Slowly and with as much finesse as she could muster, she lowered her body through the window. Once she was inside, Alex pulled out her penlight. Her night-vision goggles had been destroyed at Dr. Drake's, so she had to use the tools available to her.

She angled the small light around the room. Bile rose in her throat; it was the bedroom. She swallowed.

The sheets were rumpled.

The music was louder, coming from the other side of the door, and she stepped toward it. She held the knob in a death grip and turned it methodically. Taking a step into the hall, she hoped Jake was in position.

Alex pulled out a compact mirror and held it around the edge of the wall. The fire in the hearth reflected on the red satin of Fletcher's dress. Her sister was in a particular type of custom-made hell. Alex pulled her revolver from the waistband holster, rolled her shoulders, and swung around the corner.

"Back away, slowly." She gasped when the man's face came into view and thanked the Lord Charlie wasn't here; her sister would have freaked. "Can't anyone in this town stay dead and buried?"

"Alexandra, so happy you could join us. Please"—he spread his arms wide—"do come in. Jamie and I were just speaking about you. Weren't we, my love?"

"Yes, darling," Fletcher purred.

What in the hell? "Fletcher? Get away from him," Alex demanded. What was her sister doing?

The man clapped. "Shall we tell her our happy news? We're going to have a baby. A beautiful baby who'll be the mirror image of his mother. You don't seem happy for us, Alexandra."

"Oh, I'm thrilled." She wanted to throw up. "But I need to take Jamie home with me now."

"Absolutely not! I've worked too hard molding her to perfection, transforming her into someone eternally mine. Do you honestly think I'd allow your depraved family to ruin my masterpiece? No, Alexandra, I can't let you do that."

"You know, I like her this way. In fact, I think I prefer her this way," she lied.

“See, my love, what did I tell you?” He ran his hand across Fletcher’s cheek. “Perfect. Even Alexandra thinks so. Now…” He turned to Alex. “As a show of good faith, please put the gun down.”

She shrugged. “Sorry. Can’t. Fletcher, snap out of it!” Please. But her sister just stood there. “Everyone’s waiting for you at home. Casey and Ryan. Charlie and Craig. Mama and Daddy. Mack is too; she misses her auntie Fletch. And Jebb’s been driving me insane; you know he never listens to me. We need you, Fletcher. Jasper needs you. What did you do to her, you sick bastard?”

The man moved closer. “I fixed her.”

“Stay where you are. Do you think I won’t pull the trigger?” She cocked the hammer. “Try me?”

The man grabbed Fletcher a split second before the front door banged open. “Hey, princess, thought you could use a little help. He’s got a gun in his pocket,” Jake said as he trained his weapon on the man. “You gonna introduce me to your friend, kid?”

“What took you so long?” Alex wanted to know.

“Tripped over a dead guy.” He shrugged. “Shit happens. So you gonna make the introductions?”

“I know who you are,” the man hissed. “You’re that disgusting man Jamie was staying with.”

Jacob shook his head. “You have no tact.”

Alex bit her lip. “Jacob Keller, let me introduce you to—what name are you going by these days, hmm? Rick? I mean you did take his face, or are you sticking to Daemon? He’s a Randle, Jacob, whichever face he’s choosing to wear.”

“Now that’s all kinds of fucked up,” Jake said. “Princess, what do you say we shoot him and get it over with?”

"No!" Fletcher shouted.

"It's all right, my darling. No one's taking you away from me," Daemon said. "If we die, it will be together." He reached around his back.

"Oops. He's got a knife in his pocket," Jacob called out.

Alex nodded. "Probably the same one he used to kill Larry Hines."

"And the dude out back," Jake said.

"Don't hurt her," Alex pleaded. She should have shot him when she had the chance.

Daemon's smile was grotesque. "Don't make me."

"No one's going to kill him," Fletcher hissed, then threw her head back hitting Daemon in the face.

Alex lowered her gun while her non-brainwashed, ass-kicking sister took control of the situation. Before Daemon recovered from the blow to his nose, Fletcher had kicked him in the crotch and smashed the instep of his foot with a stiletto heel. That had to hurt. Once he was on the ground, Fletcher's fists made contact with his cosmetically altered face. Then she stopped.

"You had better have brought a blowtorch this time, Alexandra!" Fletcher said with a grin.

"Never leave home without it," Alex said, then met her sister halfway across the room and hugged her as hard as she could. "Okay, Fletcher, you're squeezing me too tight." Alex groaned, then laughed when Fletcher just held on for a second. Or maybe she was the one holding on. It didn't matter either way.

Fletcher let Alex go. "Let's get me the hell out of this damn thing."

"Which? The dress or the chains?"

"Be serious, Alex. If I had anything on under this, it'd already be off. Now let me loose!" She lifted up the skirt of the dress so Alex could get the padlock off.

Alex reached in her fanny pack and got out—

"What the fuck is that?" Jake asked.

"It's for crème brûlée. Just shut up and let me do this," Alex said and turned on the mini torch.

"Who the hell broke Alex? Jake?" Fletcher's gaze darted between the two of them. "Well, well—"

"No one 'broke me,' " Alex said.

Jake bent over Daemon, who was still unconscious. "How about we just use the key?"

Fletcher laughed. "You're a genius!"

Jake tossed the key to Alex, who then unlocked her sister. "Better than a blowtorch," she said, holding up the padlock. Sirens drowned out the music.

"Sweet Jesus, I'm free!" Fletcher looked Alex up and down. "Strip."

Alex took a step back. "Excuse me?"

"Those are my clothes you have on, and I want 'em," Fletcher said reaching for the zipper at the back of the dress; then the door burst open.

"Everyone all right?" Noah asked.

"We're good here, Reed. There's a dead guy in the back though," Jake offered.

Fletcher sighed. "Ol' Danny boy."

"Daniel Henderson?" Noah asked and radioed his deputies to check it out.

"That would be him." Fletcher rolled her eyes, then yelped when Jake picked her up. "Damn it, Jake, I swear if you don't put me down—ah, fuck it." She wrapped her arms around his neck to hug him back. "Ow."

Jake set her down. "What?'

"Nothing. Let's get the fuck out of here. Whatcha say, Alexandra?"

"Turn around," Alex insisted but her sister was stubborn. "Fletcher, either you turn around for me, or you turn around for the doctor." She was going to the hospital either way, but Alex wouldn't ruin the surprise.

"Fine! You two turn around."

Alex didn't wait for the men. She grabbed her sister's shoulders and had a look.

"See, nothing's there—hey, what the fuck do you think you're doing, Alex?" Fletcher hollered when Alex pulled the zipper down.

Alex swallowed. "Oh, Fletcher."

"It ain't as bad as it looks."

"I heard him say he punished you, but this…" Alex glanced over her shoulder to find both Jake and Noah staring. She glared at them, then held out her hand. "Jacob, can I have your sweatshirt, please?"

Jake took off his hoodie, handed it to Alex, and turned around while she helped Fletcher into it. He knocked his shoulder into Reed because he felt like hitting something and the other man was closest. The kid's back was a horror show. Jake stretched his neck and stared at the unconscious man on the floor wishing he had killed him.

"Okay, you can turn around now," Alex said.

"What do you say we GTFO?" Jake suggested.

"Yes, let's go home." Alex held out her hand to her sister.

Fletcher took it. "Sounds fan-fucking-tastic to me!"

"I'll need to get a statement…from all of you," Noah said.

"I'm taking my sister home, Noah. You can meet us there if you wish; otherwise, we'll see you tomorrow."

Jake grinned when Noah grumbled but didn't

argue. He followed the women outside.

"Oh, before I forget…" Alex dug in the fanny pack and pulled out Fletcher's locket. "I figured you'd want this back first thing."

The kid let her sister put the necklace on her, then turned with a smile. "Thanks, Alex." She kissed her cheek.

"You're welcome."

Jake blinked a couple times, then pointed to the trail. "Let's go, ladies."

Fletcher looked between the two of them. "Wait, we're walking?"

"Yes. Everyone's waiting for us at Mama and Dad's."

"Hell's bells, they'll be pawing all over me like some damned lab rat!" She grinned.

"What do you expect?"

" 'What do you expect?' " Fletcher mimicked. "I want some alone time. Just me and my show. A *Murder, She Wrote* marathon!"

Alex shook her head. "Really, Fletcher—"

"So princess," Jake began and took hold of Alex's hand. "Does this qualify as our first date?"

"Holy shit," Fletcher said stopping. "When did it happen?"

Alex narrowed her eyes. "What?"

"When did hell freeze over?" Fletcher said, then kicked off her stilettos and started running and running until Jake couldn't see her anymore.

Chapter Twenty-Four

It was almost midnight by the time Alexandra and Jake reached the B and B. All she wanted was a long hot shower and a week of uninterrupted sleep. She walked through the kitchen on autopilot, not bothering with the lights or wondering about where Jake would end up for the night. No, she had fulfilled her promise; the excitement was over and her sister was home.

Fletcher had fought them on going to the hospital, ranted and raved like a caged animal, truth be told, not that Alex could blame her. The real toll her sister would pay—physical and mental—might take time to surface…maybe years. She shivered and headed to her bedroom. What Fletcher had gone through, the marks on her—no, Alex wouldn't even go there.

The events of the evening would haunt Alexandra for some time, but she would keep that to herself. She had been uncharacteristically vulnerable these past weeks; she needed to rein her emotions in. She rubbed her face, then shut her bedroom door. The exhaustion didn't help either.

Alex entered the bathroom and avoided the mirror. She didn't need proof that she looked like she felt. She turned on the water, feeling a bit guilty that this would be her third shower of the day, and took off her clothes.

With a sigh, she stepped under the spray. The hot water slid down her body, soaked her hair, and carried the grime away. She jumped when the shower door opened, then stepped to the side without a word so Jacob could join her.

Alex took her time looking him over, and Jake reveled in her inspection. He'd done the same thing when he'd seen her fully exposed. Her breasts were full, her curves delicious, and he never forgot how she tasted. He licked his lips, then shut the stall door.

Alex turned, giving him a great view of her ass. "Let me guess…you don't know how to shower by yourself?"

Jake grunted and grabbed the shampoo bottle. He squeezed a reasonable amount of the floral-scented liquid into his hands and began washing her enticing locks. He took his time, massaging her scalp, then he kissed her neck and turned her to face him. "Rinse."

He took a moment to enjoy the sway of her breasts before he grabbed the shower gel and the squishy thing. Once he'd worked up a good lather, he began scrubbing her body. It didn't take him long to forgo the loofah and use his hands instead.

He kissed a path from her shoulder to her breasts, paying ample attention to her hardened nipples. He pulled her closer, using his fingers to rub up and down her back, then gave a gentle squeeze to her perfect ass. She moaned low in her throat and turned.

"Now you."

Jake groaned the second she laid her hands on him. She rubbed circles around his nipples, then down lower. His eyes crossed behind his closed lids as she stroked him. He stilled her fingers.

"Come 'ere." He moved her hair away from her face, then kissed her. Wanting more, Jake deepened the kiss. Their tongues danced in a delicious rhythm. He ran his hands through her hair and down her back until he had a good grip on her backside, then he lifted her up. She wrapped her legs around his waist and her arms around his neck.

Her heat made his head spin, but one thought pierced the fog. "Condom," he croaked. He spun them around to get the rubber he'd put on the toilet seat.

"I'm on the pill."

"I—"

She tightened her legs around him. "I don't want anything between us."

Her words might have been his undoing. Jake pushed her back against the stall wall and entered her with an almost animalistic fury. He'd always used protection, so without the latex being inside her was intense.

Jake maneuvered their bodies to find the best position. "You okay?"

She panted and bit her lip.

He leaned in to nibble that lip. Pulling her hips down against his, Jake pressed Alexandra harder against the tile to maintain their connection. He bent his head and manipulated her nipple into his mouth, sucking hard and using his teeth to make her moan his name.

"Harder," Alex pleaded.

Jake kept one arm around her hips, one hand in her hair, and bent his knees trying to give her what she wanted. He was so close…she tightened around him.

Jake clenched his ass muscles and pounded into her. Her small gasps tickled his ear, and her nails dug into his back. Her body went taut, and she made a noise somewhere between a moan and a scream, which sent him over the edge of orgasm with her.

Alexandra was limp in his arms. He let her down

with the utmost care, then moved them back under the spray. He closed his eyes and concentrated on their mingled breaths. They held on to each other until the water cooled.

"We should probably get out now," Alex said against his shoulder.

He nodded and kissed her temple. She sighed, shut off the water, and opened the door. He shivered as the cold air hit his skin. She got out and handed him a towel, which he then wrapped around her. A small smile played at her lips, and she gave him another towel.

He dried off, then slung it around his waist. "What do you say we get some sleep?"

"That sounds like a wonderful idea." She stood on tiptoe to kiss him softly, then dropped her towel and went into her bedroom. Jake was hot on her heels.

****

Jake whistled and maneuvered around in the kitchen. He was going to make a huge breakfast: bacon, eggs, pancakes, waffles—the works. A breakfast fit for a princess! He felt great. He felt alive. "I feel like an ass," Jake said to his new favorite spatula.

With a shrug, he danced along with the music streaming on the Bluetooth speakers, spinning around on his bare feet and using a wooden spoon as a microphone. Alexandra's laugh broke his rhythm, and he froze for a moment, then turned to her with a grin. "Good morning, princess." He turned down the music, then kissed her right off her feet.

She smiled when he put her down. "Obviously."

He poured her a cup of coffee.

"Thank you," she said and took a sip. "You got up early."

He began mixing batter. “I didn’t wake you, did I?”

“No…I’m going to take this”—she lifted her cup—“and go get dressed.”

“Don’t go getting dressed on my account. ’Cause I like looking at you in that pink thing.”

Her lips quirked up. “It’s called a nightgown, Jacob.”

“It should be an all-the-time gown.” He laughed when she shook her head. “Go then if you must, fair damsel. I shall battle the culinary dragon!” He went as far as bowing.

She laughed a real laugh that did funny things to the blood in his veins. “You do that,” she said and headed out of the room.

Jake turned the volume back up and went to work. He looked over his shoulder when the back-porch door opened. He seriously considered putting a new lock on that damn door. He’d wanted to spend the morning with Alex. Just the two of them. But when the uninvited guest showed herself, he didn’t mind so much. “Hey, kid,” he said, trying not to stare at the multitude of scars marring her flesh.

Fletcher pulled down the sleeves of her sweatshirt. “Morning, Jake. Whatcha cooking?”

He bounced his eyebrows. “Breakfast à la Jake.” Jake’s gut clenched; the kid looked like crap. Hell, she’d looked better last night than she did this morning, but he wouldn’t mention it. “You get any sleep?”

“Some. Everyone wanted their turn with me. The hacks, the quacks, and my parents.” She shook her head and poured herself a cup of coffee.

Jake couldn’t help staring at her; the night before Randle had claimed—

Fletcher growled. “What?”

He poured batter into the pan and glanced at her. "Are you—? Yah know?"

"Impregnated with the spawn of Satan?"

Jake swallowed. "Yeah?"

"No. I'm not pregnant, Jake. Don't you worry your pretty little head." She sighed. "Nothing like what you're thinking happened, Jake. Okay? He was too fucked up to get it up."

He swallowed. "Promise?" She'd never broken a promise to him.

"I promise." She looked down at her mug, then the door.

"Hungry?" He believed her, and more than that *she* needed him to believe her.

She relaxed. "Hell, yeah. All I've had to eat in the last week—never mind."

"Well, good. I'm making a big breakfast," he said and decided to mind his own damn business. She'd tell him if she wanted him to know.

Alexandra came into the kitchen wearing a dark blue dress. "Good morning, Fletcher."

Fletcher nodded and took a seat. "Alex."

"Too much excitement at Mama and Daddy's?" Alex asked while she refilled her cup.

"With both Casey and Charlie being pregnant, it's estrogen city over there—no, thanks. And it looks like Charlie's set on having a wedding, but I told her I ain't wearing a damn dress."

"We'll find you something to wear with pants," Alex said, then swatted at Jake when he kissed her.

"So you guys are having sex, huh? Never saw that one coming." She grinned.

"Kid," Jake warned with a smile.

Fletcher held up her hands in mock surrender. "I'm

not saying nothing to nobody. I know how to keep my trap shut."

Alex made a face. "Everyone already knows."

Fletcher snorted in her mug.

Alex looked at her nails. "Was there a reason you stopped by?"

Jake cleared his throat, sent the princess a glare, then looked at the kid. "Is there something you need?"

"I have to give my statement to Noah this morning and was wondering if you'd come."

Alex's eyebrows rose. "Sure, if you want. I—"

"I, ah—" She cleared her throat. "I meant Jake."

Jake winced. "We should all go. Noah needs our statements too."

"Sounds like a plan."

Alex gripped her mug. "Wonderful!"

Chapter Twenty-Five

After breakfast, they loaded up in Jake's vehicle and went to see Noah. Alex hadn't been in the sheriff's station since before her sister had quit her job. Noah had expanded the building, repainted the walls, gotten new desks and filing cabinets. Which was all normal, but he'd turned Fletcher's old office into a storage room. How odd?

Though Noah had upgraded the sheriff's private office too, it was missing something…Jasper, probably, but Alex wouldn't dwell on that. She took a seat between Jacob and her sister.

"I figured we could get this all over with at once," Fletcher said.

Noah raised a dark brow. "We don't generally let witnesses give statements together. As you well know."

Fletcher gripped the arms of her chair.

"I think you can make an exception this once, Noah," Alex said.

Noah glowered. "Fine."

"Where do you want to begin?" Alex asked.

"Fletcher needs to start by telling us what happened," Noah said reclining in his chair. "From the beginning."

Fletcher recapped her involvement with Daemon Randle before his death. Then she said Dr. Daniel Henderson had contacted her claiming Daemon was murdered, and she had to check it out. Unfortunately, everything was going down with Charlie, and she was pressed for time. "Then all the shit with Alexandra and Jasper...I had to leave. So I went to stay with him." She pointed to Jake.

"That's Jacob Keller," Jake began and gave Noah his contact information.

Alex gave her information too, then waited for her sister to continue.

"I had a feeling I was being followed. Then Daniel Henderson came to visit me and told me I was in danger. He claimed to have made some terrible mistake, and I needed to get out of Dodge. I came back to Blue Creek to get my affairs in order. There was no way in hell I was gonna run from someone who was after me."

Noah looked up from his notes. "Why didn't you inform the police?"

"Hmm…why didn't I want to tell the police?" Fletcher strummed her fingers on her chin for a second. "Oh, that's right! Because you're the law around here now."

"Fletcher." Alex glared at her sister.

"Okay, I wasn't sure how far I could trust the local law enforcement."

"Kid…" Jake warned.

Fletcher rolled her eyes. "There wasn't any time, okay? Happy? Look, I knew if someone did come after me, I needed to have things in place so I wouldn't blow my cover."

"You're not a deputy anymore," Noah pointed out. "This wasn't sanctioned by the police."

"I'm a private investigator."

Alex turned to her sister. "What?"

Fletcher grinned and pulled out her ID card to show them. "See. I was investigating a lead."

Alex turned to Jake. “Did you know about this?”

He shrugged. “Sort of.”

Alex rolled her eyes. “Well, go on, Fletcher.”

“After I put things in place, I went back to Jake’s and bided my time until Henderson contacted me again. Only it wasn’t Dan who showed up, guns blazing, at the front door.”

“Daemon Randle.” Alex shivered. She wouldn’t forget it anytime soon.

“Yeah.” Fletcher nodded. “But he had his brother’s face—I about lost my shit.”

Alex turned her snort into a cough.

Jake grunted. “He tore my place apart because he thought we were a couple.”

“Stupid, I know. He flipped the fuck out, though. I mean, he was always dangerous, but having his face changed—” She shook her head. “Extreme plastic surgery can have drastic effects on a person’s psyche, and to take the face of your own dead brother? To say he went insane is, in my opinion, putting it mildly.”

Alex shifted in her seat. She didn’t know how her sister could be so calm.

Noah fisted his hands on top of his desk. “Are you making excuses for him?”

Fletcher crossed her arms over her chest, and mumbled, “I’m not making excuses.”

Alex squeezed her eyes shut. In certain situations, victims have been known to become attached to their captors. “Stockholm syndrome—”

“I don’t have any of that, Alex. Trust me.”

Jake shifted in his chair. “How did you get him to let you write a note?”

“I convinced him you were engaged.”

“Quick thinking. I don’t have a fiancée,” Jake told

Noah.

Noah shot Jacob a droll look. “I should hope not. Continue.”

Fletcher squirmed in her chair. “Daemon asked me to go with him—”

“Now we’re getting somewhere,” Noah began. “You went willingly.”

“He was holding a gun to the back of my head. I happen to like my head where it is…so, yeah, I went with him.”

“You went directly to the lodge?”

She hesitated. “Yeah…”

“Fletcher, what is it?” Alex asked, not liking the pained expression on her sister’s face.

She shook her head and said it was nothing, then started again. “We went to the lodge to lie low. I was able to convince him I wouldn’t be able to relax until I’d emailed Jake, who needed my help with his relationship crisis. Then I worked out an email—”

“So we’d have the clues to find you.” Jake sat up. “Damn good email too, kid.”

“Thanks. I knew he planned on moving our location, but I wasn’t sure where. And when I left the clues, I only had Henderson’s warnings to go on. I knew whoever was after me was connected to Daemon, so I tried to reference every place we’d ever talked about, in a way only you guys could figure out.”

“Good thing,” Alex said. Without the clues, they wouldn’t have found her.

“What I had no way of knowing was that Larry would show up at the lodge.”

“Jasper told us why he was up there,” Alex said and dared Noah to say any different.

“He went up there to relax. I never cared; he was

Jasper's buddy. Daemon thought I'd gone behind his back and told Larry where he could find us. He interrogated Larry for a while, then slit his throat. It was quick." She rubbed her hands over her face. "I never particularly cared for the man, but he didn't deserve that."

"You saw Randle kill Larry?"

"Yes, Reed, and I'll testify to it."

"Then you went to Dr. Drake's," Alex prompted.

"Yeah…Benji. Or Dr. Benjamin Drake." Fletcher gave his information to Noah. "Course, Daemon leveled the place. He's psychotic and a pyromaniac—go figure." She shrugged. "I'd look into any unsolved arsons if I were you, Reed. Todd Mae should have a list."

"He's the fire chief," Alex told Jacob when he asked.

"Duly noted," Noah said. "Continue."

"I was there for a bit; then Alex showed up."

"I told you what happened," Alexandra said, then repeated her story with Fletcher's assistance when Noah asked her to.

"So you went to the cabin on Blue Creek directly from Drake's?"

"Well…" Fletcher's face flushed. She chewed on the cuticle of her index finger, then said, "We stayed at a hotel for a night—"

"She needs a break," Alex said and took Fletcher out of the office. They went to the break room, and Alex put money in the vending machine. "Here." She handed the ice cold can to her sister.

Fletcher sighed. "Thanks," she said, then popped the top and took a sip.

Alex smoothed down one of Fletcher's braids, then

took a sip of her own drink. They didn't say anything but stood there close together until Noah came looking for them.

"Ready?" Noah said once they'd reclaimed their seats.

Fletcher nodded. "We went to the cabin the next morning."

"What hotel was it, and what name was the room under?" Noah asked.

"He used Henderson's card. Daniel was with us from time to time. At first, he was playing doctor to his patient. Daemon hadn't needed a lot of adjustments to look like his brother, but he was still healing from his procedures. I don't think Daniel realized the effects the surgery had on Daemon until it was too late. When he showed up at the cabin, he wasn't needed anymore."

"Do you know who was buried in Randle's grave?"

"The man who was given Ian Thomas's face, Nick Flowers—"

"Wait," Alex said. "He was 'given' Ian Thomas's face?"

Fletcher nodded. "Saying Henderson was a talented plastic surgeon is an understatement."

Alex was taken aback; she had thought they had found someone who looked like Mr. Thomas. To go to those lengths to… "But why?"

Fletcher's lip curled. "It's no secret Ian Thomas stashed millions before Rick divorced Marylou. What no one knew was *where* he had hidden it. No one, that is, except Daemon. Ian had a safety deposit box in the city, and he was the only one who could open it."

"All the family would have to do is show a death certificate," Noah pointed out.

Fletcher disagreed. "You didn't know Ian Thomas;

he was a sneaky son of a bitch. He put a stipulation on his account; in the event of his death, the box couldn't be released for ten years. He'd paid up the dues and *paid off* a few people. The only person who could open the box was Ian Thomas. So they found a bum, offered him an obscene amount of money, then Henderson manipulated his face until he looked like Mr. Thomas. Then he got the money out for Daemon."

"Randle didn't kill him right away?" Jake asked.

"No, Daemon bided his time; he knew he'd need a body to fake his own death. To Daemon, Nick was expendable; plus, he had no home, no family, and no one to miss him."

Noah crossed his arms over his massive chest. "How do you know all this?"

"Firstly, I came across an Ian Thomas look-alike at Daemon's house. I followed the guy for a few days. Took a few pictures…" Fletcher let the last word linger.

Alex sucked in a breath. She knew! Not only had Marylou known what was going on, she was probably in on it. That's what Fletcher was insinuating. Alex's gaze met Noah's. He knew now too, and if he didn't do anything about it, then Alexandra McKay would.

"How do you know it's Nick Flowers, for sure?"

"Because, Reed, Daniel spilled his guts as he begged Daemon for his life."

"You saw Daemon kill Daniel Henderson too?"

"Well, one minute Daniel was pledging his loyalty and regurgitating everything he'd helped Daemon do. Then the next minute he screamed, there was a gurgling noise, and finally silence. But I didn't actually witness Daemon do it."

Noah exhaled and pointed his pen at Alexandra. "Then you two went against my orders and proceeded into the cabin."

Alexandra told him her side of the story, then sat back while Jacob told his.

"That should be all for now. I'll get back to you if I have more questions." Noah stood. "If I could have a word with you, *Ms. McKay*. Alone," he said when Alex and Jake made no move to leave.

"What do you think he's saying to her?" Jake asked once the yelling began on the other side of the door.

"If the noise in there is any indication, what he's saying to her is nowhere near as vulgar as what she's saying to him," Alex said. As smart as Noah was, one would assume he'd shut the blinds; anyone who couldn't hear the rumble of the argument only had to look at the body language to know the two were in a battle royal. Of course, Noah had sent everyone out of the station house, while they were giving their statements, so only she and Jacob were the witnesses.

Fletcher picked up a trophy.

"Oh, shit," Jake whispered.

Fletcher threw said trophy, and Alex winced as a crash resounded. Luckily, Noah had ducked.

Her sister opened the office door, and Noah shouted, "I'm not done talking to you, Ms. McKay—"

"I'll see you in hell, Reed, and we'll have an eternity to talk about it then!" Fletcher hollered back.

Noah came to his open office door. "You're obstructing justice!"

"The only thing getting obstructed here is your ass and the big stick you've got jammed up it!" Fletcher turned her back on him.

"Don't make me arrest you," Noah warned.

"Don't make me laugh. You have no grounds on which to arrest me. And you know it. Let's go,"

Fletcher said, motioning for Jake and Alexandra to start moving.

The door closed on Noah shouting that this wasn't over.

"This isn't over, McKay," Fletcher mimicked and shook her head.

"Fletcher, you do need to show him some measure of respect," Alex said as they got in Jake's vehicle.

"I'll show him something all right."

Alex shook her head at Jacob's wide grin.

Chapter Twenty-Six

Alex smiled when Jake kissed her cheek and got up from the bed. It had been three weeks since Fletcher's return, and they'd spent almost every moment together. They'd gone on long walks during the day, spent their nights by the fire, and even took a trip to the city. Jake in the city had been a brand-new experience for her. Alex stretched and rolled to her side. He'd bought her a pair of designer jeans, telling her that if they were designer, they were classy. She laughed into his pillow. No one had ever bought her jeans before.

She sat up with a sigh and moved her hair out of her face so she was free to admire Jacob as he dressed. She had bought him four pairs of wrinkle-proof, water-resistant slacks, and a few tailored shirts. He hadn't complained about any of it because when he wore the clothes, Alexandra couldn't resist him. Not that she could anyway, but he didn't need to know that.

She pushed the covers away and stood. "What are your plans for the day?"

"Craig asked me if I'd help him at the bar." He buttoned up the dark green shirt. "Does this look okay?"

Alex laughed. "Yes."

Jake winked and pulled on the pants. "What are you up to today?"

"I'm meeting Jasper for coffee at the diner." They'd been spending a lot of time with the older man, and Alex found herself enjoying his company.

"Think the kid'll be there?"

"Who knows?" Alex shrugged. Fletcher had been keeping to herself lately. She'd let everyone know she was alive, then she'd go back to her cabin and do whatever it was she did all day.

"The kid's tough as nails. She'll come around; it's just gonna take time."

"I'm sure you're right."

He nodded and buckled his belt.

"Craig may be a little disappointed." Alex walked toward him. "I have a feeling you're going to be late." She started unbuttoning the shirt.

"Oh, yeah?"

"Definitely," Alex said and kissed him.

****

"Sorry, I'm late," Jake said when he walked into Mack's.

"I was late myself," Craig said from behind the bar.

Jake leaned on a stool. "So what can I help you with?"

Craig hopped up on the bar. "I don't really need anything."

"Oh?" A fire sparked in Jake's belly.

"You're not good enough for her," Craig began. "Don't get me wrong, I like you, Jake. You're a good guy."

Jake narrowed his eyes. "Just not good enough for your sister?"

"What can you offer her? Be honest. Alexandra's a smart, talented lady."

"And I'm what? Just some lowlife?"

"I didn't say that. Alexandra has goals. Her B and B means the world to her—or it did. She hasn't even reopened since you've been here. After Fletcher came back, I mean. She's giving up her livelihood to go gallivanting around with you."

Jake had wondered why Alex hadn't reopened; he'd figured she needed some time to recoup after all they'd been through. "What is it you want me to do? Leave?"

Craig shook his head. "I'm not lying when I say I like you, Jake. I don't want to see you get hurt either. Alex has never brought a man back to Blue Creek—not once. All I'm saying is maybe you should leave before you get in too deep. I love my sister, but do you really think she could love someone like you forever?"

Jake ran his hands through his hair. He'd been thinking about cutting it. He glanced down at his shirt, at the clothes she'd picked out for him. To make him into the kind of man she *really* wants? His brother had warned him again, just yesterday.

Craig pointed a finger at him. "She's already trying to change you. Have you asked yourself why?"

"I never thought of it like that." His gut twisted. Alexandra was a different kind of woman, classier than anyone he'd ever met—outside his grandmother, of course. But Alex was falling in love with him; Jake was sure of it—pretty sure.

"Nothing and no one is going to change Alexandra. She told me once she didn't see herself ever getting married."

Never marry? He shifted from foot to foot. "I don't want to change her."

"Look, I'm trying to save you the heartache when she drops you. And from the stories Charlie's told me, it won't be long."

"You're not the first person to tell me that." Jake

shook his head. Ryan had warned him that he was playing with fire and needed to look before he leapt. Or something to that effect.

"I'm not saying you have to listen to me. I'm asking you to seriously consider what I've said."

"I have," Jake said and headed for the door; he stopped when Craig called his name. "Yeah?"

"What are you going to do?"

Jake sighed. "The right thing."

****

Alex made her way upstairs to get some photo albums from her room. She'd met Jasper for coffee, then told him to come by and look at some old pictures. She entered her room and stopped in her tracks. Jacob was packing his duffel bag. "Going somewhere?"

"Yeah"—he shoved clothes in the bag—"home."

"Home? Craig didn't need help at the bar, I take it?" Had he been biding his time until she left to make his escape?

"No, he helped *me* instead." Jake went into the bathroom without meeting her eyes.

What did that mean? "Really? How nice. Are you planning on coming back?"

Jake returned to the room and slung the duffel over his shoulder. "When Casey has the baby or Christmas, maybe."

"Wonderful," she said past the quiver in her throat. *Grow up! You're a McKay.* She crossed her arms over her chest and followed him downstairs.

He reached the bottom of the steps and looked her in the eye. "Do you want to say anything to me?"

Heat seared her cheeks, but she narrowed her eyes. "What would you like me to say?"

"Doesn't matter." He turned on a dime and grabbed

his keys from the hook.

Alexandra stood on the back porch while he loaded his vehicle.

"Last chance," Jake called out from the driver's side.

"Last chance at what exactly? Sex? I can get that anywhere." Was he testing her? She didn't—

"Happy to hear that, princess. Glad I could be of service. Maybe we could do it again next time."

Her chest tightened. "Not on your life!"

They stared at each other for a long moment; then he got in his SUV. "See you around!"

The gravel spit beneath his tires as he pulled out of the parking lot. She squeezed her eyes shut to quell the stinging.

She took a breath, straightened her shoulders, and went back inside. She never realized how empty the place was. How quiet. She'd gotten used to Jacob's chatter, the music he played when he was baking.

Her hand covered her mouth to keep in the sob. She wouldn't cry over him. Alex shook her head. She had known she couldn't keep him, but she'd gotten her hopes up. She'd started to believe…How could she be so stupid? Love was a weakness for the unguarded heart, and Alexandra McKay's heart was guarded by a thick wall of ice and steel.

So he was gone. So what? Her life had been wonderful before Jacob Keller swaggered in, and it would be even better now. A knock sounded on the porch door, and her heart leaped. He'd come back, he'd—"Oh, Jasper, it's you. Come on in."

"Don't look to happy to see me." Jasper rocked back on his heels.

"Of course I am! I was just going to grab the photo

album. Have a seat, and I'll start some coffee." She managed a smile.

Jasper took a seat. "Sounds good."

Her hand shook as she filled the coffeemaker with water. If Jasper noticed, he was nice enough not to comment.

"Saw Jake racing down the road. Good thing I ain't the law 'round here no more. I'd have given him a ticket."

"I can only assume he's in a hurry to get home. Let me go grab those pictures." She ran upstairs. She decided to switch rooms. It was good to make a change.

It only took her fifteen minutes to strip the bed, throw all her clothes into another room, and fix her face. She had rushed to a window when another vehicle had pulled in the drive, but it was only Fletcher's truck. She took another look in the mirror, pinched her cheeks, grabbed the photo album, and went downstairs.

Jasper was sipping from a mug. "Went ahead and helped myself. Had a hard time finding the album, did you?"

"Some impromptu redecorating," she said. "Was that Fletcher I heard?"

"Yep, left my phone at the diner, and she brought it to me." Jasper held up his cell phone.

She paused. She'd thought she'd seen it in his hand when he walked in, but she must have been seeing things. "Oh, okay."

He patted the seat next to him. "Let's get a look at these."

****

A week later Alex stood in Casey's bedroom with Casey and Charlie. She was trying on her bridesmaid's dress. Alex turned in the mirror. The dress was pale blue with capped sleeves and white roses embroidered on top of the bodice.

"Wow. I'm good," Charlie said, smiling. "You two look great!"

"I'm glad we're having this wedding before I blow up like a balloon. It's already a little tight." Casey waved down at her toes. "Hi, toes, I'll miss you when you're gone."

"You'll be fine. Won't she, Alex?"

"Don't worry, Casey. Ryan won't be able to keep his eyes off you." Alex gave her a small smile and took off the dress. "Your choices are fabulous, Charlie. Even Fletcher will like them."

Charlie smiled. "When's Fletcher supposed to be back?"

"She'll be here for the wedding; she promised," Casey said and shimmied out of her dress.

"Do we even know where she went this time?" Alexandra slipped on her jeans. She hadn't had the heart to—they were designer jeans, for goodness' sake. She told her sisters that often enough; hopefully she'd believe it soon.

"Jasper said she had a few loose ends to tie up," Casey said. "Why she felt the need to do it *now* is beyond me."

"As long as she's back in time. That's all that matters," Charlie said. "I need to go get Mack. Mama's been watching her so we could get some quality time. Oh, Casey, is Ryan back yet?"

Alex put her dress in the back of Casey's closet. "Where'd Ryan go?" she asked. When no one answered, she stepped out of the closet and asked again.

Casey switched from foot to foot. "To see Jake. He wasn't at his apartment, so Ryan came back home last night. Jake's landlord said Jake was paid up till the end of the month, so who knows."

"That's nice then," Alex said, proud she'd got the words past her throat. She needed to go home. "I'll see y'all later."

"Bye," her sisters said in union.

Alex headed down the steps, then remembered her purse. She went back to Casey's room in time to overhear her sisters.

"Why'd you have to ask if Ryan was back? You know damn well he went to find Jake!"

"Ugh, pregnancy brain got me again, Casey—sorry. But really it's for the best he's gone."

Alex's eyes widened, but she didn't budge from her side of the door.

"I know that, and you know that, but still," Casey hissed. "Wait a minute, why do you think it's for the best? I don't like Jake, but you do. You were jealous of Jake, weren't you?"

"I'm not jealous of anyone!" Charlie sighed. "Okay, okay, maybe just a bit. But all it took were a few words from Craig—"

"And Ryan!"

"*And Ryan* for Jake to hit the road. It's obvious he didn't care too much if he could be swayed so easily. Not that what the guys said wasn't true—"

She'd heard enough. Alex walked back into the room. "What exactly did they say to Jacob?"

Charlie's face was beet red, but she pointed at her sister. "You were eavesdropping!"

Alex motioned to the bed. "I forgot my purse," she said and took a seat. "So who's going first?"

Chapter Twenty-Seven

Jake unlocked the door of his condo and dropped his duffel bag inside. Switching his stack of mail to the other hand, he locked the deadbolt and hit the light. Then he opened the door again to make sure he was in the right place. He'd left it the way he'd found it when Fletcher had been taken—a wreck.

He walked farther inside. Someone had done a complete overhaul. In fact, the place was cleaner now than it had been when he first rented it. Jake shook his head. Ryan must have come by and fixed it up. His twin had called him a thousand times, but Jake hadn't been in the mood for idle chitchat. Instead, he'd gone to see their uncle Marty. Which had probably been a mistake.

Uncle Marty had had a field day giving Jake hell. He'd called him all kinds of names: chicken-shit being one of Jake's favorites. Maybe he was a fool. Or a chicken-shit, lily-livered, no-nephew-of-mine moron, as Uncle Marty had claimed. Jake was tired. He needed a good night's sleep and Alex. "Damn it!" He just couldn't forget her.

Fletcher ambled in from the other room. "You know, people gonna think you're crazy if you insist on talking to yourself."

"Kid!" Jake smiled and hugged her off her feet. "I didn't expect to see you here. Are you all right? Is, ah, Alexandra okay?"

Fletcher hopped up on the island. "I'm glad you

asked."

"She's not sick or anything?" Or pregnant…they hadn't used protection; sure, she was on the pill, but a guy could hope. Was it wrong to hope?

"No… Listen, I know why you left," Fletcher said twirling one of her braids around a finger. "And you were wrong."

"What do you mean?" He opened the fridge and pulled out a beer. The kid was good at keeping beer stocked, though she hardly drank. "Is it you I need to thank for cleaning this place?"

"I had to do something while I waited for you. Ryan even stopped by. He stayed for a day." She bobbed her eyebrows. "That was fun."

"You talked to him?"

Fletcher winked. "Let's just say he'll be rethinking his nosy nature."

"They're right, though. I'm not good enough for her." Jake gulped his beer.

"That's the biggest load of shit I've heard from someone sane." She shook her head. "Alexandra's never been happier than she's been with you."

"She tell you that?" He ran a hand through his hair.

The kid gasped. "You cut your hair! Why the hell did you do that?"

He shrugged a shoulder. "Needed a change."

"If you say so, but it's kinda creepy how much you look like Ryan now, except for the beard."

"We *are* twins, kid."

"If you say so."

"Did Alex say—"

Fletcher huffed. "She didn't have to *say* a damn thing. The day we went to talk to Reed, I knew."

"Knew what?"

"That y'all belong together!" She threw her hands up in the air. "Come on, Jake, I'm not blind, and I'm not fucking stupid. She hasn't smiled like that—hell, relaxed like that—since we were little. Plus, I know you well enough to know you've never stuck around this long with a woman. And you sure as shooting wouldn't spend a ridiculous amount of money on a ring unless you were sure."

He squirmed. "You know about that?" Jake hadn't told anyone. He'd planned on asking her when the moment was right; then he'd talked to his brother, and Craig—

"Jasper told me. He saw you at the jewelry store when he was in the city getting a checkup. And you know what? He thinks you belong together too."

He sat down at the kitchen table. "I fucked up."

"You shouldn't listen to what other people tell you."

Jake laughed. "Including you?"

"Well, now, I see things different from most. But, no, you don't need to listen to me either." She hopped off the counter and tapped his chest. "You gotta listen to that, Jake. Sometimes you have to listen to your heart to hear what your mind's too scared to say."

"That may be true, but it doesn't matter if Alex doesn't feel the same."

"She does!" Fletcher hollered.

He picked at the label on his beer. "She didn't say anything."

"No, but I bet her voice went real chilly-like and her eyes narrowed. Probably answered your question with a question."

He thought about it for a moment. "Yeah."

"That's how she does when she's hurting inside.

She blocks it with ice. Then buries it so deep…you get the drift. That's just Alex."

Jake stood up. "She does love me!"

"I can't say for certain, but I'm ninety-nine percent sure."

"Those are damn good odds!" Jake said, picking Fletcher up and swinging her around.

****

Alex pulled into Mack's and parked. She didn't even take the time to lock her SUV. It was still early afternoon, and the front parking lot was empty. Craig should be alone. She walked into the bar and ran into her father.

"I thought you girls were trying on your dresses," Emmit said.

"We did that already, Daddy. Where's Craig?"

"Hey, Alexandra. I thought I heard you," Craig said as he came out of the back room with Ryan.

"Oh, Ryan's here too." Wasn't this a nice surprise. Two for the price of one.

"Is it safe to go home now?" Ryan asked.

"Oh, it's safe *there,* all right." She crossed her arms over her chest. "Here, on the other hand, I'm not so sure about."

Her father took a step toward her. "Something wrong, sweetheart?"

"No, I'm fine." And she would be fine in a minute.

"Are you sure? You're acting strange." Craig came around the bar and put his hand to her head. "You look flushed, but you don't feel feverish."

Alex looked her brother in the eyes, then pulled back her arm and decked him.

"Alexandra!" Her father stared at her a moment, then helped steady Craig.

Alexandra turned to Ryan. She wouldn't admit how much looking at him hurt. How seeing a version of Jacob's face—no, there was no time for that. "As for you…I should slap you across your handsome face, but your wife would retaliate on your behalf."

Ryan held up his hands. "Now, Alex…"

"Explain yourself, young lady," Emmit demanded.

"Why don't you ask them to explain? Ask them why they felt the need to interfere in my life." She went behind the bar and filled a towel with ice.

Her father looked between the two men. "What?"

"Go ahead, tell my father how you told Jacob he wasn't good enough for me. Tell him how you told Jacob I would never stay with him. Tell him!" She stomped her foot and practically threw the makeshift icepack at her brother.

"We were trying to help," Craig said, putting the towel to his eye. "Jake isn't the kind of man who has ambition. He's reckless, Alex, and you don't need to be stuck with someone like that. Sorry, Ryan."

"You may have a point about Jake's recklessness, but he's still my brother. And he *does* have ambition."

"Let me get this straight…" Emmit crossed his arms over his chest. "You two—"

"And their wives—or wife and fiancée—your daughters," Alex added.

"So you and your better halves conspired against Alexandra and sent Jake away?" Emmit said. "Here we'd thought—"

"Thought what?" Alex stepped toward her father.

"Well…" He rubbed the back of his neck.

"You thought I made him leave?" Wonderful.

"Did you do anything to stop him?"

"Excuse me?" she asked, incredulous. "Whose side

are you on?"

"Did Jake just leave? Did he say good-bye? If it's that important to you, or if he is, why didn't you stop him?"

"He was packing his bag when I got there." Her voice caught, but she straightened her shoulders. "Why would I go out of my way for someone who'd already made up his mind? With or without help."

"But if—"

"No matter how convincing these two morons are, Jacob should have talked to me!" She tapped herself in the chest.

Her father nodded. "I see your point."

"Jake didn't give up on your relationship after I talked to him," Ryan said.

"But after he heard it from me too…" Craig shrugged. "I guess he started to believe what we said. Though, I didn't know—"

"How I felt?" Alex asked. "Because you didn't ask."

"What exactly was said?" her father asked and Craig filled him in.

"That's preposterous. I'm not too good for Jacob!" She turned to the door. "Consider this your first and only warning, boys. The next time you go messing in my life, retribution will be much, much worse."

Chapter Twenty- Eight

Alex drove around for hours thinking about Jacob. Wondering what he was doing or if he'd already found solace in the arms of…no, she wouldn't stoop that low. She decided to go home to her empty B and B.

She sighed and unlocked the back-porch door. She needed to reopen her business, but maybe she should wait until after Charlie's wedding. She hit the light switch and jumped; Fletcher was sitting at her kitchen table.

"You're back?" She almost smiled. The coffeepot was just finishing up its brew cycle. "And made coffee."

Fletcher shrugged. "I couldn't wait forever."

Alex shook her head and went to prepare them both a mug. She grabbed a bottle of whiskey from the cabinet. "Feel like adding a little Irish to this?"

Fletcher grinned. "I wouldn't say no."

Alex fixed their drinks, handed her sister a cup, sat down, and raised her mug. "To the only two sane people in the McKay family."

"I'll drink to that!" They clinked mugs and drank. "Oh, that's good."

Alex agreed. "Did you do whatever it was you needed to do?"

"Yep. Went well. So how was your day?"

"Fine," Alex began. She would blame the whiskey for loosening her lips and not her need to vent as she recapped the day for her sister.

"Damn, I bet they didn't see it coming though. Pops probably wanted to puke so bad." She shook her head.

"It felt good."

"I bet. I, ah, saw Jake."

Alex's chest tightened. "Oh? What did he have to say?"

"Not much. Asked 'bout you."

Alex took her mug and got up to find something to straighten. "Did he?"

"He loves you, yah know?"

Alex closed her eyes and bit her bottom lip. "Did he say that?"

"He didn't have to."

Alex met her sister's gaze.

"I know he does."

"Like you're the expert on love."

Fletcher shrugged. "I know the same way I know that you love him."

"You aren't being drugged again, are you? You seem to be having delusions."

"I'm not delusional." Fletcher stood and Alex had to look down. "I know what I see. I knew from the minute I saw you together in Reed's office."

"You don't know what you're talking about," Alexandra hissed.

"Don't I? Tell me you weren't the happiest you've been since Granny died. Tell me straight, Alexandra. It's just you and me."

Alexandra looked her sister up and down. "Why do you care?"

"Believe it or not, I love you. Prissy as you are. Not to mention nosy and always fucking with my head.

And never listening to me, when I know what I'm talking about."

"What happened to 'fuck you, Alexandra McKay, you're no sister of mine'? What about go to hell?" Alex crossed her arms over her chest.

"For one, you came for me—saved me. For two…" Fletcher sighed. "I know you're sorry about Jasper. Sorrier than you'll ever say. I'm sorry too; sorry I didn't stop to listen to you; I should have let you explain your side of things. And that being the case, here." She handed Alexandra a piece of paper from the front pocket of her overalls. "Just read it. I was gonna save it for your birthday. Jasper told me about your emotional blowout." Fletcher held up a hand. "Don't go all mega bitch on me. Read it."

Alex rolled her eyes and opened the envelope. "What in the world is this?" Alex asked as she read the document. "And where did you get it?"

Fletcher sighed. "Jasper gave it to me."

She reread the paper. "I don't understand."

"Jasper was the one who cleaned out Kyle Ruthie's personal effects. Don't know if you remember, but he did most of the legal work for the people of Blue Creek." Fletcher poured herself more coffee, without the whiskey. "It was never processed, but it's a kick to see."

"I never knew. Why would Granny Vaughn keep this from me?"

"She had a talent for letting people know what she wanted them to. Sound familiar?" Fletcher grinned. "Makes you feel fucking great inside, doesn't it? Knowing the Widow would have adopted you if Pops and Gracie weren't able to handle all of us."

"I wonder why she didn't?" Alex looked at

Fletcher. "Do you know?"

"Might. You gonna tell me that you love Jake now or after I tell you?"

"I'll find out for myself." She'd ask Jasper.

"Why not tell me?"

"Because it's none of your business," Alex said folding the paper and putting it in a drawer. She would think about this later.

"Alexandra, why don't you just tell me," Fletcher persisted. "One fucked-up chick to another."

Alex's lips quirked. "I never realized how alike you and I truly are."

"Kinda scary, I know."

"It makes sense though. How do you do it? How do you stay so…" She lifted her shoulders, then let them fall. "I don't know, you still have a heart."

Fletcher shook her head. "You've got a heart, Alex. You've got one of the best hearts. Everything you do is for this family. For me, or Casey, or Charlie, or the parents. Even Bullfrog. Hell, you're even giving Jasper a chance. Maybe you think it's safer not to let people in, and maybe it is, but that's got nothing to do with your heart being cold. The sweetness didn't die in you when Uncle Kyle died, Alexandra. And the love *you* have—the love *you* give—isn't the same as his either. I know that for sure."

She swallowed. Fletcher had obviously heard what she'd said to their mother.

"So that girl didn't die; she got lost 'sall. And if Jake helped you find her, then…" Fletcher shrugged. "There isn't a damn thing wrong with that."

"He did," Alex whispered, tears flooding her eyes. She took a deep breath, but it didn't stop the tightness in her chest. "It's funny, you know, I've spent my life becoming the woman I always thought I wanted to be, but when I'm with Jacob I don't need or want any of the trappings. I can just be me." She held open her arms. "Just this. And he made me feel—"

Fletcher took her hand and gave it a squeeze. "What?"

She dashed away tears and something deep inside her broke open. "Special—seen—he sees the me underneath. But that person loved him, and he left. Everyone I love leaves," she said, more to herself than to Fletcher. "What good has it done me? How am I supposed to push all these feelings down, and forget them? The happiness. How do I pretend he didn't happen? That *we* didn't happen? Because I've been trying, Fletcher. I've been trying so hard, and I can't do it—I can't!"

"You don't have to, princess," Jake said from the porch door. He moved so Fletcher could leave. The kid patted his shoulder before she left.

Alex let out a small sob. "How much did you hear?"

Jake swallowed. "I heard every word!" He walked to stand in front of her. "Why didn't you tell me? Why didn't you ask me to stay? One word from you, and I wouldn't have left. I would have said fuck everyone else. But you didn't say anything; you didn't stop me."

"I was afraid I'd beg you to stay and you wouldn't," she admitted, more tears flowing down her cheeks.

"I love you, Alexandra McKay," Jake said and placed a feather-light kiss on her temple, then her lips. "I love everything about you."

She laughed. "Everything?"

"Even when you tell me I'm a farm animal and

have no tact."

She ran a hand through his hair. "You cut it."

"Yeah." He took her hand and kissed it. "You like it?"

"I hate it," she said on a blubbery laugh.

"Now you tell me." He smiled and took her hands in his. "I heard you right, though, didn't I? What you told the kid. You meant that, right?"

"That I love you?" She sniffed, and he grabbed her a paper towel.

"Yeah. That's the one." Jake wouldn't be surprised if his heart exploded out of his chest, it was beating so fast.

"Yes, I love you, Jacob Keller. As hard as it is to believe." She put her arms around his neck. "I love you," she whispered, then kissed him.

Jake kissed her back as if his life depended on it. After a good while, he let go of her lips and held her in his arms. "God, I missed you so much. I didn't know what color went with what. And no one was there to tell me I was being a jackass."

"There's been no one here to cook," Alex pointed out. "Or ask me twenty questions."

"That's settled then," Jake said and got down on one knee. "Alexandra McKay, you're the love of my life, and I want to spend the rest of that life with you. Will you make an honest man of me? Will you be my wife?" Jake reached in his pocket and pulled out a small box. "What do you say, princess?"

"Yes. I'll marry you," she said, then gasped when he opened the box. "Holy—"

"I know. It's big!" He bobbed his eyebrows, and she giggled—actually giggled. Then he slipped the ring on her finger.

She stared at the diamond. "You picked this out?"

"Yep!" And by the look on her face he'd done a great fucking job too.

"By yourself?"

"Don't push it, princess." He took out his cell phone and picked a song from his playlist.

"What are you doing?" she asked, then yelped when he swept her off her feet.

"We're going to dance." He'd wanted to slow dance with her for a long time. "I'm going to hold you in my arms and rock."

"Sounds nice." Her sigh brushed past the collar of his shirt. "Jacob?"

"Yeah, princess?" He kissed the top of her head, then her diamond-clad hand. The ring belonged there. He was so getting laid tonight.

"If you ever leave me again—"

"Never gonna happen," Jake assured her.

"Well, if you ever do, I'll hunt you down and kill you. Okay?"

"Okay, but princess?"

"Yes, Jacob?"

"That was pretty tactless."

Epilogue

Several months later…

Jake came through the back-porch door of the B and B and hollered, "I got 'em!" He walked farther into the kitchen. "Princess?" Where the hell was she? Their last guest had left early this morning, and she'd already cleaned the room. "Alexandra?"

"Coming." She came to a stop in front of him and held out her hand. "Give them here."

"What do I get?" Jake smiled when she ran back upstairs. He poured himself a cup of coffee and leaned a hip against the counter. She came back down wearing a pair of skin-tight jeans and a slinky tank top instead of the dress she'd had on. God, he loved her in jeans.

"The pictures, Jacob." She snatched the envelope out of his hand.

"I don't see what the big deal is about some pics."

" 'Some pics'? They're our wedding photos. And I've been waiting over a month for them. I'm never trusting your uncle Marty to handle the photographer ever again!" She took a deep breath and opened the package.

Jake smirked. "I'll tell him you said so."

Their wedding hadn't been the big hoopla Jake had been fearing. Alexandra had wanted a small ceremony with family and a few close friends here at the B and B.

Course she'd planned the whole damn thing down to the smallest detail, so all Jake had to do was show up wearing the tux she'd made him buy. Easy, right?

Everything had gone smoothly until Uncle Marty had too many Irish coffees and started hitting on Mildred Lawrence, a retired secretary, manager of the diner, and close family friend. Mildred had decked Uncle Marty, and Marty lost a tooth. Jake grinned. His wife had then told his uncle that he'd gotten what he deserved, and if he ever pulled that crap again he'd be missing something much more valuable than a tooth.

"Oh, look at this one!" She held up a photo of the two of them.

"We're fucking hot!" He put up his hands. "I know, I have no tact."

She laughed. "I was going to agree with you, actually."

"As well you should. That's a good one of me and Ryan." Jake took the photo from Alex. "Good thing my hair grows fast, or I'd be as ugly as he is."

She rolled her eyes with a smile and flipped through the rest of the stack. "These are wonderful. Uncle Marty can keep his good name."

"Now, *that* I will tell him." Jake poured her a cup of coffee and handed it to her. "I saw Ryan while I was out."

Alex took a seat at the table. "What did he have to say?"

"He's taking over the hardware store." Ryan had told him that months ago, but Jake hadn't been listening. "He doesn't know anything about running a hardware store. He's just doing it because Pops asked him."

"He's been learning carpentry over the last year, and he's good too. Did you see the crib he built for the baby? It's gorgeous."

"Yeah, I saw the damn thing," Jake grumbled. "And, yeah, he has a talent for carpentry. Who knew! Our grandparents would have loved it." He took a seat next to her.

"What's wrong, then?"

"I don't know!" He pinched the bridge of his nose. "I feel useless, I guess."

"What? Why?" Alex took his hand. "You're the resident cook here, which would pay a handsome salary, if you'd take the money."

Jake kissed her hand. "You're my wife, not my boss. I cook for the guests because I like doing it."

"Noah offered you a job."

"Like I'd work for that ass hat! I've got plenty of money invested and all that crap; I'm not worried. Besides, you're my Sugar Mama." He winked at her.

She tried not to smile. He was just too much sometimes, but she'd never give him up. She didn't care if people did talk about how the McKays kept marrying inside their circle. He was and they were worth the gossip. "You could work with Craig…He did ask you."

"Nah, though, it would be cool working with Jasper."

She tapped her nails on the table. "What about doing PI work again?"

"Thought about that, but I was getting burned out anyway. Besides, with the kid being gone it wouldn't be much fun."

"Fletcher will be back soon. She needed time

away." And who could blame her sister? Between their family, Uncle Marty, and Jasper's connections, or maybe *because* of them, Daemon had stood trial for his crimes within a month of being arrested. The jury had found him guilty and sentenced him to two consecutive life sentences. After the trial, Fletcher had needed a break.

Jake nodded. "She's definitely entitled to some R and R."

"Agreed." He fidgeted with the handle of his mug. She cocked her head to the side. "Was there something else?"

"You know how you're always saying my pastries are the best?"

"Everyone says so, Jacob; you make the most wonderful pastries. I mean, you even made our wedding cake; people are still talking about it." She'd been shocked and a bit concerned when he'd said he wanted to make the cake, but when she'd seen it…well, she may have cried.

His chest puffed out a bit. "Thanks, princess. I was thinking I'd see if Charlie would want to sell some of my baked goods at the diner."

"That's a great idea! She could get one of those glass cases for pastries."

Jake grinned. "Yeah."

Alex got up and handed him his keys. "Go to the diner and ask her."

He stood up and took the keys. "You think she'll go for it."

"You won't know until you try." She and Charlie had already discussed it and agreed months ago, though Jacob didn't need to know that.

He turned at the door. “I do know one thing, for sure.”

“And that is?”

Jake pointed to her. “We’re still going steady!”

A word about the author…

W. L. Brooks likes to write like she reads with a bit of mystery, romance, suspense, and, to keep it interesting, the occasional dash of the paranormal. Living in Western North Carolina she is currently working on her next novel.

Thank you for purchasing
this publication of The Wild Rose Press, Inc.

For questions or more information
contact us at
info@thewildrosepress.com.

The Wild Rose Press, Inc.
www.thewildrosepress.com

www.ingramcontent.com/pod-product-compliance
Lightning Source LLC
LaVergne TN
LVHW020537100826
845148LV00010B/1498